STRANDED

Slocum woke the next morning with white pain knifing through his skull, and the first thing he thought was that he'd never, by God, drink again.

That was until he remembered he hadn't been drinking. A split second later, he realized his hands were bound behind him and that the Carnahan brothers were nowhere to be seen.

"Sonofabitch!" he swore while he thrashed.

A deep voice, fairly close behind him, said, "Good mornin', sunshine. Finally, goddamn it."

"I suppose you think this is funny, don't you, Sully?"

Except that once he got rolled over, he saw that Sully wasn't smiling, and that he was in a similar circumstance. Also, that the horses were gone. All of them.

"Sonofabitch!" he repeated.

"You gonna cuss all day, or do you have a knife on you somewhere?" Sully asked. "Those boys cleaned me out."

DON'T MISS THESE
ALL-ACTION WESTERN SERIES
FROM THE BERKLEY PUBLISHING GROUP

THE GUNSMITH by J. R. Roberts
Clint Adams was a legend among lawmen, outlaws, and ladies. They called him . . . the Gunsmith.

LONGARM by Tabor Evans
The popular long-running series about Deputy U.S. Marshal Long—his life, his loves, his fight for justice.

SLOCUM by Jake Logan
Today's longest-running action Western. John Slocum rides a deadly trail of hot blood and cold steel.

BUSHWHACKERS by B. J. Lanagan
An action-packed series by the creators of Longarm! The rousing adventures of the most brutal gang of cut-throats ever assembled—Quantrill's Raiders.

DIAMONDBACK by Guy Brewer
Dex Yancey is Diamondback, a Southern gentleman turned con man when his brother cheats him out of the family fortune. Ladies love him. Gamblers hate him. But nobody pulls one over on Dex . . .

WILDGUN by Jack Hanson
Will Barlow's continuing search for his daughter, kidnapped by the Blackfeet Indians who slaughtered the rest of his family.

TEXAS TRACKER by Tom Calhoun
Meet J. T. Law: the most relentless, and dangerous, manhunter in all Texas. Where sheriffs and posses fail, he's the best man to bring in the most vicious outlaws—for a price.

JAKE LOGAN

SLOCUM
AND THE CARNAHAN BOYS

J
JOVE BOOKS, NEW YORK

SLOCUM AND THE CARNAHAN BOYS

A Jove Book / published by arrangement with the author

PRINTING HISTORY
Jove edition / September 2002

Copyright © 2002 by Penguin Putnam Inc.

Visit our website at
www.penguinputnam.com

ISBN: 0-515-13384-1

A JOVE BOOK®
Jove Books are published by The Berkley Publishing Group,
a division of Penguin Putnam Inc.,
375 Hudson Street, New York, New York 10014.
JOVE and the "J" design
are trademarks belonging to Penguin Putnam Inc.

PRINTED IN THE UNITED STATES OF AMERICA

10 9 8 7 6 5 4 3 2 1

1

Slocum woke for the second time that morning, only to find the white linens pulled back from one side of the rumpled bed and Carmella nowhere in sight.

He was half-disappointed that she hadn't awakened him for another go-round before she took off, but he supposed the workings of Carson City's finest fancy house demanded her attention. And besides, he was turning pure hog, as his daddy used to say. Twice last night and once this morning—and pretty much the same all this past week—was plenty enough for any man.

Still, you couldn't rightly expect that a boar hog turned loose in a peach orchard wouldn't go just a little bit crazy.

Grinning sleepily, he worked his way up to lean back against the pillow-strewn headboard, and lifted his cigar from the crystal ashtray on the bed stand. Half left. Shame to let it go to waste.

He struck a lucifer and held it to the Cuban, and took a couple of satisfying puffs. Soft and sweet and mellow. He didn't often get truly fine cigars, but Carmella kept a secret stash of them. So far as he could tell, she hadn't broken them out for anybody else since the last time he'd paid her a call.

And then he scowled. Hell, that had been over a year ago! He wondered if she'd gone through dozens since then, if she'd simply managed to arrange for him to find the burled box with four smokes missing, just the way he'd left it last October.

He thought on this for a few seconds, going quickly from mildly annoyed to plain mad, and then wondering why he was upset in the first place. Hell, Carmella had a business to run, didn't she? And that business was entertaining men.

He'd stayed too long, that was all. The first pangs of jealousy were usually his clue to get out of town, and get on to the next gal and the next adventure, whatever that might be. Although right now, he wasn't much in the mood for adventures.

He had just concluded some business over in Bent Elbow, and had the remarkable sum of 219 dollars left in his pockets, even though a bit of frivolous spending had brought that down from its original 250. Still 219 dollars could buy a lot of living. He figured to take it easy for a month or three. Drink champagne and good whiskey. Smoke cigars and play some cards. Maybe see some old friends.

Most of whom happened to be women.

He took another puff on the cigar, rolling the smoke over his tongue before he blew it out in a narrow plume. It was a fine smoke. Carmella was damn fine too. The room around him was plush and decorated all in orangy red. Thin blades of light elbowing their way between the pulled drapes picked out a nice cherry-wood dresser, polished to a sheen, and that big red fainting couch Carmella kept at the foot of her tester bed.

"As if Carmella would ever faint," he muttered with a grin, and then tried to imagine any set of circumstances that would bring her to such a thing.

He couldn't.

"Slocum?"

He jumped, and his hand was halfway to the bedpost—halfway to his Colt—before he suddenly grinned and let his head thump back lazily against the headboard. "Jesus, woman," he drawled. "Don't do that!"

Carmella had snuck up on him, and stood in the doorway. Her dark brown hair was piled high on her head, and her plump, round figure was strapped into a very low-cut dress, the color of which matched her bedroom. Her waist was cinched in tight, and her full breasts strained against the fabric, threatening to spill over its low-cut neckline at any moment.

Lord, she was something. Just the sight of her had him well on his way to hard inside two seconds.

"C'mere," he said teasingly, with a randy gleam in his eye. "Your corset's too tight, Carmella. Let me help you out of it."

But she stood her ground, and waved a chastising finger at him. "Bad boy, sugar." Sultry-eyed Carmella was from the South—although he'd never been able to nail down exactly where—and the word came out like *sugah*.

He grinned and waved his cigar in the air. "Why, not two hours ago," he said, flicking his eyes toward the clock, "you were callin' me honey-boy."

She didn't return his smile, though, and that worried him. "We . . . we've got some trouble below stairs, Slocum. Could you come on down?"

He sighed like he was wounded, but he was already reaching for his britches.

When he came downstairs, Violet, a wispy little blonde who was barely dressed in baby-pink, raised her head from the sofa she'd passed out on long enough to point toward the kitchen, although he didn't really need the directions. He could hear raised voices—both male and female—coming from down the hall.

He followed the sound of the argument down the narrow back hall, and turned into the kitchen. When Carmella saw him, she silenced everyone with a clap of her hands and said, "At last, Slocum. The voice of reason."

He took one look around the table and said, "Coffee."

The group around the big kitchen table was an odd one. It was only ten-thirty, and most of the girls of Carmella's house weren't up and around yet, having been engaged in business until four or five in the morning. But Carmella's cook, the daunting Mary Stoddard, was in evidence, as was Fiona, a russet-haired slip of an Irish lass who couldn't be more than twenty.

At the moment, Fiona sat grumpily at one end of the table. She was clad in an uncharacteristically modest heavy robe, which she had gathered up to her chin, and she was scowling at the boys.

Slocum had never seen them before, but it was fairly clear that they were kin to Fiona. Like her, both had red hair and pale eyes with a peculiar almond slant, but both boys appeared to have just gotten off the boat. They were dressed in homespun wool trousers and jackets that had accumulated a layer of dust and grime, and Slocum figured they'd been traveling a good distance. The older turned a worn gabardine cap between his thick fingers. The younger plucked at the brim of a floppy farmer's hat that had seen better days. The older of the boys couldn't have been more than seventeen.

"Ye be Slocum?" asked the elder of the two. It came out as more of a challenge than a question.

"Not till I've had my coffee," Slocum replied as Mary handed him a cup. It was hot, and he took just a sip.

"You've got to sway 'em, Slocum," Fiona said, her voice pleading. "The daft buggers are out after killin' themselves!"

His sunburnt brow wrinkling, the younger of the two crushed his farmer's hat between his fingers. "It's our own sweet da, Fiona! Don't you care?"

"He's done what he wished," she snapped. "He was a fool, and you're bigger ones if you follow him."

The older boy said, "Don't go sayin' 'was,' Fiona. Don't go talkin' about him like he was already in his grave."

"Might be, for all you know, Tip," Fiona snapped.

"And I'll speak of him as I wish. He's my da too. Or was."

Tip, who was as thin and sunburnt as his younger brother and as freckle-speckled as a turkey egg, poked his thumb in Slocum's direction. "Don't see why ye had to call *him* downstairs for. What good's he gonna do us? He's old as the hills!"

Slocum cocked a brow.

"Why, we were only comin' to pay our respects to our dear sister," Tip went on, "and here she is, givin' us a hatful of grief and a bucket of guilt to go with it. And her, selling her own mortal body every night for a few pieces of silver!"

The younger one leaned toward Slocum and said softly, "He wasn't meanin' no offense, sir. To either you or Fiona."

Tip and Fiona, lost in their argument, were oblivious, and Slocum said, "None taken." He supposed that when you were sixteen or seventeen, everybody seemed old. And as a rule, boys didn't understand the true worth of females selling their bodies unless they were on the needy end of the transaction.

Although he supposed it was different if the female in question was a fellow's sister.

He asked, "What's your name, boy?"

"Patrick, sir." He stuck out his hand and Slocum took it. "Patrick James Carnahan, late of County Cork. I shouldn't say late, I reckon. It's been near a year since we sailed from home." He leaned in closer. "We had ourselves a terrible time comin' round the Horn." He shuddered when he said it, and Slocum didn't doubt that he was telling the truth.

"How old are you, if you don't mind my askin'?" Slocum said, and took the last swallow of his coffee. Carmella immediately snatched the cup from his hand and held it out to Mary for a refill.

"Sixteen last Thursday, sir," came the reply. "Me brother's seventeen and a half."

It was just about as Slocum has guessed it. And despite everything, he found himself liking this kid.

Patrick scooted his chair a bit closer and leaned in to be heard over the escalating battle of words between his brother and sister, both of whom were on their feet by this time. "We're not after needing your help, sir, and I'm truly sorry for Miss Carmella askin' you. We'll do just fine. But it's our da, y'see. He's been kidnapped by the most heinous of villains in the place called Arizona. That's to the south of here. And—"

Slocum held up his hand, and Carmella chose that moment to unexpectedly thrust a fresh cup of coffee into it. The coffee slopped over the side and burned its way down his wrist.

"Sorry, darlin'," shouted Carmella.

"Just a second, son," Slocum said over the din, while shaking the hot liquid from his fingers and inwardly cursing, as well as wishing that Fiona and Tip would take their shouting match into the next room. "I know where Arizona is. And why wasn't your father with you back in County Cork? What'd he do, run off and leave you?"

Patrick's round, sunburnt, hairless face puckered with umbrage. "Da had the wanderlust."

"What?" said Slocum. Tip and Fiona were screaming at each other by this time.

"I said," Patrick shouted, "it was the wanderlust. There's nothin' wrong with that. It's a manly sort of a thing. Although come to think of it," he added thoughtfully, "Fiona had it too."

"Duck!" said Slocum, and Patrick sank down in his chair just in time to avoid an airborne plate. It sailed past and crashed against the far wall.

Slocum shot to his feet. "That does it! Everybody sit down and shut up!"

The room was suddenly silent, and Tip grudgingly sat down in his chair. Fiona, who was the perpetrator, sulked into hers too, muttering, "Daft bastard made me do it."

"That plate's comin' out of your wages, sugar," Carmella said with a weary shake of her head.

Slocum—now the only one standing, since Carmella and the cook had immediately plopped down into chairs too—winked at her. "You're awful strict, Carmella."

She rolled her eyes. "So what do you think, darlin'? Can you do anythin' to help them out?"

Before Slocum could tell her that he didn't have the slightest idea what she wanted him to do, Tip folded his arms over his worn jacket and emphatically said, "We'll be thankin' you, but no, Mr. Slocum."

"We need no man's help," Patrick echoed, and aped his big brother's stance. "We've come all this way by ourselves, have we not?"

They may have got here, Slocum was thinking, but they sure weren't in very good shape. Patrick's face was round with youth, but his eyes were sunken, and his heavy coat hung on him. His older brother didn't look much better.

By now, Fiona was weeping softly, although Slocum thought it was more for effect than anything else. "Please?" she said meekly, and looked up at Slocum through her lashes. She gave them a practiced flutter. "I'm at me wit's end with these two young ruffians."

"That," Slocum said with a bewildered sigh, "I do not doubt."

Carmella stood and moved to his side, weaving her arm through his. "Tell you what, children," she said. "Why don't you—"

"We're no children!" announced Tip angrily.

"I'm a man practically," said Patrick with a little snort. The statement would have been more effective if his voice hadn't broken just at the end.

Carmella wisely ignored this, as did Slocum, mainly because she suddenly squeezed his arm so tightly that he thought she was going to cut off the circulation. She said, "Before I was so rudely interrupted, I was going to say, why don't you let Mary fix you some breakfast? Surely such big, strappin' lads like you must be hungry as wolf whelps. What's on the breakfast menu, Mary? Pancakes? Bacon? Fried potatoes? Cornpone and buttermilk?"

Tip's mouth worked around a couple of times, and he swallowed. Patrick was salivating too.

During the past week, Slocum had learned that Mary Stoddard believed there was no problem that couldn't be solved by a good, big feed. True to form, she was already tying on her apron. "I was thinkin' to start with that, Miss Carmella. Though mayhap some eggs and sausages and a bit of ham too."

Patrick leaned across the table, toward his sister. "Fi, are you eatin' like kings all the time here?" he whispered, eyes wide.

Slocum picked up his chair from the floor and started to sit down again. It sounded like a damn good feed was in the works. But Carmella pulled him up again and tugged him through the door and out into the hall.

"C'mon, sugar," she purred. "They're settled down and sidetracked for the time bein'. And you," she added, running her fingers lightly over his chin, "need a shave." She leaned back through the kitchen door a last time. "And no fightin', pets. I mean it. Mary, you have leave to whack that big skillet over the skull of the first one what raises a voice."

She returned her attention to Slocum and smiled up at him. She was a tiny thing, only five feet one. "That oughta hold 'em for a while."

"Did I ever tell you," he said as they started for the stairs, "that I have a real fancy for naked barbers?"

"Could be arranged," she said coyly, although how any woman who was practically falling out of her dress could be coy was beyond him. She sure pulled it off, though. "Course, I'll want to shave you slow, Slocum. And while I do, I'm gonna tell you all about the woes of the Clan Carnahan, late of County Cork."

Slocum stopped with his foot on the first step. "Now, Carmella . . ."

She pressed herself against him. "What, sugar?"

The round tops of her dark aureoles were just peeking above the fabric of her bodice. She shifted slightly, and one deep rose nipple nudged its way free.

Staring at it, he muttered, "Aw, hell."

"Thought you'd see it my way, honey-boy," she purred, and led him up the stairs.

2

"In the chair, Slocum," Carmella said as she locked the door behind them.

Carmella's house had one of the few privately owned barbering chairs in Nevada, and it was situated in a small room at the back of the second floor. Anything a man might need to make him smell better or feel a mite cleaner was in the room too, including a wide range of tonsorial products, a small potbellied stove for heating water, a cast-iron washtub with a spigot right over it, a massage table, and of course, a narrow bed. There wasn't much room to walk around in, but when a man was in the hands of the prettiest barber in a two-hundred-mile radius, he didn't much think about exercise.

At least, not the kind that came when he was on his feet.

Slocum eased down into the chair and settled back. It was wider than a normal barber's chair, with open arms spread out on an angle and a deeply upholstered red leather seat, back, and headrest. He eased down into its comfort, thinking that it was more like an easy chair than a barber's seat.

Fortunately, somebody had had the foresight to set

a couple of towels steaming, and Carmella wrung one out and laid it over his face.

"You just relax, sugar," she purred as she wrapped his face, then draped the tail end of the towel loosely over his eyes. It felt good. "I've got a long, sad story for you."

"And if I know you, you're gonna tell it, one way or another," said Slocum, but it came out all in a long mumble, for a fold of the towel had fallen over his mouth too.

"Can't hear you, darlin'," she said amid the sounds of rustling fabric. "Can't hear a blessed word you're sayin'."

And then he felt her hands on his belt buckle. Beneath the towel, he smiled—the little minx!—and started to help her, but she slapped his fingers away.

"You just hold still, Slocum," she chided, and he pulled his hands back to the armrests.

"Yes'm," he mumbled, still grinning beneath his towel.

She pulled his britches down and let them hover around his knees, and he was thinking that she sure had some imagination, his Carmella. Pulling him up here to listen to some cock-and-bull story, when all the time she was planning to suck him dry. Well, long live her imagination, that's all he had to say!

He was hard already, and smiling smugly beneath that damned towel when he felt the chair give a little under additional weight, then the press of flesh, and then Carmella's body, her breasts pillowing on his chest as she slowly eased her hips down upon his. He felt his shaft slowly being enveloped in the liquid silk of her.

"Better yet," he grunted, just as she lifted away the hot towel.

She was stark naked, all right, except that when he looked up at her face, she had the towel over her bare shoulder, a razor held high in one hand, and a soap brush in the other.

"Ready?" she asked brightly.

He bucked his hips a little, forcing himself deeper into her. He cupped his hands over her dark-tipped breasts, toying with the nipples, and said, "Honey, you ain't gonna shave me *now,* are you?"

She gave him a smile as sweet as strawberry jam. "That I am, darlin'," she said, and started lathering his face. "I'm gonna shave you and talk, and you're gonna listen. I figured this was the only way that you'll sit still for the whole story."

She gave his cock a tiny squeeze with her internal muscles. He groaned a little and said, "Yes, ma'am. Anything you say, ma'am."

She put the brush aside and carefully made the first stroke with the razor. "Fiona came to me a little over a year ago," she began, her eyes on the razor. "She'd come from Ireland with her father, who was a scamp and a rascal of the first water. And no, I never met him," she added when Slocum opened his mouth. "Hold still. It was just from listening to Fiona's stories. And stop stirring that big, fat willy of yours around inside me, boy."

"You're no fun anymore, Carmella," he said, but he stopped. After all, she was holding the razor. He teased at her nipples, though, pinching them, rolling them between his fingers.

She took a shivery breath, but lifted his chin anyway. "Easy, cowboy," she said with a wink. "Don't make me cut you. For some reason I'm on a hair trigger this mornin', and if I come I'll probably slash your throat."

He held very still, and she made the first pass up his throat.

"Anyway," she said, "Fiona's father dropped her off a few towns from here like so much baggage." Carmella continued to work. "Just took off in the night. When she showed up on my doorstep, some drunken cowhand had beat the puddin' out of her, and she was glad for the place to stay. And the work, of course. I never asked, but I think her daddy put her up to whorin'. A rotten thing to do, if you were to ask me."

She wiped the razor on the towel, and Slocum was keenly aware of every shift of her body. Every time he thought that maybe he was relaxing a little, she moved and he was back to solid steel again.

"Could you tell me faster, Carmella?" he asked through clenched teeth. Frankly, he didn't give a whit about the troubles of the Carnahans. They could all go hang, as far as he was concerned.

Carmella was another matter entirely. His hands dropped from her breasts and slid to her waist. He figured maybe he could hold her still. "Hurry," he said.

"Fast as I can, sugar," she purred. "Lift your chin again."

He did.

"Anyway," Carmella continued, "long about two months after that, she got a letter from her papa, tellin' about how he'd been kidnapped. Claimed the fellas that had him were goin' to kill him if he didn't come up with two thousand dollars." She ran the blade along his jaw, then wiped it again.

His hands on her waist hadn't helped a bit, and he breathed, "I'm turnin' blue, Carm." He wanted to grab her hips and started pumping her up and down in the worst possible way.

"You're not done yet, Slocum," she said firmly, and pinched his nose.

He held very still.

"She threw it out," Carmella said, squinting as she drew the razor over his upper lip in short, careful strokes. "The letter, I mean. Said it was a pack of lies. I guess he'd pulled stunts like this before to raise money. Said she didn't believe him for an instant, and even if it was true, she didn't care."

Carmella wiped the blade again, and unconsciously, he twitched inside her. She took a quick breath, closed her eyes for a moment, then breathed out slowly. "I'll tell you, Slocum," she whispered, her voice suddenly creamy. "Sittin' here on this flagpole of yours has got me hotter'n a she-cat. I mean, I'm thinkin' about you movin' inside me, and your hands all over me, pettin' me pretty, thinking about you suckin' my titties. . . ."

She paused a moment to let one hand drop to the juncture of their bodies and linger there for just an instant—an instant in which Slocum had to grip the arms of the chair so hard he thought he was going to squeeze them into splinters. There wasn't going to be a damn thing "pretty" about it if she didn't hurry up with her fool story.

But then she raised her hand again and said, "But I swear to God, if you don't let me finish tellin' you—"

"Just hurry the hell up, Carm." He practically hissed it.

"Almost finished, you big, long, horny drink of water. Let me even up your sideburns." She leaned forward again, and Slocum very nearly came. He tried to think about cards and the best way to halter-break a colt, just to take his mind off it.

"The thing is, it seems that ol' Pappy Carnahan wrote the exact same letter to the folks back home, and those fool boys of his have come all the way across the sea to bail him out of trouble. As if he'd still be in it after all this time. If he ever was." She stopped for a moment. "Course," she said thoughtfully, "I suppose he could be dead."

Slocum was doing a little better at this point, straight flushes and butt slings having taken his mind off his more immediate dilemma, and he asked, "Where the hell did those kids come up with two grand?"

Carmella gave a little shrug, and he was right back where he started. It beat him how such tiny movements could feel like the pull of the ocean's tide, but there you were.

She said, "Brought some of it from home. Worked their way over to Boston." She squinted at one sideburn, then moved to the other. "They worked in Boston at something or other and saved every cent, then crewed their way around the Horn. I take it they jumped ship in Frisco. There, you're done."

She wiped the razor on her towel, then folded it to get a clean surface and wiped the last bits of lather from Slocum's face. Slocum immediately tackled her around the waist and lifted her a few inches, in preparation to push her back down again.

Just as hard as he could.

But she braced her hands on the arms of the chair, held her arms stiff, and hovered in midair. "Hold on a minute, honey-boy," she said with a tilt of her head. Slocum knew she was as eager as he was. The pupils of her eyes were dilated with want, and her juices fairly flooded his lap, making his balls and cock suddenly cool where the air hit them. It got him even more stirred up, which he hadn't thought possible.

But Carmella had her mind set, and Slocum had learned a long time ago that when she did, you had best just go along with her.

She glared at him, and he cried, "What?"

"You're goin' with those kids, Slocum. They think their daddy's some kind of god or something, and they won't be turned back. I know because I tried, and Fiona tried, and their own mama tried before us. Somebody's got to go along and see that they don't get themselves killed."

He took air in through his teeth. "Why me?"

"Because you're the best man I know at dealin' with situations like this one," she said, and then she dipped her head a fraction lower. "You're the best man I know, period."

Slocum was human, after all. And besides, he would have agreed to his own execution at a time like this. So he gritted his teeth and said, "Fine."

She lifted a brow. "You mean it?"

"Dammit, Carmella, yes! Anything!"

She let her weight drop hard upon him with a pent-up "Yes!" Immediately, she rose with a squirm of her hips, then ground herself down, then rose and dropped again, and then stopped, drawing in her breath and arching her back in the throes of a powerful orgasm.

Slocum wasn't going to let her have all the fun, not by a longshot, and with strength he hadn't imagined he had—not after all that goddamn teasing he'd just been through—he stood right up with Carmella still impaled, still spasming, with his britches still circling his ankles, and carried her two feet to the little bed.

He dropped to his knees at its edge, pulled out, and quickly rolled her over so that she was kneeling, her belly on the bed and her knees dangling above the floor. In one motion, he spread her legs wide and plunged once again into her slippery warmth, riding her for all he was worth.

As he felt his climax racing swiftly toward him, he took two handfuls of that pale, plump, dimpled behind and drove in hard, again and again. She cried out and gripped the covers in her fists with a mighty groan as he pumped his seed deep into her.

He collapsed across her back, still inside her, and when he could talk again, he whispered, "Carm, I swear, you ever do that to me again and . . ."

He felt a chuckle go through her. "And you'll do what, Slocum? Stick that big ol' pole of yours up in me? Screw me up one side and down the other? Screw me raw? Screw me silly?"

He tried to keep his face serious. "That's about the size of it, honey."

She turned her head and looked at him over one soft shoulder. "Why, I'm just terrified, sugar," she murmured with a flutter of her thick lashes, and then she winked at him. "Why don't you scare me some more?"

• • •

Two hours later, as the clock was just striking noon, Slocum and Carmella walked into the kitchen again.

Mary Stoddard was present, as were by now quite a few of the girls, and Mary was dishing out breakfast. He noticed that the menu was far less varied than what she'd promised the Carnahans, although the dirty plates on the countertop attested to their having had a very good feed indeed.

"Ain't here," Mary said before Slocum or Carmella had a chance to ask about Fiona or her brothers. She waved her spoon toward the back door. "Boys went down to the livery, and Fiona's up to her room. Mad as a wet hen too."

Carmella sighed. "You take the boys, I'll take Fiona," she said to Slocum, and turned to leave.

Slocum, having thought better of the whole thing, began coaxingly, "Now, baby, just what the hell am I supposed to—"

Carmella whirled and set her hands on her hips. She scowled at him. "You promised, Slocum. You tellin' me you're goin' back on your word?"

He scratched the back of his neck. "Aw, hell." All those visions of long baths and cigars and good whiskey and two or three months of whoring and playing cards faded into the background with a good deal of regret. He'd given his word, and now he supposed that he had to make good on it.

Dammit anyway! He was never, as long as he lived, going to make another promise to a naked woman, that was all there was to it. He'd learned when he was a lot younger to never, ever say, "I love you," in the heat of passion, but this lesson was a whole lot harder and longer in coming.

He looked at Mary. "Which livery did they go to?" he asked resignedly. Carson City had several.

"That's my honey-boy," said Carmella sweetly—and with an irritating degree of satisfaction—as she went out the door and back up the hall.

"Jessup's," Mary said. Her back was turned and she was stirring something on the stove. Her arm shot out, still gripping the spoon, and she pointed up the street with it. " 'Bout two blocks thataway."

"I could show you, darlin'," drawled Sonia, a dark, buxom beauty who had been making cow eyes at him all week.

The girl sitting next to her giggled, then covered her mouth.

From the hall came Carmella's voice. "Do it and you'll be lookin' for new employment, girl."

With theatrical disgust, Sonia muttered, "Dammit. She's got ears like a bat."

One corner of Slocum's mouth crooked up in a brief smile. It didn't last for long, though. He supposed he'd best go see what those two numskulls were up to. The sooner he could talk them out of this fool's errand, the better.

He tipped his hat. "Ladies," he said curtly, and walked out the back door.

3

Slocum ambled on up to Jessup's. It was the same place he'd left his mare, Cheyenne, so he figured to check on her and thus kill two birds with one stone. He didn't exactly know how he was going to talk those two kids out of going on this wild-goose chase, but he was surely going to give it a try.

When he got to the livery, the boys were outside the doors and already mounting up on two of the scraggliest, plug-ugliest horses he'd ever seen. Probably a couple of the oldest too.

"Whoa up there, Patrick," he said, catching the bridle of the boy's shaggy swayback. It wasn't difficult. The poor nag could barely lift her head, and once he had hold of it, she leaned on his shoulder, closed her eyes, and gave out a grateful groan.

Tip glared at him from atop the other horse. Well, Slocum thought, it had once been a horse anyway.

"Beggin' your pardon, Mr. Slocum, but I'll be askin' ye to leave go of me brother's mount. We're bound and determined to be on our way," Tip announced grimly.

By now Patrick's horse was *really* leaning on him, and with some difficulty Slocum said, "Tip, if these nags get you ten feet past the city limits, it'll be a miracle. Where'd you come by 'em anyway?"

"They were the cheapest Mr. Jessup had," Patrick explained from beneath his floppy hat. He was looking worried, and turned to his brother. "I told you they weren't fit, Tip. My mare's half dead, and that one'a yours has the heaves, as sure as you're sitting up there on him."

Slocum noted the thick ring of muscle that circled the gelding's rib cage and said, "Believe he's right, Tip." And then he looked up at Patrick and said, "Hang on a second." He pushed his shoulder back into the old mare (who had gone to sleep by this time), and she grudgingly took her weight off him. He took a step away, lest it happen again.

As they talked, he studied the boys more closely. Tip was taller and leaner of face, and his unkempt hair was a slightly deeper shade of russet than was his brother's. His burnt and freckled cheeks were hollow from lack of good, daily food, and his russet brows nearly grew together in the center. Unlike Patrick, he was shaving, but didn't look to have done so in a spell. Sparse, wiry hairs a half inch long jutted from his chin and cheeks like burnt trees after a forest fire. If somebody had painted the burnt trees red, that is.

Despite his unkempt appearance, there was a singular look in his eyes, a look Slocum had seen before in the faces of eager, cocksure young shootists, or kids going off to war certain it would only last a week or two. Slocum knew that look all too well: Tip Carnahan was poor but exceedingly proud, and with a very heavy chip on his shoulder. He thought he'd live forever.

It was a combination that was likely to get him killed.

Now, Patrick still had his baby fat, although how anybody whose limbs were so starved and scrawny could still own a round face was beyond Slocum. But the face wasn't what made him look softer. It was his eyes. More thoughtful than Tip's, they gazed out over a world that probably seemed impossibly hard, harder than any boy should have to deal with.

And so far, it had been exactly that, Slocum thought.

"Get down," he said.

He thought Patrick was inclined to follow his suggestion, but Tip remained in the saddle. After some hesitation, during which he bobbled up and down in the saddle like a fishing float, Patrick followed his brother's example and stayed put.

Slocum sighed. He tried another tack and decided to distract them. Maybe Tip's pride would cinch it.

"Boys," he said, "I hate to tell you, but you've been cheated. I don't know what Jessup charged you for these horses, but it was too much."

Tip's chin jutted forward even as his gelding cocked a hind leg and closed its eyes. "They're fine. Just need some limberin' up, that's all."

"I told you, Tip," hissed Patrick.

"Shut up," said Tip.

"No, there's no way these nags'll get you down to Arizona," Slocum coaxed. "These horses are twenty if they're a day. Patrick's mare is swayed and she's got popped knees. That gelding you're on, Tip, has got a bowed tendon that ain't all the way healed, on top of the heaves. Ain't no way could he jog for so much as twenty feet. Now, why don't you get your money back from Jessup, then come on down to Carmella's and have some lunch. Be that time pretty soon. We'll talk about it."

Slocum thought he'd made a pretty good case for himself, but Tip wasn't having any of it. He had his mind made up, which Slocum had known pretty much from the start.

Tip gathered his reins. "Be that as it may, sir," he said in that overly polite fashion that was beginning to wear on Slocum's nerves, "there'll be no further talkin'. We're off to free our da, and that's the end of it."

With a theatrical sigh, Slocum let go of his younger brother's bridle and stood back. "All right," he said evenly, crossing his arms over his chest. "I wish you luck."

The boys got their horses moving after a good bit of coaxing, then kicking, and started down the street at a weary plod. Slocum noticed that Patrick's mare staggered every few steps, and he slowly shook his head. He had figured they wouldn't make it much past the city limits, and now he was beginning to wonder if they'd make it two blocks down the road.

Just then, Jessup himself came out of the barn, wiping his hands on a rag. A balding, wiry man of middling height, Jessup was good with horses and all right with people, so long as he didn't have business dealings with them. He squeezed every nickel until it screamed, and Slocum knew Jessup was charging him seven cents more per day to board Cheyenne than any other stable in town would have. He knew she was getting the best care, though, better than she'd get at the Tip Top Stables or Harbin's Livery. She was worth it. Besides, wasn't he rich? At least, for the time being.

Jessup strolled up to stand next to Slocum, and followed his line of vision to the two boys before he said, "I told 'em them horses was only fit for glue 'n hides 'n mucilage, Slocum, but they wouldn't be turned. Couple'a loons, them boys."

"Mornin', Jessup," Slocum drawled, although he continued to stare after Patrick and Tip, who had made it a good block. He reached into his pocket for one of those good Havanas of Carmella's. While he was striking the lucifer, Patrick's mare went down to her knees, then all the way down, and just lay there on her belly.

Slocum lit the cigar, shook out the match, and took a couple of puffs. "Believe you're gettin' your horse back, Jessup," he said.

Down the street, Patrick was out of the saddle, and Tip was too. While they struggled to get the mare back on her feet, Tip's gelding wandered over to the hitching rail and proceeded to lean his backside against it. They were drawing quite a crowd.

"Aw, crud," muttered Jessup, and gave a shake to his head. "That ol' Susie mare. Once she gets it in her mind that she's tuckered, she just lays down, *splat*, where she stands."

"Reckon that long walk from the barn was what wore her out," Slocum commented dryly, then more thoughtfully he added, "Suppose we ought to give 'em a hand." He gave no indication that he was inclined to move, though. He took another draw on the cigar and blew out a haze of smoke.

"Reckon you're right," said Jessup, but he didn't move either.

"How the hell'd they get here?" Slocum asked. The crowd down the street was getting rowdy and shouting a few catcalls, although a couple of well-meaning cowboys had stepped down off the walk to help the boys.

"Oh, I bought 'em a couple weeks back from Cal Jenkins," Jessup said. "Ain't had the heart to butcher 'em yet. That's all they're good for. I told them kids."

Slocum said, "I meant the boys."

"Oh. Come in on the stage, or so they said," Jessup replied. "By the looks of 'em, I would'a said they come in on the back of a freight wagon."

With a huge effort from the boys and the two men assisting them—and a mighty groan from the mare that Slocum could hear plainly clear up the street—Patrick's mare regained her feet.

"I'll be diddly damned," commented Jessup with a scratch at his age-spotted scalp. "She usually stays down a good bit longer."

Slocum didn't answer. He merely watched as the boys carefully remounted and started off again.

"Want to check that Appy mare of yours?" Jessup asked at last.

"Yeah," Slocum said, and gave a final glance to the two young fools slowly plodding down the street.

They'd be back.

An hour later, Slocum was back down at Carmella's place, and heartily wishing he was anyplace but. He'd fully expected the Carnahan boys to have come back by now, dragging their tails between their legs—and possibly dragging those horses too—but there was no sign of them.

"What do you mean, you just let them ride out?" Carmella railed for roughly the sixth time. Fiona was curled in a chair across the parlor, weeping, and the other girls had wisely fled the scene. "You promised me, Slocum!"

"Carmella, honey, if you'd just let me explain . . ."

"Don't you 'Carmella, honey' me!" she spat, and her eyes were as black as those little stones the children called Apache tears. "Here I thought you were trustworthy!" she went on. "Here I thought you were a man of honor!"

"You sent me precious baby brothers out into the wasteland all on their lonesome!" Fiona cried, and blew her nose loudly into the hem of her skirt. "How could ye do it? They'll be beset by banshees or worse! They're but babes in the woods!" She began to wail anew.

Slocum tried again. Over the keen of Fiona's weeping he said, "Now, Carm, if you'd seen those old nags they were ridin', you'd know that—"

"All I know is that you're about as likely to spend another night under my roof as—"

"Excuse me?" said a new voice. "Beggin' your pardon?"

They all twisted toward the front door and the voice, and Slocum allowed himself a cocky smile. "You were sayin', Carmella?"

Patrick stood in the doorway, his hat in his hands. He looked a good bit more tired and dusty than he had before. Although Fiona burst from her chair with a shriek and threw her arms around him, the boy ignored her. Over her shoulder, he said to Slocum, "You were right about them horses, sir. We left the poor mare in the wilderness and come on back. I'm fair worried about her, I am. I was wonderin', could you see your way to—*Jaysus,* Mary, and Joseph, Fiona! You're about to strangulate me!"

She stepped back and pressed the flat of her hand to his chest. They were of a height, and Slocum guessed that Patrick still had a few inches left to grow.

Fiona, her nose attractively red from crying and her hair all falling in a mess of red fairy curls, said, "Oh, Patrick! If you lads had gone out there and got yourselves killed dead, I don't know what I would've done."

And then, quite suddenly, she scowled and slapped him across the face. "Never again be doin' that to me!" she shouted, and Slocum blinked in spite of himself. "Never in your life or mine, Patrick James Carnahan!"

And with that, she turned on her heel and stormed up the stairs, weeping loudly.

Sheepishly, Patrick shrugged his shoulders as the red handprint on his cheek bloomed bright. "She's always been changeable as a freshening wind," he said apologetically. He rubbed at his face, then stared at his fingers to see if he was bleeding.

"Sorry I doubted you, Slocum, darlin'," Carmella said contritely, and just a little too late.

Slocum wasn't one to hold a grudge, though, especially when the offender was about five feet one and the half-moon tops of her nipples were just peeking over the neckline of her dress, and especially when that offender had given him the barbering of his life that morning.

He said, "Forget it, Carm," grinning, and reached over to give the front of her dress a little tug to make her decent. There was a child present, after all.

He turned toward the boy. "It's all right, son," he

said soothingly. Somehow, even though these bull-headed kids had come halfway around the world to ransom their horse's ass of a father—who was most likely drunk on his ass in some Sonora saloon by now—even though they'd come all that way on their lonesome and had managed not to get themselves killed, he couldn't help but think of them as a couple of kids that were in need of protection. Especially Patrick. He figured that Tip just needed to be protected from himself.

"I had a little talk with Jessup," Slocum went on, "and he tells me that mare of yours'll get up when she's good and ready. I'll ride out and pick her up, if that'd make you feel better."

Patrick brightened a good bit. " 'Twould. I'd be beholden to you, sir."

"And I'd be beholden to you if you'd quit callin' me 'sir.' Slocum's the name."

"Aye, Mr. Slocum, sir," said Patrick with a nod.

Slocum muttered under his breath, but he said, "C'mon, let's go get that old mare of yours," winked at Carmella, and walked out the door.

When they arrived at the stable, Tip's gelding was snoozing up against the inside wall of the stable, oblivious, and Tip was in the midst of a heated argument with Jessup. Slocum gathered that Tip wanted his money back, and Jessup wasn't budging.

After telling Patrick to wake up the gelding and put him away, Slocum waded into the fray, which had nearly escalated from a shouting match to blows.

"Knock it off!" he roared, and put one hand on Tip's chest to hold him away. "You too, Jessup!"

"Goddamned shanty Irish kids," Jessup spat, but he stayed put, holding his ground. "I warned 'em, Slocum! I told you I did. But would they listen? Hell, no, they was too full'a themselves."

"I'll show you some shanty Irish tricks, you cheatin' English bastard," Tip shouted, and hauled back a fist.

Which Slocum caught in midair.

"Don't you be callin' me English, you mick whelp," Jessup cried. "I were born an American, and my daddy before me too!"

Tip shook his fist free, and Slocum made no move to stop him. "Fine, you pair of idiots," he said. "Go ahead and pound each other into next Christmas. Patrick and me are goin' out to pick up Susie."

Tip forgot to be mad long enough to ask, "Who's Susie?"

"Your brother's mare," Slocum said in disgust. Hadn't they even asked about these nags' names? "Jessup, you got a decent horse I can rent for an hour or so? For the boy."

Without taking his eyes off Tip, Jessup said, "Bay in the end stall, name's Orion. That'll be four bits."

Shocked, Slocum blurted out, "For an *hour*?"

"Day or an hour, it's all the same," replied Jessup, still glaring at Tip, who was dancing a fighter's jig now, his bony fists cocked.

Slocum dug into his pocket and tossed a few coins at the stable owner. He muttered, "Go ahead, slug yourselves senseless," and then said to Patrick, "Throw that tack on the bay, and hurry up about it. Let's get saddled and get goin'."

4

The boys hadn't gotten far, and by the time Slocum and Patrick reached old Susie, she was up on her feet and lipping halfheartedly at a clump of spring-green bunchgrass. She made no attempt at escape, and seemed grateful to be led back toward town.

Patrick hadn't said much on the way out, other than to comment admiringly on Slocum's mount. This was all well and good, for the leopard mare was well worth anybody's admiration as far as Slocum was concerned, and he was proud of her. But he was at a loss as to just how to coax Patrick into talking about his daddy or his errand.

How did you talk to kids anyway? Did you cajole them, yell at them, fool them with lies? He wasn't much good with youngsters. He liked them, all right, but he hadn't been around all that many, except back when he was one too, and that didn't count. Mostly, outside of the mare and a few worried comments about his brother, Patrick's conversation had been limited to "This way, sir" or "Over there, sir" or "I'll get her, sir."

It was just as well, Slocum supposed. After all, talking to these boys could prove tricky. A fellow couldn't ask right out how it was to see their sister again, when that same sister was working in a whorehouse. Any mention of their father seemed to get everybody's smallclothes in a knot. And when Slocum had asked what it was like to crew a sailing ship across the wide Atlantic—a question he'd deemed reasonably safe—Patrick had only answered, "I'm supposin' it was all right, sir, save for the grubs gettin' in the meal," and then shut his mouth again.

But now, as they headed back to town—at a slow plod, to accommodate doddering Susie—Patrick spoke up once more.

"Are ye sure me brother'll be all right, sir?" he asked again.

Slocum had about had it with this "sir" business—which always came out sounding like "sore" when it sprang from either of the boys' lips—but three instances of asking the kid to cut it the hell out had fallen on deaf ears.

He ground his teeth and said, "I told you, Patrick. Jessup's a cheapskate, but he ain't no killer. He won't beat your brother into the ground. He'll just teach him a little lesson."

Still, the boy looked worried. "But supposin' Tip doesn't quit. He's a fool for scrappin', that Tip. And Mr. Jessup's old."

"He ain't all that old, boy," Slocum said testily, but didn't add that Jessup had been a damn fine boxer in the Army, having been the company champion. At least, he seemed to remember Carmella telling him so between rounds of playing house the past week.

The conversation was going round in circles, and Slocum decided to rein it to the side before it took the bit completely in its teeth.

"Tip's a funny sort of name," he said. "What's it short for, Patrick? Don't reckon I've ever heard it before."

"It's for Tipperary, sir," Patrick said right out, and then he colored. "Aw, blast me hide! Please, don't go tellin' that I told. Tip'd have me head."

Slocum smiled. "Why's that?"

Patrick's eyes widened. "Why, it's a sissy name! Tip says it is anyway. Mum named him after the locality she came from. I don't believe Tip'll ever forgive her entire," he added with a serious shake of his head, and Slocum held back a chuckle.

"Why doesn't he use his middle name then?"

Patrick's head kept shaking and his eyes grew bigger. "Oh, that'd be worse!" he said, and said no more, so Slocum didn't push him. But the subject of the boys' mother was breached at last, and he thought he'd best plunge ahead while he was able.

"Why'd you run off and leave your mama?" he asked. "I know you were worried about your daddy, but seems to me that—"

"There were three others t'home to be taking care of her, and her of them," Patrick cut in defensively. "We was just two extra mouths to feed, that's all, and after Tip got . . . after Tip had his troubles . . . Well, it was time for us to be takin' off on our own, that was the gist of it. Da's letter just put the capper on the whole thing."

That Tip had been in trouble, most likely with the law, didn't surprise Slocum. A boy that proud and that eager for a scrap was bound to see a good deal of trouble, most of it of his own making. Tip had likely fled the vicinity with Patrick tagging after, and the law on his tail.

It was something Slocum could relate to, having been in that circumstance several times himself.

"How much of that ransom have you put together?" he asked casually. "Two thousand, wasn't it?"

"Aye," Patrick said, and gave Susie's lead rope a tug to hurry her along. "She's gettin' balky again, sir."

He didn't answer the first part of Slocum's question, which Slocum chalked up to prudence on his part. Patrick probably didn't want to confide how much money he was carrying, much less confide it to a stranger with whom he was alone in the middle of nowhere. For all Slocum knew, the boy had the cash hidden on his person, and was scared to death that Slocum was going to club him, rob him, and leave him for dead.

"She goes better without a rider in the saddle," Slocum commented, nodding back toward Susie, who appeared to be half-asleep but was still plodding along, dragging her platelike hooves in the dust. Nobody'd shod her for a long time.

"Aye, that she does," replied Patrick, who seemed relieved that Slocum hadn't pressed his point about the ransom money. He all but breathed a sigh.

"I'll see that Jessup pays you back for those horses," Slocum offered, thinking that if Jessup wouldn't reimburse them, he'd fork it over out of his own pocket. After all, the boys couldn't have paid more than five bucks a head for these nags. And if they had, he'd slug Jessup himself.

Patrick made no reply, and they rode on in silence until Slocum saw the edge of town coming into view.

"Didn't see any packs on your horses," he said conversationally. "No bedrolls either. What were you fellas plannin' to do for food and water?" They hadn't even had a canteen between them.

"Oh, Tip says that there's plenty of water to be had, and we'll eat what we shoot." He turned slightly in his saddle and said, in a confidential tone, "Tip has himself a pistol."

"That's good," said Slocum, although when the boy turned away, he rolled his eyes. Whatever gun Tip had was likely as old as the hills they were riding through, as worn out and antiquated as the clothes on the Carnahans' backs. Hell, it'd probably blow up in his hand the first time he tried to use it.

"Course, there's the water question," Slocum added after a moment. "South of here it's mostly desert. You can go for days without seein' a drop of water or a speck of shade."

Patrick looked at him as if he were out of his mind. "I can hardly believe that, sir. Why, in the mountains we've just traveled over, there were creeks and brooks galore. And back home, ye can't go two feet without trippin' over a spring or a waterway!"

"That's Ireland, kid," Slocum said with a shrug. They were in Carson City proper by this time, and traveling slowly down the center of the street. "This here's America, and it sure ain't east of the Mississippi. The farther south you go, the more you see the devil's own handiwork. There ain't no roads to speak of—"

"Faith!" the boy interrupted in disbelief. "We're on a blessed thoroughfare right now! We were on a road all the way out and back!"

"That's because this is Carson City, Patrick," Slocum said. "The road runs out eventually, and there ain't no roads where you plan to go. I know, because I just been there. And don't interrupt me, boy! Hell, where was I?"

"No roads," Patrick answered dully.

"Right. There ain't no roads, and towns are few and far between. Plus, you and your brother would be better off steerin' clear of half of 'em. They're full'a thimbleriggers and trash. If you don't die of thirst out in the wilderness, you could fall off a mountain, get shot full'a arrows, or murdered by bandits. You could break your neck sliding down an *arroyo*—or bust up your leg, which is just as bad if you're on your lonesome and don't have nobody there to tend you."

He was on a roll now, and was actually enjoying himself. "You could get lost in the Grand Canyon and wander till you die of loneliness or sun poisoning, or drown in the Colorado. The Colorado floods about every five minutes, y'know, and when she does, she's a bitch and a half. And then there's the animal population to consider. You could end up dinner for a bear or a puma, run into a rabid raccoon or badger, die from a rattlesnake bite or a scorpion sting—or swell up and *wish* you'd died if a black widow or a fiddle spider gets you. And that's just the tip-top of the list."

"I think you're just havin' your sport with me," Patrick said leerily, but he had the sense to look a tad worried. "Me brother has a map and a compass. He says the journey's all open plain and soft mountains, not like the mighty Rockies we just traveled over. The plains look to be real friendly. Besides, Tip says the Arizona mountains are but bumps in the earth."

Slocum sighed. "Those mapmakers were downright optimistic, boy," he said just as they pulled up in front of Jessup's livery. "And your brother's full'a sheep dip."

As it turned out, Jessup was nowhere to be found, and neither was Tip Carnahan. And once Slocum's eyes adjusted to the dim interior of the stable, it told the story of a free-for-all.

Hay bales had been toppled, and a wooden crossbar lay in splinters. Buckets were overturned. A one-ear bridle hung precariously from the rafters, a hackamore teetered on the back of a bewildered rental horse, and assorted tack was strewn this way and that—half of it partially covered by the straw from the floor, which in spots had been kicked loose clear down to the dirt.

"Faith," breathed Patrick when they stepped inside. He closed his eyes for a moment, muttering, "Ah, Tipper, ye've done it again."

"I'll say he has," growled Jessup, who was just limping through the door and out of the sun's glare. His left arm was in a sling, and his nose was beginning to swell. One eye was already dark red and puffed up: the certain sign, Slocum knew, of an impending shiner. It was going to be a beaut too. If young Tip Carnahan had done this to Jessup on his own, maybe he'd better have another think on the boy.

"Where is he?" Slocum asked.

"Where the little bastard belongs," spat Jessup, and there was a gaping hole where Slocum could have sworn there had been a snaggly left incisor a couple of hours earlier. "In jail."

"At least they won't be tryin' to go anywhere for the next few days," Carmella said later that night. She was naked, curled in the crook of Slocum's arm, and gazing dreamily up at her bed's canopy ceiling. "How long did Sheriff Metzger say he'd hold Tip?"

"A week," Slocum said. He'd told her several times over the course of the afternoon and evening, but she liked to rehash things to death. It was her only real drawback, but one look at her stripped down made him forgive a multitude of sins.

He reached for the champagne flute on the bed stand, moving his cigar back between the crotch of his first and second fingers so that he could more easily pick it up. His other hand was occupied with Carmella's breast, which he lazily kneaded and petted while he drank. The champagne was warm now, but it still tasted fine, and he drained the glass. That breast felt pretty damn good too, and his cock stirred beneath the covers. It was about time for another go-round.

He was just wishing that he had another bottle of champagne—cold this time—because he'd like to pour it over those breasts of hers. He'd like to watch them tighten with the cold, and then he'd like to lick it off, every last drop. Maybe he'd pour it a few other places too. . . .

Just then, Carmella turned on her side and snuggled up against him, cocking one leg over his crotch and pressing her female parts, still damp from their last bout of lovemaking, against his hip. Slowly, she began to rub him with her thigh, and he immediately went from mildly interested to downright eager. Who needed cold champagne anyway?

He put his empty champagne glass down.

"You gonna stay put till he gets outta jail, sugar?" she asked as she toyed with the hair on his chest.

"Right in this bed, darlin'," he answered, and rested

his cigar in the ashtray. Then, shifting slightly, he put his arms around her and kissed her long and soft.

And as he did, he let one hand wander down her belly and between her legs. He slid his fingers over her moist curls, cupping them for a moment, then between her silky lips. Deftly, he began to stroke the tiny button of flesh that gave her so much pleasure.

She swirled her hips, squirmed down against his hand, and groaned, and when he switched to gently rubbing it with his thumb so that he could open her with his fingers, she arched her back and made a little burbling sound.

"Mmm," she whispered when he broke off the kiss— and the petting—at last. "That's my honey-boy."

Shifting his arm, he rolled on top of her. She needed no invitation to open her legs to him. Hands on his shoulders, her eyes vaguely unfocused with desire, she could still ask, "You sure you talked Patrick out of it?"

"Did my best, baby," he said, and reached between their bodies to tease her velvety slit, now drenched with moisture, open again. He pushed just the head inside her, and she gave a tiny gasp of pleasure. He kissed her again.

"Told him stuff that should've scared the pee-waddin' right out of him." He eased in another inch. If she wanted to talk about the Carnahan boys at a time like this, he reckoned he could give as good as he got.

He said, "Didn't seem to make much difference on the surface, but he's a smart kid. Sort of." Another inch. "He's got all week to think about it."

Her eyes had gone to slits, and he kissed her once more before he raised himself up from his elbows to balance on his hands. He hovered over her in the gold glow of lamplight, staring down at those lush breasts, centered with deep rose, that he had suckled not a half hour ago, and would surely suckle again; the little hollows of her collarbones; the smooth column of her neck; the full lips that he had already kissed the rouge from; and her hair, all that mahogany hair, that fanned out over the white pillows like the darkest silk.

She brought her knees up as if to urge him on, but he hesitated. She was beautiful, he thought. They were all beautiful, the women he'd known. They were all flowers, from orchids to cactus blooms and everything in between, all fragile in their own right, each having a beauty all her own.

But right at this moment, Carmella was the fairest.

She reached up, twining her forearms about his, cupping his elbows in her palms. "Please?" she said so softly that he barely heard her.

"We done talkin'?"

"Slocum . . ."

In reply, he slowly pushed his hips forward, sinking the length of his shaft into her moist, welcoming warmth with a calm leisure that was almost excruciating. He buried himself, and then pushed farther still, so that she raised her hips off the mattress and hovered as if she were held up by little more than the strength of his cock inside her.

She moaned softly and gripped his arms tightly. Eyes still slitted, she whispered, "It's going to be like that, is it?"

He didn't answer, only slowly drew back until just the tip was within her again. He waited until she whimpered, and then he allowed himself to glide back into her, burying himself to the root. He dipped his head and snagged the knotted tip of a dusky rose nipple in his teeth, then sucked it into his mouth before he pulled his hips back once more and hovered.

Eyes closed now, her head craned back against the pillows, Carmella hissed, "I . . . could . . . kill . . . you . . ."

Letting the nipple drop from his lips, he suddenly drove forward. She gasped, and her eyes popped open.

He grinned at her. "You might want to wait till I'm finished, darlin'," he whispered, and at last began to stroke into her smoothly, rhythmically.

Carmella was wild, but then she always was. Teeth grazed flesh, nails found purchase. Slocum's rhythm increased, and she moved beneath him like the proverbial cat in heat, meeting his every thrust, gyrating her pelvis and pulling at him with invisible muscles, so that each time he ground his hips into her was slightly different than the time before.

They ended together with an explosive, contorted, animal gyration that left Carmella nearly unconscious and Slocum short of breath, and both of them slick with sweat. It took him a second to realize that somehow, they had gotten themselves crosswise on the bed. Carmella's legs were locked over his backside and her head hung off the edge. Her long hair brushed the floor.

"Dear God," she croaked, her internal muscles still gently thrumming, still rhythmically squeezing him. Slowly, she unlocked her legs and let them slither down his sides.

He eased out of her then, and drew her up to the safety of the mattress, where she kissed him sweet and slow and filled his ears with tiny sighs, then curled up against him. Almost immediately, she went to sleep with a smile on her lips.

Sated—for at least the time being—he gently stroked her naked body from the curve of her breast to the indentation of her waist, over one round, dimpled buttock, and down her thigh.

All beautiful, he thought contentedly. *Each and every one.*

He slid his hand over velvet flesh to her backside, and gave it a little squeeze. Slowly, a grin spread over his face. *I suppose I could put up with this for another week,* he thought as he too feel asleep.

5

Destiny just ain't on my side, Slocum found himself thinking the next day as he cinched up his saddle. It was seven in the morning, much too early for a man of means to be up and about, and the horse that he was angrily saddling wasn't his.

Jessup stood behind him, clinking a bag of coins up and down in his palm. "I ain't forgettin' this, Slocum," he was saying, but there wasn't a kind note in his voice. "You may'a paid for this here horse and the one them boys stole, but—"

"They stole two," Slocum interjected as he gave the latigo a grim, final jerk. "And when I bring 'em back, I expect my money back. That there's just to shut you up and hold you off from filin' charges. That damn plug they stole from you wasn't worth a hundred dollars, and you know it."

Jessup grinned nastily, then winced and put a hand to his jaw. "And that one you're saddlin' up weren't worth it either. I know it and you know it. But when a feller's in a hurry and—"

"Shut up, Jessup." Slocum stuck a foot in the gray's stirrup and stepped up into the saddle with a creak of leather. He turned a final time toward the stable man.

43

"Just don't go spendin' that money," he warned again, and rode out into the morning sun.

The Carnahan boys had exited town sometime during the night, after Patrick had knocked the deputy on duty unconscious and sprung his brother. They had taken two horses from Jessup's—Orion, the bay rental horse that Patrick had ridden the day before, and Slocum's own good Cheyenne—and they'd beaten a path out of town.

If those boys had planned and schemed ten years in advance for the best way to piss Slocum off, they couldn't have made him any madder than he was right at the present. Just thinking about one of those plowboys sitting on his Appaloosa mare had him ready to knock them into next year. Very possibly, the next century.

When he caught up with those two idiots, they'd be lucky if they lived through the grief he was going to give them.

He was just coming up on Carmella's place when Fiona ran out into the street, waving her arms. It had been Fiona who had discovered Patrick's untouched bed at dawn, and Fiona who had come hysterically pounding on Carmella's door, ruining what promised to be a very fine encore to last night's proceedings.

Despite the urge to just run her over, he reined in the gray gelding.

"What!" he snapped just as Carmella herself, dressed all in blue today, emerged from the front of the house. She was lugging a very large flour sack, and she was followed directly by Sheriff Metzger, who stayed back up on the walk, leaning his spare frame against a porch rail.

"Oh, bless you, sir," keened Fiona, who apparently hadn't stopped weeping since he'd stormed out, first to the sheriff's office, and then to the livery. She grabbed his hand and held it to her face. "Bless you for all your kindness."

She wasn't going to bless him for bringing them back to face assault charges, but he was too angry to mention it. Also, too worried about that leopard mare of his. He extricated his hand just in time to take the bag, which Carmella was holding up to him. It was heavy, and it clanked.

"Some provisions," she said simply, and gave him a worried smile. "In case it takes a bit longer than you think, sugar."

He knotted the bag's end around his saddle horn. "Be back by tomorrow," he said curtly. He hadn't yet decided if he was bringing the boys back in one piece or several. First, he'd have to see what shape Cheyenne was in. If those jackasses had hurt her, if they'd so much as touched a spur or a whip to her . . .

Beside him, Carmella tugged on his sleeve. She was standing on her tiptoes, although it did little good in helping her reach his ear. Her hand hugged his thigh.

"I'm sorry, Slocum," she said contritely. "I'm so sorry I got you into this."

"Hurry back, Slocum," called the sheriff sarcastically. His arms were folded over his chest, and his hat was pulled low, shadowing his thin face. "Got a nice, warm cell waitin' for the both of 'em."

Fiona's wail's lofted to a new pitch, and she buried her face in her hands. Carmella deserted Slocum to put a comforting arm around Fiona's shoulders and said, "You stop that, Ike Metzger. That's just plain mean."

The sheriff gave a shrug. "Ain't the case at all, Carmella. Said it was nice and warm, didn't I? Them boys is lucky I ain't sicced a whole posse of gun-happy, by-the-day deputies on 'em."

Slocum threw him a scowl, and Metzger caught it.

"Oh, you'll do just fine on your own, Slocum," he drawled. "A man with a thieved horse has a lot more incentive workin' for him than a pack of dollar-a-day hired badge-polishers. You change your mind about filin' charges yet?"

Fiona peeked up at him from behind her hands, a look of abject horror on her face.

"No," he said, and Fiona closed her eyes in relief.

Carmella mouthed a silent thank-you. Metzger had made the trip up to Jessup's with him, although his stay there had been quite a bit shorter than Slocum's. Obviously, he'd hoofed it up here and filled the ladies in on the situation, mentioning that Slocum had refused to press the matter.

So far, at any rate.

"Well," drawled the sheriff as peeled himself off the porch rail and stood erect, "reckon you can always do 'er later on." He took a step forward. "Miss Carmella? You reckon one'a them gals is up for a little diddlin'? It's kinda early, but this here hoorah has got me plumb awake and a tad itchy. If you know what I mean."

Carmella helped Fiona back up to the walk. She gave Slocum a last glance over her shoulder and mouthed, "Good luck." As he gathered his reins, he heard her wearily say, "Sure, Ike, it's on the house. I think Bertha's awake."

Slocum snorted softly. When it came to officers of the law, it was always on the house, wasn't it? He dug his heels into the gray, and cantered down the street and out of town, headed south.

At noon, Tip and Patrick chose to rest their purloined horses in a little draw. The vegetation had thinned a good bit since they left Carson City, but there were still enough trees to make shade here and there, and the draw had the advantage of owning a small, shallow creek.

Patrick, who, unlike Tip, had always seemed to know just what to do with a horse, took care of them as he had each time they'd stopped. Tip squatted by the creek and took out his map again.

He was worried, but that would pass. He'd been worried lots of times since they sailed from Ireland, and they'd been all right every time, hadn't they? The coppers that had nearly gotten them on the docks before they set to sea, that giant of a seaman who'd taken a dislike to them on the *Derry Breeze,* the hatchet-faced man who'd tried to cheat them of their money in Boston: All these—and quite a few more—had been taken care of by the good grace of God, in many instances aided by Tip's blarney-laced tongue. Or Tip's brass knuckles.

He shrugged. It was a gift, the way they always managed to slip free of trouble. It was God's way of telling them they were doing right.

Patrick knelt beside him. He was a comfort, was Patrick, although he could most certainly be a pain in the arse too. Last night he'd been a godsend, coming in the door like that, hat in his hands, asking the deputy—pretty as you please—if he couldn't just talk to his poor brother for a moment. And then lambasting him with a chair.

It had been a thing of beauty.

Patrick squinted at the map and asked, "How much farther is there to go, Tipper?"

Tip put a grubby finger to the worn paper. "We're here." He moved it slowly downward in a straight line, disregarding such petty nuisances as mountain chains and canyons and deserts and the like, until he paused at a spot very near the Mexican border. "And we're goin' here."

Patrick squinted and pointed up higher, close to the place they were at the present. "What's this?"

Tip folded the map. "Some canyon," he said with a nonchalant shrug. "We'll be cuttin' across it." He stood up. "We'd best be eatin' now."

" 'Twas the Grand Canyon I was pointin' at, Tip," Patrick said. He rose too, and his round face was puckered with worry, his brows knitting. At times like this, Tip could see Mum's face strong in Patrick, and it always made him feel a little guilty. She'd cried a river the night they'd left.

"Slocum spoke of it as if it was a dangerous place," Patrick continued apprehensively. After a moment, he stuffed his hands in his pockets and announced, "I'm thinkin' we'd best be ridin' around it."

"What, and lose weeks?" Tip asked with an arch of his brows. "That old saddle tramp filled ye up with nonsense and fairy stories, Patrick. Why, I have it on peerless authority that a man with his jaw set good and firm can hop, skip, and jump his way across the silly thing with no trouble a'tall, a'tall."

Patrick relaxed a little, but not much. He said, "Be ye sure? Hand to the Bible?"

"Holy Mary, Pat, I've got you this far, haven't I? Near halfway round the world we've come! We've both still got our skins on, and we're still livin' and breathin', aren't we?"

"Barely," said Patrick, and pointed at Tip's face. "That old Mr. Jessup gave you a bruise the size of a draft mare's hoof."

"Aw, stop your exaggeratin', Patrick." It felt bigger than a hoofprint, though. He refrained from touching it. "And don't you think poor Da is hurtin' worse, trapped as he is and held prisoner by armed brigands and filthy foreigners?"

Patrick didn't reply, only stared down at the little creek.

Tip touched his shoulder. "Didn't mean to pain you, Pat," he said softly.

"I know," said Patrick. "It's just that it's takin' us so bleedin' long."

"Can't be helped," Tip replied stoically.

"And we still don't have all the money."

Tip pressed his lips together for a moment. "Aye, but we've got as much as could be got. They're bandits, Patrick. They'll bargain, don't you think?" He drew himself up and grinned. "Besides, Da's likely drunk 'em out of house and home by this time. They'll likely pay us to take him!"

Patrick brightened a little. "If they do," he said, "maybe we can give some of it to the man at the stable, and Mr. Slocum as well. Rent, don't you know. For the horses. Faith, I'd hate to be hanged for a horse thief, Tip."

Grinning, Tip cocked his head. "Sweet Hades, Patrick! Sooner or later, all us Carnahans has got to be hanged for somethin'. Though I can see your point. I surely wouldn't want to go to the gallows for something so hellish-lookin' as that paint-spattered mare you're ridin'. Never seen the like. Why, back home, Toby Kennedy'd shoot her on sight!"

Patrick's hands came out of his pockets, and they were balled up into fists. "Toby Kennedy knows about as much about horses as I do about the far-off land of China, which is precisely nothin'. That's what they call an Appaloosa horse," he said proudly, pointing at that mare. "She's a fine specimen too, and Mr. Slocum has her trained just sparkin'. He pitched a holy fit when he found her gone, I'll wager."

Tip snorted. "You're sayin' that like it was a good thing."

"I'm hopin' so," Patrick said cryptically, and left Tip behind to stare after him as he went to retrieve the food he'd stolen from Carmella's kitchen.

The boys had made no attempt whatsoever to cover their tracks. Slocum wasn't surprised. A pair this green was apt to make all sorts of rank mistakes, and therefore be easy to overtake.

As he trailed them through the hills, he found places where they'd stopped to rest the horses, and this gave him some comfort. They were stopping often, perhaps more often than their mounts required, but they were making surprisingly good time for a couple of jack-asses who didn't know where the hell they were going. If they kept on like this, they were bound to ride straight into the Canyon and topple off the edge.

He didn't like to think about that. Not the Carnahans so much, but the idea of somebody casually dumping his horse off a mile-high cliff was likely to ruin any man's day.

"Get up, Flannel," he said, urging the gray on.

He rode well past dusk, the moon being full and the sky being cloudless. He rode single-mindedly, keeping an eye to their trail, with only the sounds of his creaking saddle, the plods of his horse's hooves, and his anger and worry about the leopard mare to keep him company.

And then, along about nine o'clock, when he was just about to give up and make camp for the night, he spotted it: a flickering pinpoint of light in the distance, a light that he figured could only be their campfire.

Muttering, "Lousy little sonsabitches," under his breath, he rode forward at a careful walk. It would be just like those idiots to do something smart for a change, like post a guard.

But he needn't have worried. When he rode in through the low, sparse trees, they were both snoring in their blankets. They didn't even wake when he got down off the gray and led him to the picket line.

Although he was mindful that Tip had a pistol—and he was certain he was using the term loosely—he hadn't seen one anywhere. If the Carnahan boys did have a gun, and if they were running true to form, they'd likely left it in a totally inaccessible place.

After all, they'd camped on a hillside where their fire could be seen for a good half mile. They'd piled their spare firewood down by the horses instead of up by the fire, and they hadn't put their food pack up a tree. Jars of jelly, part of a small ham, and a half loaf of Mary Stoddard's bread lay on napkins inches from the fire. A corner of one red-checkered cloth was slowly singeing.

Shaking his head in disgust, he left them to sleep. Oh, he was going to wake them up, all right, and he was going to give them holy hell, but there was more pressing business to get to first.

Once the gray was unsaddled and fed, he checked on Cheyenne. He went over her carefully, running hands over her spotted coat, feeling her legs with expert fingers, lifting her hooves. And miraculously, she seemed none the worse for wear.

He scratched the Appaloosa's pretty forehead, and she responded by ducking her head and nuzzling his hand, as if to ask just where the hell he'd been.

"Right behind you, old girl," he whispered, and straightened her forelock. "Never very far."

The click of a gun's hammer being cocked got his attention quick enough, though.

"I'd be pleased if you wouldn't be movin' around, Mr. Slocum." Tip's voice came from behind him. He heard slow footsteps as the boy approached.

Slocum closed his eyes and gave himself a good mental kicking. All this, from a lousy promise he'd made in a barber chair.

He had no more than opened his mouth to ask Tip just what the hell he thought he was doing—and Tip had no more than crossed the distance between them—when a second pistol's hammer clicked back. He flicked his eyes to the side, to the location of the sound, and saw nothing but scrub trees and shadows.

"Dammit, come outta there, Patrick," Slocum snapped. Yesterday, the boy hadn't said he was armed.

But then, maybe he'd snagged a pistol out of the sheriff's office, one Metzger hadn't noticed until after Slocum had left town—and Metzger had finished up at Carmella's.

From back at the fire, Patrick's breaking voice said, " 'Tisn't me, sir."

Slocum heard Tip mutter, "Shite!"

Before Slocum had time to build up a whole new worry, a slow, deep, bass chuckle emerged from the shadowed trees, and a voice, round and resonant, said, "Drop that iron, boy."

Slocum knew that voice. It was unmistakable. Nobody in the world but Sully Washington, the biggest, baddest bounty hunter ever to come out of the Great State of Texas, could talk up out of the bottom of a well like that. Just the sound of Sully's mellifluous vocalization had seduced countless females from the Gulf to the blue Pacific, and set the rest to swooning. Slocum had seen it happen.

Slocum said, "You'd best do what the man says, Tip. Sounds to me like a killer with no conscience."

Tip ignored him entirely. His voice quavering, he said, "No, sir, I won't. You'll be droppin' yours, you lurker in the bushes! Come out where a man can see you proper!"

"Tip, for the love'a God!" pleaded Patrick.

Slocum felt the barrel of Tip's gun nose against the back of his neck.

"Shut up, Patrick!" Tip shouted, and Slocum felt him shifting about. "Come out, you lurker in the bushes. Toss your pistol out where I can see it, and ye'd best be right behind it."

But nobody came out, and Tip, in a nervous fit of

mock bravery, shouted, "Come out with ye! Hands in the air, if you please! This is the last time I'll be askin'!"

There was a short pause, and then the man in the bushes said, "Why?"

Despite the fact that a lunatic boy was holding a cocked pistol to his neck, Slocum smiled. Damn that Sully anyhow! It was exactly how *he* would have played it had the situation been reversed.

"What?" cried Tip in a flustered voice. "Because . . . because if you don't, I'll surely shoot this man in the neck, that's why."

"Go ahead," said Sully's rumbling voice, and there was a shrug in it. "Better odds."

"Jaysus, Mary, and Joseph!" called Patrick, who had lost all vestige of control over his breaking voice. It switched octaves twice with each word. "For the love'a Mike, Tipper!"

From the shadows, Sully said, "Listen to your brother, boy."

Slocum felt the pressure of the gun barrel ease off, then disappear.

"Let it drop."

He heard the thud as the gun hit the ground.

"Back off. There, that's a good little fella. Slocum?"

Slocum turned and bent to pick up the gun. It was ancient, just as he'd imagined it would be. Tip had probably snagged it out of some dealer's junk pile.

" 'Slocum'?" Tip said, his blue eyes full of sparks. "Is he callin' you by your name? He's a friend of yours?"

Slocum ignored him and turned the old pistol over in his hands. "Where'd you get this damn thing anyway?" He thumbed out the chamber, lifted the gun to his eye, and took a look through the barrel, sighting across the clearing to the fire.

Just as he thought. Irritated at the boy's stupidity, he looked back at Tip. "This gun ain't been cleaned in a coon's age, you jackass. The barrel's all full'a crud."

He thumbed out the cartridges and snapped the chamber back into place with a flick of his wrist. "Probably would'a blown straight up, and you would'a taken off your own hand, not to mention my damn neck."

But Tip Carnahan—world traveler, horse thief, brawler, and would-be assassin—wasn't looking at him at all. Instead, the little bastard was staring at the brush, which crackled with the movements of Sully Washington as he shouldered his way into the open.

Slack-jawed and obviously disgusted, Tip breathed, "Jaysus, it's a damned nigger!"

"That does it," said Slocum.

He hauled back and slugged the boy square in the jaw.

6

" 'Better odds'?" Slocum said as Sully Washington joined him.

Thoughtfully, Sully rubbed long, dark fingers across his chin. "Well, they would have been," he said, and then he roared out a laugh and gave Slocum a bear hug that lifted him off his feet and nearly broke his ribs.

Now, Slocum hadn't seen Sully in two years or better, but it could have been yesterday as far as the man's appearance went. He hadn't aged a mite. He was still wearing a pale blue, open-necked, drop-sleeved shirt, the kind that laced up the front, the kind Slocum had heard folks call a pirate's shirt. It couldn't possibly have been the same one, could it? Maybe Sully'd had a whole slew of them made at one time, all alike. It would be just like the narcissistic sonofabitch, and Slocum knew that he headquartered in New Orleans. That pirate shirt looked suspiciously French to him.

Or maybe Spanish.

Sully still wore a silver concho-circled black hat and black trousers with conchos running down the legs in a line. He still had the Mexican-style ammunition belts crossing his chest, which were currently embedding the marks of every single cartridge into Slocum's chest. An Arkansas toothpick was strapped to his belt, and a

silver-trimmed, pearl-handled, eagle-butt Colt rode
each hip. His Winchester, which had been swinging
easily from his fingers, had slipped to the ground in
his enthusiasm.

Six feet four in his stocking feet, Sully was a good
two inches taller in his boots. He also had shoulders
as wide as a draft mare's backside, and many a badman
had simply thrown down his guns and started begging
for mercy when Sully appeared on the scene.

"You don't need to kill me," Slocum managed to
croak out, and Sully let go. Slocum nearly fell over.

"How the hell you been, you old bushwhacker?"
Sully boomed happily, oblivious to Slocum's distress.
"And what the devil are you doin' with these whelps?"

"Long story," Slocum said, once he could breathe
again. He bent to pick up Tip, who was, for the moment at least, out cold. He started dragging him toward
the spot where Patrick waited, cringing, and said,
"More to the point, Sully, what the hell you doin' out
there in the bushes? What you doin' in Nevada, for
that matter?"

"Well, I've got paper on a couple of kids that held
up a bank in . . . Here, let me help with that." Sully
grabbed Tip's arms from Slocum and began to drag
him as easily as Slocum might have dragged a gun-
nysack full of feathers. He slung Tip's inert body at
Patrick's feet, and when Patrick just stood there, shaking, he raised his brows, tilted his head back, and said,
"Boo!"

Poor Patrick dropped to his knees and clasped his
hands before him.

While Sully laughed, Slocum said, "Relax, Patrick.

Your brother ain't dead, and there's no good whatsoever can come from prayin' to Sully."

For some reason, this struck the big man even funnier, and he only laughed louder.

"He's not the Devil?" Patrick said, gulping. His voice was still skittering all over the place.

"He's a bounty hunter, boy," Slocum said, "and out of Texas, not hell. Although I'll admit you ain't the first one to make that mistake."

Still chuckling, Sully waved a huge hand. "If y'all have got things under control for the time being," he said as he walked away, his rifle swinging, "I'm gonna go get my horse." He disappeared into the darkness.

"Was . . . was that a regulation rifle he was carryin', sir?" Patrick whispered.

Slocum's brow creased. "Regulation?"

"It looked for all the world like he was carryin' a toy."

Slocum supposed it had. "Throw some water on the gunslinger here," he said, pointing down at Tip. "If I'm awake, everybody's awake."

A few minutes later, while Tip sat sputtering wetly in the dirt, Slocum crouched down, rocking on his heels.

"I'm gonna say this just one time, Tip," he began softly, but dead serious. "I'm an easy man to get along with most of the time," he lied. "Just ask anybody. But there's one thing I won't put up with."

He paused, flicking his eyes between Tip's and Patrick's. Patrick was watching him like a cornered rabbit with a coyote bearing down on him, watching Slocum like he was the last thing he was going to see on this earthly plane.

Tip glared at Slocum through slitted eyes and damp hair, and with a cold, biting hate that might have been appropriate on the face of a man going to the gallows, but not on that of a seventeen-year-old boy.

Slocum gave an inward sigh, but plunged forward. If Tip had grown to hate that hard this young, there wasn't a damn thing Slocum could do about it except lay down his rules and see what happened.

"Nobody, and I mean *nobody*, steals my horse," he said flatly. "Men have tried it, sure. And those men have died, most of 'em, by my hand or the law's. You try it again, and you'll end the same way. I won't be easy on you a second time. Got it?"

Tip scowled at him and said nothing.

But so softly that Slocum could barely hear him, Patrick stammered, " 'Twas . . .'twas my idea, sir." He shifted his gaze from Slocum's eyes to the dirt at his feet, and his hat shadowed his eyes. "I was thinkin' that maybe, if you were to follow us along, that maybe . . . maybe you'd come to our aid. You know, help us free Da from these kidnappin', godless cowards."

Slocum just stared at him. He was a good kid, this Patrick, but he had a hell of a one-track mind.

"The only thing I'm gonna aid you in, kid, is gettin' your sorry asses back to town. You've got a whole heap to answer for, to both your sister and the sheriff. And Jessup."

"Aw, bugger that sorry Englishman," Tip said suddenly. "You'll not be takin' us back to town, Slocum. You'll not be takin' us anywhere."

His half-starved features were grim with determination and, Slocum thought, a good bit of desperation.

It wasn't the best partnership on any man's face, let alone a kid's.

Slocum said, "Patrick, go down to the picket line and bring me my rope."

Patrick swallowed hard, and tears came to his eyes. "Good Christ, sir! Is there to be a hangin'?"

Slocum rolled his eyes. "Just go get the damn thing."

After a good piece of time, Sully brought up his mount, which, he explained, he had left in a hollow about four hundred yards out. He still rode the same horse too: a black bay sixteen-hand gelding he called Old Scratch. While the horse was too tall for Slocum's personal taste, he was well built and tractable, and he fit under Sully just fine. Slocum had always admired him except for one little detail: He was proud-cut.

A proud-cut horse is one who hasn't been gelded just right and who, although incapable of siring, is still a randy bastard. If left to his own devices, Old Scratch would have mounted—and bred, however unproductively—every mare in the country.

In fact, two years ago, Old Scratch had bred the little red mare that Slocum was riding back then. *While* he was riding her. He still had a dent in his skull from one of that damn gelding's hooves.

"Old Scratch sends his regards," Sully said as he joined them at the fire. "He asked particularly after your head-bone."

"Very funny," Slocum replied dryly. With a fork, he turned over the ham he had frying in the skillet.

Sully regarded first the sizzling ham, and second the trussed Tip. Slocum had tied him hand and foot, and he wasn't about to go anywhere. "Get frisky again?" Sully asked.

Slocum nodded. "Somethin' like. You want your ham hot or cold? Figured we'd best eat the bread before the ants got the last of it."

"Hot." Sully picked up the ham and began to saw off a thick slice. "Coffee brewed yet?"

"Give 'er a minute," Slocum said.

"That's our food you're eatin'," said Tip accusingly, although Slocum noticed he didn't do it very loudly. Funny how the presence of ropes could cut down a man's volume.

"Nope," Slocum corrected. "It's Carmella's food, and you nearly let it go bad or get hauled off by critters. You're lucky some big ol' puma didn't wander in and eat the ham and you too."

"That, or a grizzly," offered Sully happily. "Or a wolf. They've got some big lobos in these parts."

Tip didn't reply in words. He merely spat on the ground and glared.

Apologetically, Patrick quietly offered, "Beggin' your pardon, sir, but me brother's only testy because of the beatin'. Well, the bonds too."

Slocum frowned.

"Oh, not the beatin' he got at your hands, sir! That was just a wee tap. I'm meanin' the one he took from Mr. Jessup. I'm thinkin' he suffered some cracked ribs besides what shows."

"Shut up, Patrick," Tip snarled.

"Part badger, that boy," Sully remarked, and tossed his ham into the skillet that Slocum's had just vacated. "Or wolverine. Surprised you didn't gag him so's he couldn't bite."

"He's more part mule. Mule-headed leastwise," Slocum said, and took a big bite of his sandwich. The ham was fine and the bread was good, even if it was a little dried out. He hadn't eaten since a little past noon, and in truth, would have eaten a live prairie dog had there been one handy.

Around a mouthful, he said, "You were tellin' me what the hell you were doin' out there."

Sully deftly jerked the skillet, and his ham flew up in the air, flipped over, and landed perfectly with a sizzle that impressed even Slocum. Patrick stayed silent, but his mouth gaped. Tip was staring at the ground and didn't notice.

"Had paper on a couple of boys," Sully said, "like I was sayin'. Saw these two young gentlemen and followed along at a discreet distance. You know how it is, Slocum. A dreary life of watching and waiting."

"Uh-huh," said Slocum. Shoot-outs and womanizing was more like it. He had finished his sandwich in four bites and was ready for another, but Sully was still using the skillet. He poured himself a cup of coffee. It was still weak, but drinkable.

"Anyhow," said Sully, "I had just about decided these lads were far too fresh from the old soil to be a couple of dastardly young gunslingers out of Montana, and then you showed up." He slid the ham onto his waiting bread and slapped a second slice on top.

"The minute I saw you on top of that ewe-necked gray, I figured you must have something to do with the nice little Appy they had. Decided to stick around and see what was what. So, Slocum," he asked, sandwich poised inches from his mouth, "what *is* what?"

•   •   •

While Slocum and Sully talked at length over new times and old times (and a few times they had only imagined having), the boys whispered on the other side of the fire.

"Faith, Tipper, but I believe we're in the presence of greatness!" Patrick murmured.

"Only in the presence of a champion knot-tier," grumbled Tip, who had been straining at his bonds for the past hour and a half. Due to the good fortune of having been born with two double-jointed thumbs, Tip could slither free of most anything, but Slocum had hog-tied him good. He finally gave it up as hopeless.

"But have ye been listenin'?" Patrick whispered. "That Sully fella's a great, grand-lookin' bastard! Why, he appears like he came right out of a storybook, and he talks more melodious than a Dublin actor. What tales they're tellin'!"

"What bunk and ballyhoo, you mean," Tip said in disgust. "And you've never heard a Dublin actor in your life."

If the truth were told, the stories being bandied about by Slocum and Sully had impressed even him, but he wasn't about to admit it. "It's all lies, Pat. Why, one of them's a nothin' but a lowly saddle tramp, and the other's a filthy nig—"

"Stop that!" Patrick hissed. "Jaysus, Tipper, sometimes I'm thinkin' ye hate and detest every livin' person what isn't Irish, and three quarters of them that are. It's always the filthy niggers or the filthy Chinese or the damn froggy Frenchmen or the blasted English. I was gettin' to like that nice Italian feller on the ship. He had a bit of whalebone, and he was teachin' me scrimshaw. Don't know why you had to take after him with a length of kindlin'."

"Greasy wop bastard," grumbled Tip.

"See?" said Patrick. "There you go again, callin' people names!"

From across the fire, Slocum leaned forward a little. "You boys gettin' restless?"

"No, sir," said Patrick.

Tip glowered. Why his little brother had to be such an arse-kissing little twit was beyond him. It must be their mother's blood coming through.

"Slocum tells me you lads were headed southeast," Sully said. "How were you plannin' to straddle the Canyon?"

"We'll still do it," Tip said tersely.

"Somehow," said Patrick, although he sounded less sure.

Sully leaned back, a thin, black cigarillo in his mouth and coffee cup in one hand. He shook his head. "It's a hellish thing, that Canyon," he said, the cigarillo gripped between his teeth. "The way you were goin', you'd have to ride near to Colorado to get around it. Hell, maybe all the way back to Missouri, right, Slocum?"

"Mayhap." Slocum grinned a tad, which led Tip to believe he was lying just as generously about this canyon as he had about all the other deeds and people he and this Sully had been jabbering about. Capturing rogues and killers indeed! Fighting wild Indians, his foot! They were nothing but a pair of prevaricating tale-spinners.

Telling lies was a subject he knew something about.

"Tuck up, you two," Slocum said, and tossed his

remaining coffee onto the ground with a *splat*. "We're headin' back to town at dawn."

Sully followed suit, then stood up to a nearly monstrous height and stretched. It wasn't natural, a man being that tall. "Believe I'll give the nags a last check, Slocum," he said, and wandered down to the picket line.

Slocum stood up too, saying, "And I believe I'll make sure you two idiots don't try to kite out during the night."

Tip threw a look at Patrick, and his brother replied with a nod just before Slocum started tying Patrick's hands, too.

"Sorry to make you suffer for your brother's sins, boy," Slocum muttered as he snugged the knot, "but it can't be helped."

"I understand your predicament, sir," Tip heard Patrick say as Slocum tethered him to a stunted tree a few feet away. He watched as Slocum carried Patrick's bedding to him, and said, "Get some sleep, kid."

When Slocum looked over at him, Tip simply turned over and away from him.

"Fine," Slocum grumbled.

There came the sounds of a bedroll being laid out, a saddle being shifted, and a body easing down, trying to find comfort.

"Mr. Slocum?" Tip asked, still staring out into the stunted, foreign trees and the brush.

"What?"

"Did you . . . did you have your way with Fiona?"

There was an unbearable silence before Slocum said, "No, kid. Carmella's my gal."

Despite the fact that as far as Tip was concerned

Slocum was a liar and a rogue, he felt an odd sense of relief. Not enough that he'd meekly go back north in the morning, though. Not nearly enough to sway him from his errand.

He listened while Sully walked back up from the horses and settled down by the fire, waited for the men's breathing to settle into snores, and then he listened for the soft sound of his brother's pocket blade, working slowly on the ropes.

In another hour, Patrick would have worked his magic again, and they'd be shed of these two men. Let them tell their stories and be full of themselves in a barroom someplace distant. Let them pick on fellows who didn't have urgent missions to the south.

Let them go their way. If they didn't, by God, he'd see them dead.

7

Slocum woke the next morning with white pain knifing through his skull, and the first thing he thought was that he'd never, by God, drink again.

That is, until he remembered that he hadn't been drinking. An instant later, he realized his hands were bound behind him and that the Carnahan brothers were nowhere to be seen.

"Sono*fabitch*!" he swore while he thrashed.

A deep voice, fairly close behind him, said, "Good mornin', sunshine. Finally, goddammit."

"I suppose you think this is funny, don't you, Sully?" Slocum asked through clenched teeth as he struggled to roll over. Waking up was bad enough on any given day, what with old injuries and bones long busted and healed all waking up at different times, but waking up hog-tied and helpless—and being laughed at, however silently—was worse.

Except that once he got rolled over, he saw that Sully wasn't smiling, and that he was in a similar circumstance. Also, that the horses were gone. All of them.

"Sonofabitch!" he repeated.

"You gonna cuss all day, or do you have a knife on you somewhere?" Sully asked. "Those boys cleaned me out. They must've hit me with an anvil, the way my head feels." He shifted a bit, winced, and added, "When I catch up to those rotten little bastards, I am gonna put such a world of hurt on them that they'll wish they'd never left the home sod."

"Yeah, you and me both," muttered Slocum, and stuck out his leg. At least the boys hadn't tied their legs too. "Can you reach my boot? There's a blade stuck down in it."

"You sure? I'd hate to do a whole lot a wrigglin' and come up empty. Might make me testy, Slocum. You don't want to see me testy."

Slocum almost smiled, but not quite. He thumped his leg against the ground, and felt the knife's grip dig into the outside of his calf.

"It's there, all right," he said, and tried to keep the relief out of his voice. They'd gotten his guns and Sully's guns, and Sully's knife as well. Goddamn those little shitheels anyway! Being hanged for a couple of horse thieves was too kind a fate.

A half hour and a good bit of sawing later, both men were free and surveying the campsite. The Carnahans had left them their tack and a bit of food, but that was all. Having stomped the last bit of sleep and ache from his bones, Slocum grabbed his bridle, blanket, and saddlebags, and hefted his saddle over a shoulder.

Sully did the same, and without a word, they started out on foot, following the track of the horses.

Now, walking for a lengthy distance is not the strong suit of any man who lives in the saddle. His boots aren't built for it, and his calf and thigh muscles are trained for gripping a horse, not for bearing weight. He doesn't like it, not one bit, and Slocum and Sully were no exceptions. But when you plop a man down in the middle of nowhere and you take away his mount, that man has got to walk.

And walk they did. They walked for three hours, by the end of which time Slocum's calves were on fire, and his thighs not far behind. Although Sully must have been going through much the same thing, he didn't mention it. He was too busy carping about his reputation and what he was going to do with those damn-fool kids once they caught up with them.

It was all talk—well, mostly—and Slocum knew it, but if he had to listen one more goddamn time to Sully saying, "I'm gettin' too old for this shit!" he was going to take his life into his hands and slug Sully square in the nose.

After all, he was a couple of years old than Sully.

A little past noon, with heads pounding and legs cramping, they at last came to a place where the boys had stopped to rest. They found trampled weeds and crumbs from the last of the bread, the ham bone left to draw ants, and a cache of their weapons—minus Slocum's Colt, which didn't please Slocum one bit.

More importantly, however, they found that the boys had turned a couple of the horses loose, probably so that they could make better time. Sully, who pulled out his spyglass, picked them out first, lipping at the sparse brush down the valley.

"Sawed-off peckerwoods did one thing right," he said as he collapsed it and stuck it back in his saddlebag. "They left us Old Scratch and your mare." He stuck two fingers in his mouth and whistled, two long and two short. "You'll have those guns back by nightfall."

Slocum whistled too, then sat down in a grateful heap while he waited for the horses to slowly amble their way toward them.

Sully remained standing. "Course, you could just write off the loss," he said as he watched the horses' progress. "I'd think about it if I were you. Those kids are more trouble than they're worth, if you ask me."

"Don't recall posin' the question, Sully," Slocum said. He was rubbing his calves, both of which seemed to have seized up at the exact same moment. "Besides, you're forgetting those nags they're ridin'."

Sully nodded. "Your investment."

"Yup."

Just then the horses wandered up over the hill. Old Scratch was arching his neck at Cheyenne and generally making a fool of himself. Cheyenne's head lashed out at him, and she snapped, clicking her teeth on nothing but air. Slocum figured it had been going on for some time like this—the gelding talking sweet to her, and her telling him in no uncertain terms to get lost. She wasn't anywhere near in season, but that damned horse of Sully's would try to breed a swamp log if he could get it to hold still long enough.

Slocum whistled softly to the mare, and she broke into a trot. She was glad to see him.

He went to stand up, but his legs weren't having any of it. He said, "Shit. Gimme a hand, Sully." The big man stuck down a paw-sized mitt and hauled him to his feet.

"You shouldn't've sat down," Sully said brightly as he bridled Old Scratch with a dull *clank* of bit on teeth.

"Oh, shut up," Slocum growled, and started tacking up his mare.

• • •

"Jaysus, Mary, and Joseph," breathed Patrick.

"You already said that," whispered Tip.

They didn't look at each other as they spoke. Their eyes, wide and staring, were transfixed by the impossibly immense chasm that lay before them.

Dressed in the colors and shadows of afternoon, striated hummocks and soaring rocks jutted from the canyon's floor, which had to be, Tip thought, a good mile straight down. Blue shadows going to purple lurked here and there, teasing around rocks, sending dark fingers into chasms. Rock layered in red and yellow and white and beige, dotted with green, reminded him of some gargantuan version of his mother's fancy tortes, the eight-and twelve-layer ones she made for special holidays. Standing on the rim and gazing down on to the distant floor of it, he felt very big and very small all at the same time.

It's what God must feel like, he thought. *What he must feel like when he looks down at the earth.*

"The other rim's got to be miles off," said Patrick, and his tone was awed, yet hopeless. "I've never seen anythin' so enormous in all me born days, Tip. Never seen anythin' quite so grand either. Faith," he whispered, and slapped a hand over his heart. "I could die right now a man fulfilled, for I've seen everything."

"Don't die yet, Patrick," said Tip. "I'll wager there are a few more things you'll be needin' to experience before you're fulfilled all the way." He turned and walked back toward the horses, and after a moment, his brother followed him.

"Well, we'll be goin' back up to Carson City then," Patrick said, and his voice carried equal parts relief and resignation. "We can always be sneakin' these horses into their stalls in the middle of the night and scuttle our way out of town. Nobody'll be the wiser, and then they can't go callin' us horse thieves, can they? But first, we've got to get some sleep. I swear, Tip, I'm so tired that I'm about to keel over right here. We haven't had our heads down but two hours in the past two days."

"Stop your exaggeratin'," Tip said wearily. "It's been closer to three hours." He fiddled with his reins while he thought, which was becoming harder all the time. He couldn't seem to get his brain's attention.

He managed it, though, by digging grimy nails into the palm of his hand, and said, "No, brother, I think we'll just follow this monstrous big ditch along for a while."

Patrick's brows shot up. "What? Are ye daft?"

Tip sighed. "Maybe yes, maybe no. But I'm thinkin' there has to be some kind of way down. An animal trail, or some natural way."

Patrick looked ready to cry. "But Tipper! What if there isn't? What if we have to travel all the way to Missouri, wherever that is? Da'll surely be dead and buried if he isn't already! Mr. Slocum said—"

"Mr. Slocum's a bold liar, and so's that heathen, black-skinned friend of his. They were havin' you on."

Patrick gave a slow shake to his head. "I don't think so, Tip. I think we ought to be turnin' around. Maybe we could follow this canyon, but let's follow it back west. The ground's got to come together someplace. It can't go all the way to the bleedin' Pacific Ocean!"

Tip gathered his reins. "Perhaps it can't, Patrick, but you're forgettin' something."

"What's that?"

"Your friend Slocum's back there, and that big African bastard too, if I'm not missin' my guess."

Tip flailed his legs into the tired gray, and after a moment it started moving east, following the rim.

He didn't need to check over his shoulder. He knew Patrick was coming too.

Dusk found Slocum and Sully still riding slowly along the north rim of the canyon. Each time Slocum saw it, he was impressed all over again. It was so huge that it was almost beyond description, and now, cloaked in deep shadows, its depths had gone to indigos and violets and deep blues and purples as far as the eye could see.

It was a picture that no man could ever truly capture on canvas, the one singular earthly feature for which, he was certain, the word "grandeur" had been invented.

Despite what he'd told the boys, he knew there were ways to get down to the bottom of it, and ways to get back up again, if only a man knew where to look. Indians, the occasional white man, and countless animals had been doing it since time immemorial. But still, he hoped that those idiots wouldn't try it. He figured they were too dumb and too green to know a path down when they saw it anyway.

There were a whole world of things he'd rather do than skitter endlessly toward the canyon's floor, praying that Cheyenne wouldn't make a misstep. There were plenty of places where a single hoof—placed the wrong way on a steep incline covered in the most unsure of footings—could ruin a man's day.

Slocum and Sully hadn't spoken for more than an

hour, and darkness was falling fast. Although night would take longer to find them up on the rim, it would be only a few more moments before shadow would overtake the depths of the canyon entirely. The black at its bottom would begin to rise up at them like dark water filling up the world's biggest well.

"Why the hell are these peckerwoods going east anyway?" Sully suddenly asked, and Slocum jumped in spite of himself.

"Because they're peckerwoods," Slocum said sullenly. The canyon was filling up with shadows, all right. He could no longer see even a scrap of its floor. Rocks rose up from it as if from a bottomless, black, and endless sea.

And then he reined in Cheyenne. Sully nearly rode into her back end, whose proximity got Old Scratch all excited. It took Sully a minute to convince him not to do anything stupid.

"Goddamn, you're a bonehead sometimes!" he hissed, and reached out an arm to swat at the horse's ears.

Slocum had his spyglass out by this time. He hadn't been seeing things. There it was, a tiny flicker in the blackness.

Once Sully had Old Scratch settled down, he'd aped Slocum, and was staring through his own glass. "Might be Indians," he said, his voice rumbling. "Might be a rock-breaker."

"Might not," replied Slocum. He closed his spyglass down with a rapid *click*. "How they managed to get down there without breakin' their fool necks is beyond me. I'm gonna skin those little bastards."

"I'll help," said Sully.

As the light faded, they kept following the trail along the rim, and finally found the place where the boys had gone down. It was an old Indian path, Slocum thought, for when he left Cheyenne with Sully and climbed a few yards down on foot, it seemed to him that portions of the topmost part of the trail had been artificially carved into the ancient limestone.

He didn't go more than a few yards, though. To have ventured further in the gloom would have been suicide.

And so they made camp. They picked a place well back from the rim and built a small fire, and as Sully whipped up some dinner and Slocum tended the horses, he was thinking about Carmella—and how much nicer it would have been to be having supper served in her bedroom, possibly on her bare backside.

But no, he had to go and make a stupid promise, didn't he? And here he was, out in the middle of nowhere, his legs still aching from that goddamn walk he'd taken this morning, and he had a goose egg on the back of his skull that he was pretty sure made his hat ride funny. Sully had given them both some powder for the pain, but it was wearing off.

"Just you wait," Slocum muttered toward the canyon and the far-off boys. "Just you wait till I get my hands on you. . . ."

He staked the horses well apart, lest Old Scratch get any more ideas about breeding his mare. He watered and fed and rubbed them down, and by the time he ambled back to the fire, Sully had biscuits and flour gravy waiting for him.

"Boys didn't leave any meat except the jerky," he said as he handed Slocum a plate. "Which, as you will recall, we ate the last of around noon. We're gonna have to start shooting game tomorrow."

Around a mouthful of food, Slocum said, "Hope you don't mind me tellin' you that this is pretty damn bad, Sully. Tastes like hot wallpaper paste."

"Beggars can't be choosers," Sully replied, and took a bite of his own. He made a face. "Christ Almighty." He reached into the bag at his side, mumbling, "Maybe some more pepper . . ."

They passed the salt and pepper, and Slocum couldn't tell that it made much difference. But he was hungry, and the biscuits and gravy at least filled the hole in his belly. Sully finished first, scrubbed his plate clean with a handful of sand, and set it aside. "Least the coffee's decent," he muttered as he poured himself a second cup.

He took a sip, and leaned back. "Believe I'll be sayin' good-bye tomorrow, once you throw a rope on those two numskulls."

Slocum arched a brow. He'd sort of hate to see Sully go, but the man likely had business to attend to, and plenty of it. Sully Washington made himself a real good living bringing in badmen, and you didn't do that sitting on your backside.

Slocum said, "Suppose you've got a fistful of paper. Appreciate your keepin' my company as long as you have. Who's next on your list?"

Sully smiled wide, showing white, even teeth. "Oh, I've got several to pick from. Wendell Pugh is supposed to be down in Arizona."

"Wendell Pugh?"

Sully nodded. "Killed a man over in Santa Fe. He's runnin' with a fellow named Bob Token, who did the same in Texas. Figure to kill two birds with one stone, as it were. Bob's poster says dead or alive, and the authorities don't care one way or the other about Wendell either."

Slocum knew just exactly how those boys were going back to Texas and New Mexico respectively—over the backs of their horses. They'd likely be pretty ripe and falling to pieces by the time Sully got them there too. He deserved every dollar he made.

"Thought I might make another stab at pickin' up Paolo Martinez while I'm down there too," Sully continued.

Slocum's head came up. "You goin' after him all on your lonesome?" he asked, and when Sully nodded, he added, "That's crazy!"

Sully laughed, deep and booming, and the sound of it was eerie. Even the coyote who'd been creeping closer—and who was just sneaking into Slocum's rock-tossing range—spooked and slunk away at a fast trot.

"Aw, you'll never find that bastard," Slocum said, and set aside the rock with no small degree of disappointment.

Sully cocked his head. "Oh, you never know, Slocum. I got a tip that he was holed up down at Pima Wells."

Slocum reached for the coffeepot. "Don't mean shit. He moves about every five minutes, I heard."

Sully shrugged. "Same tip said that old Paolo broke both his legs. Sonofabitch got drunk as a skunk and fell off somebody's roof. I don't think he's gonna be moving for some time. And if he does, it won't be far."

"A couple of busted legs won't stop him," Slocum insisted.

"It will when he's got a girl in Pima Wells," Sully said. How the hell did he know these things anyway?

"I figure," Sully continued, "that Paolo's evaded the arm of the law for so long that he thinks he's immune. He's gotten sloppy of late, and cocky on top of it. I heard that he even wrote a letter to the territorial governor, braggin' about taking that Army payroll down in Tucson last month."

It didn't sound a bit like Paolo Martinez to Slocum. The man was a killer, not to mention a thief, and he'd always been a slippery sonofabitch. His gang consisted of anywhere from seven to fifteen compatriots, depending on who was telling the story, and they were on the constant move. It was how Paolo Martinez had managed to evade the law for the last eight years. Slocum couldn't see him changing now, and he said as much.

"Well, men sometimes get soft through the years," Sully replied, then corrected himself. "Not soft so much as careless, I reckon, which comes from not getting caught. They start to think they're supernatural. It's Paolo's turn. Besides, I heard that he's come under some new influences of late."

Slocum scowled. "For instance?"

"Not sure. Might have hooked up with another gang. The grapevine's pretty quiet about that. Jumpy too. But he's surely changing his methods." Sully drained his coffee cup and stretched out on his blanket. "Either way, sooner or later, that old Mexican bandit's gonna be money in my bank account."

8

Slocum and Sully were up at dawn, saddled by a quarter to six, and by one-thirty they had skittered precariously down the long canyon wall.

This wasn't as easy as might be imagined. It was nearly a mile straight down, but the trail, which looped back and forth, sometimes gentle and wide enough that it could have accommodated two horses riding abreast at a soft downward slant, was nearly seven miles long. Often, it descended in a steep incline that had the men clinging to their saddle horns, leaning hard toward the left or the right, and swearing. Sometimes they had to dismount and coax their nervous mounts down suicidal slides, while the loose rock their boots and horseshoes dislodged bounced down sickly and disappeared into the abyss.

"Christ," muttered Slocum once they finally reached the bottom. He swung down off Cheyenne and began checking her for rock cuts. She'd come down one slide on her haunches. "I'm not gonna go through that again if I can help it. The south rim's got better trails."

He opened his saddlebags and found a tin of salve, which he proceeded to apply to the two small gouges he found on her hide. That the boys had managed to get down to the canyon floor in one piece was a pure miracle. Every few feet he'd expected to see one of their horses—one of *his* horses, by rights, until he got them back to Jessup—lying dead, with an Irish pup in the same condition lying next to it.

"Salve?"

Slocum looked up to find Sully holding out a hand. He wiggled his fingers, and Slocum tossed him the tin.

"Picked up a nice gash on his hock," Sully explained as he went back to the gelding. "Those damn kids have got the angels on their side. That's all I can figure."

"More like the devil himself," Slocum replied. It had been coolish up top, cool enough that he'd started the journey down with a jacket, cursing that it wasn't heavy enough to keep him warm. Now he peeled it off and rolled up the sleeves of his sweat-soaked shirt. It had to be at least a hundred degrees down here, maybe more.

He'd hate to be stuck in this canyon come June. Or July or August.

"Any water left?" he asked Sully.

"Not unless you've got a couple canteens you haven't told me about," came the reply. He tossed over the salve tin in a gentle arc, and Slocum caught it and snapped the lid in place. "We'll come on the river before too long."

"Hope we don't have to strain it for mud," Slocum grumbled. Down here, the Colorado was brown and muddy about three quarters of the time, maybe more. Unless it was flooding, of course, which it did with disconcerting frequency, and on a schedule that Slocum had never figured out. Those times, the river was pure, roiling filth.

For millennia, the Colorado's wandering waters had

cut this canyon, cut it right out of the living rock. A long time back, maybe fifteen years, Slocum had weathered a flood down here. He'd lost his good Appy gelding, Traveler, and nearly lost his life too. He didn't want to be anywhere in the vicinity if the river decided to take another whittle at the stone walls.

"I wanna get up and out of here as quick as possible, goddammit," he groused. "I've had it with this wild-goose chase."

Sully had already mounted up again. From the lofty height of Old Scratch's back, he leaned back and hiked his eyebrows. Grinning, he intoned, "Bitch, bitch, bitch."

Slocum swung into the saddle. "Hang it all, Sully, that's real easy for you to say. Hell, when you bring in your man, you actually get paid cash money for him. I got two'a these jackasses to bring in, and I'm losin' money on the deal."

Not to mention time with Carmella, he thought.

Sully laughed, blast his hide. "Well, what's life without a little adventure, Slocum?"

Having crossed the vast expanse of the canyon floor, Tip and Patrick trudged beneath a blasting sun, searching for a way up and out. They weren't having much luck. Tip led the limping gray, and Patrick, astride the bay, Orion, kept pace.

Tip had taken a tumble about halfway down the last slide, and Patrick told him it was a miracle that both he and the horse hadn't been killed.

He didn't need his brother to tell him that. He'd been reciting Our Fathers in triple time for the whole of the time he was flying through the air. It had seemed like hours when it was happening, but Patrick had said it had only taken half a second. Funny, that.

The horse had done something to its leg—Tip couldn't recall exactly what Patrick had said it was, but he'd said it wasn't broken. Tip remembered that part anyway. He himself wasn't in much better shape, having landed on his shoulder and given it an excruciating wrench. He was fairly well bruised too, although his heavy jacket, which was now tied behind the gray's saddle, had saved him from major bodily damage.

"We're never goin' to get out of here," Patrick said for perhaps the twentieth time. "We're never goin' to get to Da. We'll be roasted to death in this inhospitable place if we don't starve first, and not a soul will know it or find our poor bones."

"For the love'a Christ, Patrick, stop singin' that tired song," Tip snapped. "I'm tellin' you, I'm goin' to get us out. I'm the one on foot, am I not? I'm the one with the terrible torn-up arm. Do ye hear me complainin'?"

Patrick's features bunched indignantly. "Not till now," he said. "Although you were doin' your share of it last night."

Tip stopped walking and faced his brother. "Patrick, who held your head when we had that bad patch of sea coming round the Horn and there you were, pulin' and pukin' to beat the band? Who yanked you into the alley right from under the copper's nose before we sailed from Tralee? When we were on the Barbary Coast, who crowned that fearful Hawaiian hooligan when he was about to go knockin' you silly? I could keep listin' 'em, Pat. Don't ye trust me after all that?"

Patrick didn't answer for a terrible moment, but then

he said, "Course I do, Pat. But then, I'm thinkin', who got me into this mess in the first place? Could've been Da, with that daft letter of his. But I'm thinkin' it was mostly an excuse. 'Twas mostly you, wasn't it, Tipper? You were runnin' so fearful of Moira's father that you ran clear across the sea and took me for company."

There it was, out in the open at last. How many miles had they crossed, by sea or by foot or by horse? And this was the first time Patrick had mentioned the why of it.

Slowly, Tip said, "That must have been weighin' on you somethin' fierce, Patrick. For your information, 'twasn't Moira Banyan at all, nor her father. Ours either, I suppose," he admitted.

"Finally," said Patrick, and his shoulders sank. "Why'd ye do it, Tipper? Why'd you drag me from me bed in the middle of the night to die in this terrible place? Jaysus, Mary, and Joseph, I'm about to cook in me clothes! If I'm about to die, you've got to tell me, Tip. What ran you from home?"

Tip almost said it out, nearly confessed. But he couldn't. It was too terrible. So he said, "There was some trouble at Murphy's Tavern, that's all. And we're not goin' to die. I'm goin' to find us a splendid trail any minute now, and—"

"Trouble at Murphy's?" Patrick shouted. "Are ye daft? We left kith and kin and everything that was sweet because you owed Murphy for a bleedin' pint or two? Because you got into fisticuffs with a surly patron? Jaysus, Tip, what'd you do? Toss a rock through his bleedin' window again?"

Patrick stopped for a moment and closed his eyes, but before Tip could get a word in edgewise, Pat was off again. "Da's letter had been sittin' there for near two weeks, read and ignored, when you came home with a fire lit under you and said it was tonight or never. I thought sure it was Moira, thought sure you'd got her in a family way. I thought you were afraid of her father takin' out after you with his ax. And now you tell me it was a little trouble at Murphy's!"

"Patrick . . ."

"Don't hinder me now, Tip, I've a head of steam," Patrick spat. "Was there no good reason why we robbed that poor man on the docks?"

Tip scowled and tilted his head. "He wasn't poor, Pat," he said indignantly. "He had fifty-six pounds in his purse!"

"That's neither here nor there. And you wouldn't have had to pull me into that alley if he hadn't got up and screamed for the coppers. Was there no good reason why we had to work our way over on the *Derry Breeze,* lyin' like a couple of parlor rugs about how we were such fine, experienced seamen?"

Tip drew himself up. "I'd been on fishin' boats."

"The two-oar kind!" snapped Patrick. "That's a different thing entirely. I was fair dizzy with fakin' it for weeks!" Tip had never seen him in such a mood. "And stop interruptin' me," Patrick went on angrily. "Why'd we work so hard in Boston Town, savin' and scrimpin' with hardly a cent left for bread for our bellies? Why'd we undertake that perilous journey round the Horn?"

"Well, by then we *were* experienced seamen," Tip offered.

Patrick threw up his hands. "You're missin' the point, brother, darlin'. Why in the name of Sweet Christ did we do all those things and more, when all the time you were just runnin' from some small trouble at Murphy's? When you thought all along that Da was dead?"

Tip inhaled sharply. "I never thought he was dead!" he hissed. "Never! Shame on you, Patrick! Shame on you for thinkin' it, let alone sayin' it."

"I've said it before."

"Aye, but ye weren't so terrible serious. Our da's alive. I feel it in me bones. If you don't," he added imperiously, with hands propped on his bony hips, "you can just take yourself on back. I'm not much carin' at this juncture. Just hand over what ransom money you're carryin', and I'll be on my way."

Patrick just sat his horse, his arms folded, staring down at Tip. Tip stared back. It was a standoff if ever there was one, but they were two stubborn lads from a stubborn family, born of a stubborn race.

Just when it seemed that neither of them would give in, and that Tip would die of old age or heat prostration in that selfsame spot, Patrick suddenly said, "I'll be walkin' for a while. You take Orion." And he got off the horse.

Tip knew better than to pick at things when he was getting his way, so he simply nodded, said, "Aye," and changed places with his brother.

Patrick set out ahead of him, leading the gray. Over his shoulder, he said, "It's gettin' late, and this canyon'll be thick with shadows inside of two hours, if yesterday was any clue. Five more miles, that's all I'm goin', Tipper. If we haven't found a trail, it's back to the other side for me. Trouble at Murphy's, my arse!"

Tip didn't answer. He just rode along behind in grim but grateful silence.

They hadn't gone three miles when he spied a twisting, whipstitch path that looked like it would take them all the way up.

The river was clean and clear on this occasion, and Slocum and Sully filled everything that would hold water before they cantered off along the boys' trail. This was fairly simple, as the Carnahans were doing nothing to obscure it, and for the most part, the canyon floor was amenable to holding a track.

For a place as sere and unwelcoming as the canyon floor, there seemed to be abundant wildlife. Their cantering horses sprang several jackrabbits from their hiding places. Slocum caught a glimpse of a coyote peering from its rock den, and he spotted a small herd of wild burros—the descendants of burros long ago abandoned by solitary rock-breakers—in the distance.

There was a puma track too. It appeared several times on top of the boys' tracks, sometimes following along for a couple hundred yards, sometimes veering off again, only to reappear. It had Slocum worried, but that was the least of it.

One of the boys was leading a horse, and they were moving slow. Slocum hoped that they hadn't banged up the horse so much that Jessup wouldn't pay for it.

And he hoped it wasn't the gray gelding, Flannel. He'd actually managed to bring back a fairly decent rein on the horse in the time it had taken him to overtake the kids. He figured old Flannel must have had some training at one time or another, and might have even been a pretty fair cow pony. His owner must have fallen on hard times to let him go. At least, it was the only way Slocum could figure an almost decent mount like that would end up as a rental horse.

He was thinking about this and a number of other things when Sully, who was riding just ahead, pointed up and called out, "Here!"

Slocum rode up to the place where Sully had stopped. The Carnahans had headed up this way, all right. The trail started on a steep angle before it disappeared from sight. But it was coming dark, and the question on the table was whether they should ride up and try to beat the night, or stay down here and wait until morning.

Sully frowned at him. "I said, this is the place."

Slocum stared up. "Yup."

Sully rolled his eyes. "I swear, Slocum, you're about as excitable as a rock. The next time I track some no-payout boys across this canyon, I'm gonna take along a fellow who has a little zest for conversation."

Slocum eyed the trail. It was man-made too, but no men, save the two he was tracking, had used it for a long time. The rounded pad prints of the cougar overlaid their tracks and those of several burros, although the latter were probably three or four days old. He could see only the first part of the path, but the boys' tracks hadn't come down again, so they must have gotten all the way up.

Well, there was no time like the present.

He reined Cheyenne past Old Scratch, pointed her at the steep incline, and grabbing the saddle horn, fanned his hat across her rump. She sprang ahead, scrambling up the first thirty feet until she came to a place with better footing. It was only the first increment in what promised to be a very long haul.

Behind him on the canyon floor, he heard Sully boom up a laugh, then say, "Now, that's more like it, you sonofabitch! Here I come!"

Shadows chased them all the way up as they zigzagged ever higher, and the canyon beneath them was a vast, black velvet pool by the time they climbed out of it. The safety of the south rim, where they dismounted at last to rest the horses, was deep in the shadows of dusk.

Slocum had been right about the relative ease of traversing the trails on the south side of the canyon—this one anyway—but he'd be damned if he'd do it again voluntarily. There were a whole lot of easier ways to get across the Colorado River.

The meter of her gait, telegraphed through his backside, had told him that Cheyenne was all right while he was riding her, but once he got off he felt her legs anyway. He couldn't see too well, but his fingers didn't find any gaping wounds. Sully seemed satisfied with Old Scratch's condition too.

"Wish that old moon would hurry and come out from behind the clouds again," Sully said as they watered the horses. "I do believe it's bright enough that we could track another two, maybe three hours before I keel over from lack of vittles. We might just catch up with them."

"Yup," said Slocum.

Sully leaned an arm across Old Scratch's saddle. At the moment, it was dark enough that about all that showed above that pale blue pirate shirt was eyes and teeth. Sarcastically, Sully said, "Listen, Slocum, if you don't stop being so goddamned loquacious, I'm gonna have to cut you loose. Talk, talk, talk, that's all I get outta you."

Slocum grunted.

"See what I mean? Why, a fellow can hardly get a word in edgewise!"

In truth, when Slocum hadn't been concentrating on navigating the uneven trail or keeping his balance (or trying to avoid sliding off Cheyenne's backside on the steep parts), he'd been thinking about those cougar tracks. The cat was following the boys, all right. Although Patrick and Tip had been incredibly lucky so far, he doubted that all the shamrocks in the world would dissuade a hungry mountain lion.

He tightened his girth again just as the moon slipped free of its cloudy cover, and swung up into the saddle with a squeak of leather.

"Let's go," he said.

Sully shook his head in a slow complaint. "Talk, talk, talk," he said with a straight face. "When's it gonna end?"

9

"Don't move!" Tip hissed. Their horses were long gone, thundering out into the brush. They had gone wild-eyed for no apparent reason, and bolted into the darkness. Shocked, the boys had just leapt to their feet when they heard the cat's first heart-stopping screech.

Now they stood, quaking, on either side of the little fire they had built amidst the boulders, twisting their heads like owls and searching in vain for some sign of their tormentor. Tip didn't know about Patrick, but he was shaking so hard that his teeth were rattling.

"Is it a b-banshee, Tip?" Patrick croaked, and his words came out in a fog on the chilled night air.

"A lion, I'll wager," Tip whispered. He heartily wished he'd brought the guns from his saddlebag when he'd retrieved his jacket. Not that he could have hit the bitch of a beast, but the sound might have scared it away. "Maybe a leopard."

The cat screamed again, and it sounded like something come up from hell. It was close enough that Tip felt the sound as much as heard it. Every hair on his body was standing on end. Why didn't it just come in and have its way with them? Was it toying with them like a barn cat with a mouse? He had absolutely no idea what to do.

93

But Patrick did.

"Open your coat, Tipper," he breathed as he edged closer.

This struck Tip as being so ludicrous that, for a half second, he forgot to be scared. "And give the bleedin' thing an easier path to me vitals?"

"Open it, I'm tellin' you!" came Patrick's whisper. "Hold it wide! We'll look bigger."

By this time, Patrick had moved slowly to Tip's side of the fire, and the boys stood arm-to-arm, jackets held wide, waiting, holding their breaths.

This was all his fault, Tip thought in a rush. His fault they'd left home, his fault they'd nearly gotten themselves killed countless times on sea and on land, and this time it looked like there was no escape. Their luck was up. There were no alleys to duck into, no firewood to club a fellow with (save what was already burning), and no fellow at all, just a mindless wild beast. Patrick had been right all along.

I'm even too dense to have brought the pistol to where I could get at it, Tip thought, and wanted to die. Well, he would soon enough.

When the cat, invisible in the darkness, shifted and a pebble bounced down from the boulders above, Tip nearly wet his britches.

"Maybe it's goin' away," Patrick hissed hopefully, and then, suddenly, he gave a shout and flapped his arms.

Tip jumped back involuntarily, letting his jacket fall closed and yelling, "What are you doin', you daft bugger?"

And in the time it took him to get the sentence out, the monster leapt into the ring of firelight, sailing straight over Patrick—who ducked with a thin shriek and hit the ground—and right for Tip.

The second it took the cat to spring at him seemed hours long. He couldn't move. There was a blur of teeth and claws, mingled with pictures of his life as it flashed before his eyes, and the stench of the beast itself. He felt his poor bladder give way just as the heavens thundered so loud that he thought his ears would burst, and then the beast was upon him.

Its weight thudded into him, knocked him sailing. He went down screaming, one arm over his face and the other held out straight, as if he thought he could fend off those terrible claws and fangs by the force of his bare hand. And when he landed, the weight of the beast knocked all the air out of his lungs.

But the animal didn't rip at his throat or tear at his innards. Instead, it shuddered once, made a small, mewling sound, and went still.

Air flooded back into his lungs, and with it, the foul stink of the beast. Mindless relief coursed through him, followed directly by the realization of the horror of what might have been. This last was too much for him to handle. To the distant sound of Patrick shouting, "Tip! Tip!" his eyes rolled back in his head, and he passed out.

Slocum rode into the firelight a few seconds later, his rifle still out and ready.

Sully, right behind him, drawled, "Dead?"

Slocum dismounted and gave the cat a nudge with his toe. "As a doornail," he replied. He reached down, grabbed the lifeless puma by the scruff of its neck, and dragged it off to the side. A quick drop to his knees and a scan of the boy's body told Slocum that Tip was unhurt. He raised his face to Patrick. The boy lay panting on the ground, tears staining his freckled face.

"Get some water," Slocum said.

"Suppose I should round up their horses before they get all the way down to Prescott," he heard Sully say as a trembling Patrick crawled forward and handed him a canteen.

"W-will he live, sir?" Patrick asked in a whisper. Brusquely, he scrubbed at his face with his fists.

Slocum poured water on Tip's face, then slapped him. He came to in a sputter.

"Just long enough for me to kill him," Slocum replied through clenched teeth.

Patrick swallowed, his Adam's apple bobbing.

Tip, who was still caught in that never-never land of semiconsciousness—and was therefore still trying to avoid the cougar—immediately began to thrash and scramble.

Slocum was ready for it, though. He pressed his hands on the boy's shoulders and shouted, "It's dead, boy! You're all right!"

Well, not completely. The poor kid had soaked his britches. Slocum couldn't say that he blamed him.

Tip quieted down, but he leerily eyed the big cat's body. "Be ye sure, Mr. Slocum?" he said.

There was a little respect in the boy's voice at last, but Slocum knew he couldn't count on it remaining for long. He stood up, and there was nothing more he wanted than to pound the Carnahans into next week. They'd dragged him from Carmella's arms, dragged him clear across the goddamned Grand Canyon, and nearly gotten themselves—and him—killed. And even though Tip was meek at the moment, the minute he came back to himself all the way, he'd be just as mule-headed and jackass-stubborn as always.

Of this, Slocum had no doubt.

"Get up," he said.

Slowly, feeling at his body to make sure he was all still there, Tip did. When he felt his damp pants leg, he had the good grace to color deeply.

"Get changed," Slocum said. "You leave those pants on, they'll chafe at you."

Wordlessly, Tip took the canteen from Slocum and wandered back into the shadows.

"Jaysus," said Patrick, looking after him. To himself, he said, "If I hadn't just taken a piss, I would've done the same." Then he turned to Slocum and whispered, "He'll just be washing up a mite. We haven't a change of clothes."

"Uh-huh." Slocum pulled the saddle off his mare, who was eyeing the dead cougar with some trepidation. He could hear Sully out there in the distance, in the dark, slowly coming in with the horses.

"I didn't know ye had the lions in America," Patrick continued, although his conversation was somewhat strained. "I thought they were just on the African continent."

"It's a mountain lion," Slocum said. He dug out his brush and curry comb. "Puma. Catamount. Cougar."

"Which is it then?" asked Patrick.

Slocum began currying the mare's back. "All the same thing," he said. "Just depends on where you are. You used to see a jaguar around here every now and then too. Ain't seen one'a them for a lot of years, though. They're pretty much killed off."

"Ah," said Patrick, although he still sounded puzzled. He was trying not to cry too, Slocum knew. "I saw a lion once, in a travelin' carnival. Gypsies, y'know. 'Twas some bigger, and had a grand mane of hair all round its neck. But it wasn't nearly so fierce as this one."

"Might want to drag it off somewhere," Slocum grumbled. "Throw some dirt over it." He could hear Sully close by now, but he could also tell he was having some trouble with the horses. "Go on, Patrick. Get that cat-stink covered up, or the next time I'll let you chase down your own horses."

Patrick took the small folding shovel that Slocum held out and made it two steps away before he stopped and turned. "Your pardon, sir?" he said quietly.

Slocum had the brushes back in his hands, but he paused and propped an elbow on the mare's shoulder.

"Sir, I'm just wantin' to say thank you, thank you very kindly. After what me and Tip done, thievin' your mounts and all . . ." The boy's voice was breaking again, and he cleared his throat. "We're not deservin' of it. We're in your debt."

Slocum nodded in acknowledgment, then said, "Where's my guns?"

"Saddlebags, sir," Patrick said and pointed, and when Slocum didn't reply, only bent to their meager pile of belongings and started digging through them, he mumbled, "Right then." The shovel under one arm, he went to the cougar. After a few hesitant, abortive moves toward it, he finally grabbed hold of it and began dragging it away.

A moment later, Sully rode in. Old Scratch looked bored, but the two geldings trailing behind him on lead ropes were skittery as hell. It took both men to settle them down, although Slocum attributed their quieting more to the sound of a shovel working off in the dark—and the puma scent fading—than anything he and Sully said or did.

Besides various minor cuts and scrapes on both the horses' lower legs, Flannel had picked up a stone bruise, and Orion had a nice dig out of his off hip. Slocum brought out the tin of salve again and began smearing it on.

"Who's takin' care of the cat?" Sully asked. He was wearing his scuffed leather jacket, which had been dyed black—right down to the fringe—to match his pants and hat. Sometimes Slocum just wanted to slug him on general principles.

"Patrick's throwin' some dirt over him."

Sully sniffed. "Too bad. If there was more time, I would've liked to skin that cat out. It was a big one." He cast his glance about the little camp. "If Patrick's on shovel duty, where's the other half of the family?"

"Off," said Slocum. He figured he wouldn't tell Sully about the boy wetting himself. The kid didn't have much dignity left, after all.

Don't care what anybody says about me, Slocum thought with some degree of irritation as he put the salve away. *I've got a heart, goddammit.*

Tip had shucked his britches, rinsed them as well as he could, and thrust his shivering legs back inside. The wet part felt like ice in his crotch and all down his leg, but he steeled himself. He deserved to freeze. He deserved it if his testicles froze solid and snapped off.

He'd made up his mind. He was going to go back

out there and apologize to both Slocum and Sully, and then he'd apologize at greater length to Patrick. He'd probably be saying he was sorry for years.

They'd come a good long way, his brother and he, but it was far enough. That cat could have just as easily hit his younger brother as himself, and it had been miraculous indeed that Slocum had been there to shoot it.

And that he hadn't missed.

A shiver, completely unrelated to the cold in his britches, raced up Tip's spine.

"It's a fool you've been, Tipperary Carnahan," he muttered to himself. "Ye should've just stayed home. Left Da to his fate. And faced the music for what you did at Murphy's."

He'd always been too quick to scrap, always eager for a fight. Always pigheaded and hotheaded, which was a dangerous combination, and undoubtedly wasn't a thing you bragged on. But he supposed that he'd always been that way, and a man had to play the hand he was given.

Well, this hand had played out. He had no more cards left. What had been a lark for him in the past had now turned dark and dangerous—for his brother as well as himself. That was the most frightening part of it.

For a moment, he'd thought that he could go back with these men. He'd act the repentant sinner, and then he'd run out on them at the last minute, thus saving himself from the jailhouse. Fiona would take care of Patrick, after all. And Patrick still had half of what ransom money they'd been able to raise. He'd do fine.

But now he was thinking that if he was going to do

the right thing, he'd best do it all the way round. It wasn't the thing that Da would have chosen for him, not by a long shot. No, Da would have been prouder if he'd shot the both of these men and run off in the night, with Patrick in tow—and likely all the mens' belongings to boot.

But Da wasn't here. Da was down south someplace and likely long dead, though Tip was loath to admit it.

Da made his own bed, he thought. *Let him lie in it.*

He straightened his shoulders, stepped out from behind the rock, and looked toward their little camp. All three of them—Patrick, Slocum, and that Sully—were gathered about the fire. The horrible beast that had nearly killed and eaten them was nowhere in sight, and the horses calmly ground oats from their feedbags at the farthest reaches of the firelight.

It was almost a homey scene.

Tip wiped at his eyes. Whether it was abandoning Da—or maybe it was abandoning the dream of Da—after all this time, or finally facing up to what he himself had done . . . Well, that was of no importance. What was important was that he was going to do the right thing, the best thing. For Patrick as well as himself.

But when he strolled into the glow of the fire and sat next to Patrick, the mood was not what he had expected. He'd assumed that Slocum would read him the riot act for running off again, for thieving those horses and the guns—and for not thinking to keep them close to hand.

But Slocum was intent on a letter—the selfsame letter, worn and dirty from so many readings, that he and

Patrick had been carrying all the way from Ireland. Da's ransom demand.

"Shit," Slocum grumbled. He folded it up and fairly threw it back to Patrick, who, for some reason known only to God, was actually smiling.

Beside him, the great, black giant of a man was chuckling, and the short fringe on his black coat trembled with it. "Small world, isn't it, Slocum?" he said.

If he lived to be a hundred, Tip was sure he'd never get used to Sully Washington's voice. It was a wholly supernatural thing.

Tip whispered, "What is it?" to Patrick, and Patrick leaned toward him.

"It's Da, Tipper!" came the answer.

"Actually, it's Paolo Martinez," said Sully happily.

Tip scratched at his head. "I'm comin' in too late."

"The brigand Paolo Martinez is the one what took Da," Patrick explained, as if Tip were simple.

"Tell me somethin' I'm not already knowin', Pat."

"And Mr. Sully Washington here is on the trail of Paolo Martinez!" Patrick grinned from ear to ear. "Don't you see? We're all goin' together to save Da!"

10

"The hell we are!" Slocum snapped. He shook his fist at Patrick. "I'm gonna hog-tie you and your addlepated brother, and I'm gonna tote both your hides back up to Carson City. You got no business goin' after Paolo Martinez. Hell, if I'd known it was him you were trailin', I could've saved us all some time and shot you back up at Carmella's. A bullet's a bullet."

Flinching, the boy opened his mouth to speak, but Sully beat him to it. "Easy, Slocum," he said. "It's not such a bad idea. Why, these young lads have come halfway round the world to find their daddy. Doesn't seem right that you should deny them when they're this close."

Slocum snorted. "Stop takin' their side! You saw the date on that letter as clear as I did. It's almost a year and a half old. The only thing they're gonna find is a ghost."

The camp went suddenly silent. Patrick looked as if Slocum had squashed him flat as a bug, and Tip just stared at the ground.

Well, hell, it had to be said, didn't it? Somebody . had to have some sense!

But Sully was glaring at him.

"What?" Slocum cried. "You mean to tell me you

103

want these two jackasses in your way when you corner Paolo? Hell, Sully, you'll likely get them killed and yourself too. They can't shoot, for Christ's sake! They can't even sit a horse decent!"

"I can, sir," Patrick offered meekly, but Slocum ignored him.

"They don't know what the hell they're doin'," he railed. "They don't even own the damn nags they're ridin'!"

Quite suddenly, Sully grinned. "Why, Slocum," he said grandly, "you can be downright garrulous when you want to be."

Slocum stood up. He stared down at the three of them, saying, "Fine. Go right ahead. But me and Cheyenne and those two horses the kids are ridin' are goin' back up to Carson. Period."

He stomped out into the darkness and sat on a boulder, angrily rolling a quirlie. Damn them anyhow! It was a fine time for Sully to all of a sudden feel the urge for fatherhood, or whatever it was that had set him on this track. It'd be a pure miracle if they managed to cross the mountains alive and with no major bones busted, and then there'd be the desert to contend with.

Not to mention Paolo Martinez and about four thousand armed *bandidos*.

Was everybody crazy but him?

But by the time he'd finished the quirlie, he was pretty much resigned to the idea. Those boys had the scent deep in their noses now, and they'd likely get down south no matter what it took. And common sense to the contrary, he understood that. He could understand why a fellow would undertake a project when all signs told him he was sure to fail. He'd fought a war on the doomed side, hadn't he?

And about a thousand things since then.

He didn't know that Carmella would understand, let alone Fiona. He didn't know that he rightly understood the whole thing, only pieces of it. But he supposed he'd have to go along with them.

Dammit.

For days, they traveled a roundabout path through the mountains, heading generally southward. Once Flannel was healed and fit to ride, which took a few days, they made better time. But not much, for the boys were green and the going was slow. They slapped at bugs, cursed low-hanging pine boughs (which swept poor Patrick from the saddle more times than Slocum could count), led the horses half the time, and skittered up and down slides of shale or mud or crumbling granite.

Sully took pity on the boys, and taught them to shoot, using his rifle. Inside a week, Patrick had shot a squirrel, although it was more luck than anything else. Still, he was proud, and put together a squirrel stew for them that night; he turned out to be a pretty fair trail cook.

Tip was nipping off the ends of distant branches, and had brought down his first deer. Slocum and Sully agreed—although not in front of the boy—that he was a natural with a firearm.

Patrick could indeed ride, Slocum grudgingly noted, and was actually a great help with the horses. He didn't exactly look at home in the stock saddle he was using, and for a while the slapping tree branches had him on the ground nearly as often as on Orion. But once Slocum figured out that Tip was shoving the branches out of the way—and then letting them swing back full force—instead of lifting them and going under, he put Tip to riding drag. Patrick never got smacked from the saddle again.

By the time they were almost down out of the last of the foothills and ready to stop and pick up more provisions, the boys had developed something of a sense of ease with their adopted country. Or they had, at least, come to some sort of truce with it.

Slocum let them feel a little cocky. The desert would take that out of them without any help from him.

He bypassed the town of Prescott completely. The town was too big and swarming, and operated twenty-four hours a day. There were too many ways a couple of green kids—especially these two—could get into trouble. Slocum had seen enough trouble in the last couple of weeks to last him a long time.

Instead, they pulled into Dirty Dog, a town that boasted two saloons, one whorehouse, a mercantile, a feed store, and little else, save for a small, broken-down hotel, with a seedy restaurant attached, and an assay office.

"This is a town?" Patrick asked when they rode in. He scratched beneath his floppy cap and stared at the yellow and white bitch asleep in the middle of the rutted path that passed for a main street.

"I'm not carin'," said Tip, "so long as they've got an eatin' place that serves anythin' beyond venison."

Since Tip had shot that buck, they'd been eating venison stew and venison steak and venison pie until they were all sick of it. Slocum nodded his head in agreement.

Sully and Slocum had hammered it into the boys that they were to make no mention, while they were in town, of Paolo Martinez—or their father. Neither were they, by word or act, to get themselves into any trouble whatsoever. The last thing Slocum needed was Patrick breaking Tip out of yet another jail by knocking some lawman cold. Of course, Dirty Dog had neither a jail nor a sheriff, but Slocum figured that was beside the point.

After they got a room in the hotel and turned their horses loose in the pen behind it, Sully and the boys set off for the mercantile, list in hand. Slocum, however, went straight to the whorehouse.

It wasn't much. When he walked into the parlor, he found it deserted, although he heard springs squeaking away in the back room.

"Anybody to home?" he called hopefully.

The springs kept on squeaking, but a little blonde poked her head out from behind another door. She was dressed in her underwear, and had her hair loosely piled up on top of her head in a riot of untamed, honey-colored curls. Her green eyes twinkling, she smiled at him. Dimples sank into her cheeks.

"Howdy," she said. "You lookin' for a good time, handsome?"

"Been on the trail for over a week," he said, and his mouth crooked up in a smile. Dirty Dog had come up in the world if it could boast whores as pretty as this one. "What do you think?"

She sashayed out into the parlor and took his hat. Toying with the brim, she said, "Well, you got Little Fawn. She's half Navajo and real purty. She's with a feller right now, but she oughta be done any time. It's

Bob Billings, and he never stays for more'n one ride. Or you got Cherry. She just run up the street, but she'll be back any minute now. Or," she added, trailing a finger over his jaw, "you got me. I'm Tillie."

He put his hands on her shoulders and skimmed them down her arms. "You'll do fine, Tillie."

She smiled wide, exposing small, straight, white teeth. "Suits me fine." She took his hand and led him back through the door, down a short, dim hall, and into a small bedroom fitted with nothing but a cot, a crude washstand, and a curtainless window covered in soap.

She slipped the pins from her hair, saying, "No cornholin', no askin' me to put my mouth where the Good Lord didn't intend it to go, and no rough stuff, okay?"

She was so tiny, yet so businesslike, that Slocum grinned. "Oh, yes, ma'am," he said.

Her hair fell down around her shoulders in a riot of golden curls, and she pulled off her camisole. Her skin was pale, and her breasts were small and high. They looked to him to be as firm and round as a pair of pippins. Centered in pale pink nipples, the tips had tightened in the chilly air the moment she lifted her top.

"It's a buck a go," she said, pausing. "That okay with you, mister?"

He was hard already. He dug into his pocket and pulled out two dollars. He said, "Start me a tab."

Tillie didn't have much imagination, but after the first time, after he'd made her explode with an earth-shattering orgasm, she panted, "Jesus, mister!"

She didn't look a bit unhappy. Actually, she looked like he'd just told her there was going to be an extra Christmas this year.

Slocum was feeling a good bit better too. He'd been starved for female company for so long that he was about to burst. Which, come to think of it, he just had.

He fingered one shell-colored nipple, and she made a tiny sound.

"You paid for twice," she said almost shyly, which was quite a trick for a naked whore lying spraddle-legged and half underneath him. "You think . . . you think maybe you'll want to go again pretty soon?"

He chuckled and bent his head, sucking a nipple into his mouth. He hadn't taken much time to fool around with her before, that was how great his need was. But now he began to suckle her in earnest. She was firm, all right, tight everywhere. If he'd opened his mouth all the way up, he thought he might just be able to get her whole breast into it. He rolled the nipple between his teeth, and heard her breathe, "Oh, mister!"

With a hand on one breast and his mouth busy with the other, he ran his other hand slowly up and down her body, stroking her, teasing her, and at last dipped it between her coltish legs. Expertly, he began to pet her, to play with her, and she squirmed beneath him on the coarse sheets.

"Please," she whimpered, her eyes closed, her neck straining.

He pulled the pillow from beneath her head, saying, "Turn over, Tillie."

Her eyes slitted open and she weakly recited, "No corn-holin', mister. This place has got—"

Before she could say "rules," he flipped her onto her belly and positioned the pillow beneath her hips. He heard her softly mutter, "Aw, the hell with it, just do me. . . ."

But Slocum wasn't one to get whorehouses mad at him. He liked to leave them wanting more of his business. He spread her legs wide and easily sank into her in just the right spot.

As he'd hoped, she rose up on her knees to meet him, then pushed her narrow ass back into him with a little sigh.

As his hands traced her spine, squeezed at her lean flanks, toyed with her breasts, he began to ride her. He went slowly at first, knowing that when he'd entered her she was on the brink.

But he couldn't hold her off for very long. Before he was ready, she spasmed beneath him. He paused to hold her until she stopped trembling.

"Ain't nobody like you ever come in here before," she whispered. She was taking in air in big gulps.

In reply, he simply started pumping his hips again. Now he pounded into her, and she gave as good as she got, her head down on the mattress, her arms braced, her fanny up in the air, and her pelvis tilted just right.

Evaporating sweat rose in tiny tendrils of steam from them both. She met him thrust for thrust, twisting back into him, getting more creative by the moment. And just when he felt his own jolt coming, coming, she groaned and shook and quaked beneath him again. This time he didn't hold her, only rammed deep and fast until he'd spent his seed.

Panting, they collapsed in a heap on the cot. She immediately curled to face him, and buried her face in his chest.

"Holy cow, mister," he heard her breathe as the steam rose from their slick bodies. She shuddered. "Holy cow!"

• • •

When at last he walked up to the hotel, having spent a total of four dollars with Tillie—and a better four he hadn't spent in a long time—he found their room and the rest of his party. Tip, mad as a bag full of badgers and with a brand-new shiner just starting to color his left eye, was tied and gagged in the corner chair.

Sully was not in the best of moods.

He didn't offer any explanation, just rumbled, "Whores any good?"

When Slocum said, "Yup," Sully strode past him and went out the door. Which left Slocum to figure out just what the hell had been going on.

He decided against taking off Tip's gag just at the moment, and turned to Patrick.

"Well?" he said. "I'm waitin'."

" 'Twasn't our fault, sir," Patrick began.

His brother shouted something against the gag, but it came out as, "Mrph! Mrph, mrph!"

Slocum held up a silencing hand, and Patrick continued. "Y'see, we were in this pub they've got up the road a bit, and the fellow that was tendin' bar—his name was Flannery—he asked us what part of Ireland we were from. Course, we didn't tell him we were Irish," Patrick confided. "You suppose he was recognizin' us from our speech?"

"Man's a genius," Slocum muttered.

"So we said we hailed from County Cork," Patrick continued, his bony hands balling into fists, "and then he says as how only highwaymen and horse thieves come from there—"

"Got that right," Slocum muttered.

"And how the worst excuse for a thimbleriggin' reprobate of a sneak thief he'd ever had the displeasure to meet came straight from County Cork," Patrick said.

Slocum glanced at Tip again. "That when your brother hit him?"

" 'Twas not," Patrick said, and stood up a little straighter. "We did like you and Mr. Washington said, Tip and me, and held back. But then he said the name of the man he'd been defamin', and it was then that Tipper hauled off and slugged him." He smiled just a little. " 'Twas a grand roundhouse punch, it was." He demonstrated, and Slocum leaned back to get out of the way. "Knocked him clear into the mirror and cracked it!"

"And the name of this fella he was runnin' down?" Slocum asked, although he had a pretty fair notion what the answer was going to be.

"None other than Seamus Rafferty Carnahan," Patrick said proudly. "Our own sweet da."

11

Three days later they were approaching the Salt River Valley, and Slocum was still peeved. Sully, who had been in a better mood once he returned from Dirty Dog's sole whorehouse (after spending a few dollars with Little Fawn), had untied Tip against Slocum's wishes, but spent the night sitting up, guarding him. Slocum sure as hell wasn't going to lose any sleep doing it.

Unfortunately, it seemed that Seamus Rafferty Carnahan has passed through Dirty Dog nearly two years prior, only weeks after having abandoned his daughter up north. The barkeep had remembered him because Seamus had taken him for sixteen dollars and change and two bottles of rotgut, and left him with a lump on his head that hadn't gone down for weeks.

"You bring them kids on back," he had grumbled at Slocum, while he held a slab of raw beefsteak to his face. Slocum hadn't seen it, but his guess was that Tip had returned the favor of a black eye before Sully stormed in and broke it up. "You just bring 'em on back," the bartender groused, "and I'll take that sixteen bucks outta their hides!"

Slocum declined, and had a empty beer keg heaved at him for his trouble.

As mad as he was at Tip, he had to admit that the kid had guts, if not too many brains. Tip was tallish, but he was sure skinny, and couldn't weigh more than 120, maybe 130 pounds. That bartender had been six feet tall if he was an inch. The crude forge and smithy set up next to the saloon attested to the reason he had an ironworker's arms.

Tip was brave, all right, but foolhardy. If Sully hadn't been there, the boy would have ended up dead. Or would've wished that he were.

Tip was Patrick's hero, though, and all the lecturing and shouting Slocum and Sully did could do nothing to dampen that. It was worrisome.

Additionally, Slocum couldn't figure out what the devil was going on with Tip. Maybe it had been something to do with the cougar attack, or maybe the boy had had some kind of revelation earlier on. But whatever had done it, Tip had seemed different after they caught up with the boys at the canyon.

If Sully hadn't seen their daddy's letter and gotten all enthused about bringing them along, would Tip have turned back? Slocum had pondered it, off and on, these last couple of weeks, although it was a moot point. But the kid had surely changed.

He'd actually been polite while they were coming down through the mountains. Well, polite for Tip. He'd seemed grateful when Sully took the time to teach him how to use that Winchester, and he'd been honestly thrilled when he brought down the deer.

But now his surly edge was back, full force. Not exactly in the same manner as before, but it was present. Slocum wanted to get shed of the Carnahan brothers in the worst way, and it didn't help his mood that the farther south they went, the longer it would take him to haul them back up to Carmella's.

Well, that wasn't exactly true. It was Tip he was anxious to be rid of. He'd actually grown sort of fond of Patrick. He just wished the kid didn't worship his big brother like he was some sort of idol—an idol with a big old ruby planted in the middle of his forehead and sixteen golden arms.

Another day passed, and they came to Phoenix. It wasn't much of a town, but they stocked up on provisions and had dinner. Slocum had a bath and a shave, and set out for the local house of ill repute. Sully had gone down there an hour before.

"I'll be going' too," Tip announced. Slocum had shelled out a dollar apiece for a bath for the boys, and he barely recognized them. Both their freckled faces were clean and shiny, their hair was slicked back and neat, and Tip had shaved what few chin whiskers he had. They both reeked of bay rum.

"Go back to the hotel," he growled out of habit. "Whores cost money, you know."

Tip set his jaw. "I'm thinkin' that we could be sparin' a dollar or two, seein' as how we'll be bustin' Da free and all. And Patrick here has never had the services of a female."

Beneath the painted sign for Baker's Bath House, Patrick flushed. "Why, you've never either, Tip!" he blurted out.

Well, if Tip was keen to come along, Slocum couldn't think of any good reason to stop him. If the sonofabitch was busy with a whore, Slocum reasoned, he couldn't start any fights. Patrick was a little young, but then, Slocum had been young too when he first sank into the softness of a woman.

The boys stared at him intently.

"Aw, hell," he said. "We'll see if they don't have a couple of hobby-horse gals. Hate for you two to get bucked off and busted up right away."

Tip's expression went from a glower straight to a look of triumph. Patrick appeared a little worried. As Tip set off ahead at a brisk walk, Slocum said, "Patrick, is there something gnawin' at you?"

As he expected, the boy stammered, "I didn't suspect you'd capitulate so easy, sir." Patrick turned his head away and whispered, "I don't . . . I don't exactly know how ye go about it."

Slocum bit back his smile, and put a hand on the boy's shoulder. "Well, we'll pick you out a real gentle one, Pat. You just tell her she's your first, and she'll lead you right straight through it."

Patrick turned toward Slocum. "She . . . she won't be laughin' at me?"

Slocum shook his head. "Promise. Why, these gals probably break in half the boys in the territory!"

Patrick seemed to take that under advisement, and as they walked up the steps to the place beside the sign that read "Miss Elvira's," Slocum said, "You pay for two go-rounds, Patrick. The first one's fast and don't count when a boy's as green as you." He opened the door.

"Huh?" said Patrick.

"Trust me," said Slocum, and shoved him inside.

Tip had already vanished up the stairs, and Slocum pulled the madam, Miss Elvira herself, aside. Miss Elvira was a buxom brunette who looked to be a little over the hill, but who had no compunction about displaying her merchandise anyway. Her breasts were all but falling over the top of the low-cut camisole she was wearing, which was snugly cinched in by a whalebone corset ribboned in pink. Below that, she wore thin pantaloons that stopped above the knee, and her dark stockings bulged here and there with varicose veins.

"Got a young'un here what's never rode the bronc," Slocum confided. "You think you got a gal willin' to be a mite gentle with him?"

Miss Elvira took a look at Patrick, who was standing in the middle of a room filled with lounging whores and looking a bit peaked.

"Got just the gal," she said, and called out, "Verdette! Get in here, girl!"

Slocum cringed at the volume of it, and Patrick, who was nervous as a cat anyway, jumped a foot. But the girls seemed used to it, and a half minute later, Verdette poked her head out of the back hallway.

They had interrupted her during her dinner break by the looks of it, because she was holding a half-eaten chicken leg. But she was petite and honey-blond and pretty—and very young—and a smile slowly spread across Patrick's face.

"You called, Miss Elvira?" she said.

The two women had a few whispered words, and then Verdette handed her chicken leg to Elvira. Grinning, she came into the parlor and took Patrick's hand. He swept off his hat, and said, "Evenin', miss." His voice only broke once.

"My name's Verdette Crenshaw, sweetie-pie," Slocum heard her say as she walked Patrick up the stairs. "What's yours?"

"How about you, handsome?" Miss Elvira's hands were on her hips. She wiggled her chest at Slocum and batted her eyes.

"Oh, I've got mine all picked out, ma'am," he said quickly, and held his hand down to a slim Mexican gal. Miss Elvira looked daggers at him for a second, but then the expression vanished.

"Have fun, you two," she chirped, and turned her attention to the cowhand who had just come in the front door.

"Got a name?" Slocum asked as, in front of him, the girl climbed the steps. *"Cómo te llamas?"* She had a round backside that jiggled and swayed just right, and he stayed two steps behind her just to watch it.

Over her shoulder, she grinned and giggled, "Juan-ita, señor."

"Juanita," he said as his eyes went back to that swishing ass. "That's a right pretty name."

They were all pretty, the girls he'd known. Every damned one of them.

Slocum had Juanita panting and pressed hard against a wall—with her legs locked behind him and her nails gouging his shoulders—when he heard a god-awful ruckus.

It wasn't just one of those "cowboy-having-a-good-time" ruckuses either. He heard a lot of shouting and, if he didn't miss his guess, most of it was coming straight from Tip Carnahan's mouth.

"Screw him," Slocum muttered just as Juanita gasped, dug her claws into his neck, and shuddered.

He chose to ignore the argument raging down the hall. He pumped up into Juanita again and again until he came in a roaring rush. Stuttering to a halt, well-spent and sated, he brushed a kiss over the girl's forehead, then eased her down to the floor.

She looked up at him with half-lidded eyes and slid her arms around his waist. "Again?" she asked softly in Spanish, standing on her tiptoes.

"Two times a night's my limit, darlin'," he lied, and bent to scoop his britches from the floor.

A minute later he was headed down the hall, britches, boots, and guns in place, but his shirt open and flapping. He followed the sound, muttering, "I'm gonna kill him, I'm just gonna murder him where he stands."

It seemed to him that an extra voice had been added to the argument somewhere along the way, and when he pushed open the door, he saw that he'd been right. There was Tip, in the middle of the room in his underwear, and he was faced off with a redheaded girl (who was stark naked save for a pair of pink pump shoes) and Miss Elvira.

Both the women were madder than hornets, but Tip was holding his ground.

Slocum shouted, "Stop it!"

They paid him not one whit of attention.

He was about to pull his Colt and fire up into the ceiling when behind him, Sully boomed out, "Shut up, goddamm it!"

That was one thing about Sully's voice: It might sound plumb eerie when you were out in the middle of nowhere and he snuck up on you, but it was a handy thing to have around when there were a bunch of women squawking at the tops of their voices and about to shatter your eardrums.

Everybody shut up, and the redhead looked like she'd just heard the voice of doom.

Maybe she had.

"Thanks," said Slocum.

"No problem," replied Sully.

Tip shot an arm out and pointed to the redhead. "Trina stole my money!" he shouted. "I had it here, in me shoes, and she's thieved every last penny of it! She's a robber and a skulker!"

"Well, now, that's sure the pot calling the kettle black," muttered Sully.

Slocum didn't look at him. He arched a brow at Tip. "You kept your money in your shoes?"

Trina cried, "Did not, did not!" Her small breasts bobbled with every denial.

Slocum slid a quick glance down her body, and saw the new wet streak slowly running down her leg. Tip had done one thing right tonight anyway.

"Well, I had it when I came in this very door, and I've been no place since!" Tip shouted.

"Calm down!" Slocum shouted right back at him, then asked, "Did you go to sleep after?"

Tip cocked his head, as if Slocum had accused him of something heinous. "For a few minutes," he admitted grudgingly. "After the first time. Then I woke up and done her again, and when I reached for me clothes . . . Well, me shoes were light!" He bent and picked one up, then turned it upside down. "See? The girl's a thief, I'm tellin' you!"

Trina ducked beneath Miss Elvira's arm, prepared to dash into the hall stark naked and go God knows where, but Sully moved his bulk in front of the open doorway and slowly shook a finger in her surprised face. "Tut-tut, my dear," he said, eyeing her up and down. He was grinning. "Nice titties."

Trina scowled at him, but made no attempt to cover herself.

"I won't stand for this," Miss Elvira said angrily, her arms crossed over her heaving bosom. "You fellas stop accusin' poor Trina! Why, that idiot boy probably lost his cash out on the street somewhere. He'd just come up from the bathhouse, he told me so. Maybe he lost his stake down there!"

Trina nodded her head rapidly. "That's right! He said he come straight from Baker's." She plopped her hands on her naked hips. "He was prob'ly so hog-dirty that the water turned all black. That money's likely down in the bottom of the tub under two feet'a Irish slime!"

"I'd like to hit you," growled Tip, and he cocked a fist. "I think I will!"

"No, you won't," said Slocum, and it was more on the order of a command than a comment. "Get your clothes on. Both of you."

"And I was so enjoying the scenery," said Sully. His eyes were on Trina's breasts.

"Get out!" screeched Miss Elvira. "Get outta here this instant, all three of you!"

"Not yet," said Slocum, and with Sully standing guard at the door, proceeded to open every drawer in the little dresser. He emptied the chifforobe. He looked under the washbasin, under the bed, and shook out the covers.

"See?" Trina said through clenched teeth. She'd pulled a robe around her by this time. "I didn't rob nobody. I told you."

"I'm callin' for the sheriff," Miss Elvira said nastily.

Slocum stopped scratching at his head and smiled. His eye had just lit on the tiniest corner of a piece of paper. It jutted from under the back of the dresser, and he wouldn't have seen it at all if he hadn't bent just then to toss the covers back on the bed.

"Well, now, that's a right good idea, Miss Elvira," he said. "You just go ahead and call him."

He swung the dresser out with a screech, and bent down. Sticking out from under the back of the thing were the crumpled edges of three five-dollar bills.

Trina forgot that Sully was there and bolted. He caught her against his body, and when she started kicking at him, he simply picked her up, twirled her around, and held her against his broad chest and off the floor.

Slocum went to the front of the dresser then, and crouched down. Sure enough, there was the money on the floor. Trina had probably slid the lowest drawer out while Tip slept, jammed the cash back behind it, then quietly put the drawer back in again.

"Weren't you goin' for the law, Miss Elvira?" Slocum asked as he scooped out bills and coins. They were making a nice little pile on the floor.

Miss Elvira didn't answer, but Trina, flailing helplessly at the amused Sully, cried, "That's mine! I saved it!"

Slocum looked up at Tip, who had a very self-satisfied smirk on his face. "About how much were you carryin', boy?"

There was no hesitation. Tip spouted, "Eight hundred and fourteen American dollars and seven cents, and a tuppence."

Slocum pulled out a few more coins. "You had all this in your *shoes*?" he asked.

"That I did," came the answer.

Slocum had it all by then, although he turned the dresser on its side and gave it a thump, just in case. "All right," he said, pulling over the room's single chair. He sat down. "Now, I'm gonna count this and you're all gonna watch," he said. "And whatever's left over after I get to eight hundred and fourteen dollars and seven cents, you can keep."

"Don't forget the tuppence," added Tip.

"And a tuppence," Slocum said, and began to count.

"Bastards," growled Miss Elvira. "Saddle trash."

Trina hung in Sully's arms, defeated.

As it turned out, there was a grand total of three dollars and eighty-four cents remaining when Slocum finished, and he presented the sum to Trina. Who ripped it from his hand.

"Nobody says thank you anymore," Slocum commented with a shake of his head as the three of them walked down the stairs. " 'Thank you for giving me my money when you could just as easily have taken it all, Slocum.' 'Thank you for not calling the sheriff and having me tossed in the hoosegow, Slocum.' 'Slocum, thank you for—' "

"We get the idea," Sully said. "Whoring surely loosens your tongue."

"You know, you're never goddamn happy," Slocum growled as, with a thump, Tip ran right into his back.

"Where's Patrick?" Slocum asked once he'd regained his balance. Another go-round of "Where's the money?" was about the last thing he needed tonight.

But Verdette, Patrick's choice for the evening, appeared on the other side of the staircase. Gooey-eyed and still flushed, she looked up at Slocum and said, "Oh, he just left. He was darlin', just darlin'." She sighed happily, then asked, "Was that you doin' all the shoutin' up there?"

Sully squeezed past Slocum to say good-bye to a pretty sepia-skinned gal waiting down below.

Slocum, however, stayed put and tipped his hat. "Yes'm," he said, and gave her a wink. This girl was no thief, he'd bet the ranch on it.

But just the same, when they emerged on the walk to find Patrick sitting on the steps all dopey-eyed and grinning like an idiot, Slocum insisted that the boy take off his shoes.

Patrick sent a look to Tip, who nodded, and Patrick went to work on the laces.

It was all there, as Slocum had expected. Patrick shoved the cash back in and they started up toward the hotel, the boys about ten feet ahead and Sully and Slocum bringing up the rear.

"Did you know that gal you were kissin' good-bye?" Slocum asked. "Know her before tonight, I mean."

Sully nodded. "I visit Maybelle from time to time," he said with a smile. "Didn't know she was working here, though. Fortuitous."

Slocum looked at him.

"A happy accident. You want to know what really bubbles my brain?"

"What?"

"How in the name of Hades those kids can walk with all that cash in their clodhoppers."

Slocum laughed. "C'mon," he called ahead to the

boys. He motioned toward a saloon. "Let's get us a beer, and I'm buyin'. The first time deserves a little celebratin', even if you did nearly get yourselves swindled blind."

12

Smoke hazed the noisy barroom as Tip leaned his elbows on the scarred table, watching Patrick and sipping his beer. He didn't bother straining to listen as Slocum talked to the man at the next table, who he seemed to know. Sully Washington had wandered away directly after they came in, and was hunched at a table in the rear, engrossed in conversation with a redheaded man dressed entirely in fringed and beaded buckskin.

At any other time, this would have fascinated Tip, for he had read stories of frontier men and, according to the authors, they all dressed that way. Not in plain pants and shirts like Slocum.

He wasn't begrudging Slocum his manner of dress, however, nor Sully Washington, whose apparel was some finer, albeit stranger. He'd changed his mind about Sully. He supposed there were filthy black men in the world, all right, just like there were filthy Irishmen. He himself had been one of the latter up until a few hours ago, when he'd immersed himself in one of the tubs at Baker's. Christ, he felt half a stone lighter!

But Sully was, well, just grand! He'd nearly kissed the man when, with his help, he'd shot that buck. Sully had shoved him out of that timber rattler's way when

they were coming down through the mountains, and
taught him how to listen for their sound. Like the hiss
of a teakettle on the boil, it was. Of course, Slocum
had pulled his fat out of the proverbial fire a few times
too—saved his very life, in fact—but Tip's own da
had never been so patient with him as Sully Washington. Nor so nice, nor so generous.

In a manly way, of course.

Why, Sully had even let him use his own personal
rifle, which he'd told Tip had been a gift from the
territorial governor of Colorado. On the stock, there
was even a little brass plate with an inscription. It had
the governor's name and Sully's, and it said, "In Gratitude."

It was glorious just to hold it.

He was sorry he'd made Sully so mad up north in
that little hole of a town. Dirty Dog, that was the name
of it. Where did these Americans find such hideous
names for their towns anyway? But he was sorry for
grieving Sully anytime or anyplace.

Slocum wasn't such a bad fellow either, he supposed. Oh, he scowled a lot and made a show of being
irascible, but hadn't he paid for a bath for both him
and Patrick? Hadn't he taken them to that house of ill
repute when he could've locked them up in the hotel
and been rid of them?

Tip had to admit he was deserving of that sort of
treatment. But Slocum didn't even threaten it. And
hadn't he brought them into a tavern? Not that Tip and
Patrick couldn't have gone right in there, bold as you
please, all by themselves. But he'd invited them. And
hadn't he bought them each a pint?

All right, it was dishwater compared to the good

dark ale he could get back home, but it was drinkable enough. And despite that tussle with that thieving bitch Trina, he felt like celebrating. It wasn't every day a man had his very first poke.

Two of them, in fact!

Christ, what a grand thing! He was ready to go do it again, save for the fact that the whorehouse was full of robbers. Maybe in another town . . .

"Tipper?" said Patrick, pulling him away from his thoughts of new towns and new conquests. Patrick was looking all mushy and moony again, which he had, off and on, since they'd left Miss Elvira's, and which was usually a bad thing. "Tipper," he said grandly, "it's in love I am. I'm considerin' marriage."

Tip rolled his eyes, but Patrick didn't see. "Patrick, I told ye before. Just because ye gave the girl a poke, ye don't have to—"

"No," Patrick cut in, "don't be treatin' me like a know-nothin' babe. I'm a man now, by Christ, and she was awfully nice to me, Tipper, awfully nice. I'm thinkin' that she was a lot nicer than she had to be for two dollars cash. I'm thinkin' that she felt it too." He clasped a hand over his heart.

"I'm supposin' she did, Patrick," Tip said with a straight face. "I'm supposin' she felt it when ye gave it to her hot and strong. Tell me, did she go all writhey on ye?"

"Stop that, Tip!" Patrick said. He'd finished his beer and called for another. "Don't be demeanin' it like that. It was . . ." He raised his eyes heavenward and dreamily added, "It was sacred, I swear it. Like bein' in church."

"And I'm certain Father O'Brien would be thrilled

to hear ye say it," Tip said dryly. "You're drunk, Pat. Things'll look different come the mornin'."

"Drunk, am I?" Patrick asked as a barmaid slid a fresh glass onto the table. He took off his shoe and paid her.

"Aye, sozzled. That's your fourth beer, by my count, and you're not accustomed to the drink."

Patrick was having trouble getting his shoe back on, and Tip pushed his hands away and laced it up for him.

"Thank you, Tipper," Patrick said grandly when Tip had finished. Patrick took a swallow of his fresh beer. Foam covering his upper lip in a thick mustache, he said, "You're the most darlin' brother a man ever had. Will you be comin' to my weddin' then?"

With a sigh, Tip gave up and said, "Aye, Patrick, I will. Now, don't you think you'd be happier in your own sweet bed back at the hotel?"

A dreamy look came over Patrick's face. "I'd be happier in me darlin' Verdette's."

Tip pushed back his chair. Muttering, "I'm thinkin' that's already occupied several times over, Pat," he bent and looped his brother's arm about his shoulders, then heaved him to his feet. Da had always said it'd be a cold day in Hades when a Carnahan man couldn't hold his spirits, and Tip suddenly smirked. "I wonder how they're likin' the ice-skatin' down there," he said to himself.

"Skatin'? Who's skatin'?" mumbled his brother.

Tip poked Slocum in the shoulder, pointed to his brother, then pointed out the door, and Slocum started to stand up.

"Keep your chair, sir," Tip said, and waved him

down. "I've got him." Slocum raised a brow, but eased back into his seat.

"Are we goin' to visit Verdette?" Patrick asked with a woozy sort of animation.

"Aye, Patrick, aye," Tip said soothingly as he half-carried his brother toward the batwing doors. "In a while. But first, I think you'll be havin' a little nap."

Slocum didn't connect with Sully again that night. He lingered when Sully left the bar, being engrossed in a very interesting conversation with a fellow called Crazy Earl Lemke, and when he finally got back to the hotel, Sully was still out. Slocum didn't waste time worrying about him. He knew that Sully could take care of himself.

And about six other people besides.

When he woke the next morning, Sully's bed had been slept in, but the man was already gone.

"Hope the goddamn gadfly paid the hotel bill," Slocum muttered before he woke the Carnahan boys. He was getting pretty low on cash. The kids' horses—and the women he'd bought, and the drinks—had nearly cleaned him out.

He tugged on his boots and loudly said, "Wake the hell up, girls." Tip sat up right away and swung his legs over the side of the cot he shared with Patrick. Patrick simply pulled the covers up over his head and groaned sickly.

"Had more of a night than he bargained for, didn't he?" Slocum commented. He stood up, tucked in his shirttails, and began to strap on his guns.

"He has no head for spirits, does Patrick," Tip answered, yawning. He rubbed at his head, then ground the sleep from his eyes with his fists. He looked up. "Mr. Slocum? I'd like to voice my gratitude for your generosity last night. It was real fine of your, buyin' us the drinks and all. And . . . the other. Well, you didn't pay, but you know what I'm tryin' to say. And I'm especially grateful for your actions with that thievin' wench."

Slocum settled his hat on his head. "Well, now, Tip," he said dryly, "I'm right grateful that you didn't just haul off and break her jaw."

A smile tickled at the corner of Tip's mouth, and he flushed. "I suppose I deserved that."

"You can be a rowdy little bastard sometimes."

Tip shrugged. "Take after Da, I suppose."

Slocum crossed the little room and put his hand on the latch. "Breedin' only counts for half of it, Tip," he said. "What you do with what the Good Lord gives you—that's what matters."

Tip was silent for a moment. "How much longer will it be till we find the villains? By my calculations, it's four days, more or less, till we reach their lair at Pima Wells. But then," he added with a small sigh, "I'm not the best at readin' these American maps. When they're drawin' in all those bumpy doodads, they don't give a fellow a clue what it's like to cross 'em."

Slocum chuckled softly. "No, reckon they don't. But we're not goin' to Pima Wells."

Anger crossed Tip's features in a hair-trigger rush. It was a familiar expression, and one Slocum wasn't a bit happy to see. The boy opened his mouth, but Slocum cut him off before he could fall back on bad habits and get himself into a world of trouble—which Slocum was more than willing to provide.

"Hold on, kid. Your daddy ain't in Pima Wells unless he's buried there. Paolo Martinez and his gang have moved on a whole bunch of times since then."

"Where then?" Tip demanded.

Slocum opened the door. "Mission Springs."

"Mission Springs?" boomed Sully. "Not on your life."

"That's what Crazy Earl said," Slocum repeated testily.

It was late morning. They had exited Phoenix, Sully having paid both the hotel and the livery bills. They had forded the wide and shallow Salt River, and were now headed south toward Tucson over one of the most deserted, dry, and downright boring strips of territory known to man. In the distance, twin dust devils danced over the featureless landscape, bowing and turning as they spun.

Sully had sprung for a donkey back in Phoenix. Loaded with water bags and grub, it trotted dully behind them at the end of a long rope. Perhaps thirty feet back, the Carnahan boys followed. The last time Slocum had looked, Patrick was still holding his head. Part of Slocum hated to do this to the kid, but the other part said he had to.

"Don't care what Crazy Earl said," Sully insisted. "Red Granger says Paolo's holed up at Indian Cliff."

"Fine," snapped Slocum. He was growing weary of the conversation. "But Mission Springs is closer. We're goin' there first."

"It's twenty-four goddamn miles out of the way!" Sully roared, and the donkey behind them skittered to one side, nearly yanking Slocum's arm from its socket and pulling the rope hard across Sully's back.

Slocum got him hauled back into position, then tossed the lead rope to Sully. "If you're gonna bandy that goddamn voice'a yours about," he said curtly, "*you* lead the sonofabitch."

Sully's mouth stretched into a slow grin. "All right," he said. "Mission Springs. But I'd hate to think that I bought Red Granger all those drinks for nothing." He clasped his hands on the saddle horn. "Went up to the sheriff's office before breakfast. Had an interesting talk."

"And?"

"And our friend Paolo Martinez hasn't been blamed for any burnings, kidnappings, robberies, murders, or mayhem for nearly three weeks," Sully said. "Course, there was somebody hit a payroll over around Gallop. That got blamed on Paolo, but the sheriff is inclined to think northern New Mexico's just a little out of his territory."

Slocum nodded. The dust devils were spinning closer now. He said, "Sheriff make any sounds like he was wantin' to mount up a posse and come along with us?"

Sully snorted.

"Figured." Slocum paused a moment before he said, "Maybe Paolo really did bust up his legs."

"I'm inclined to think so," said Sully thoughtfully. "And so was Red Granger. Who didn't offer any assistance either, in case you were going to ask. Course, I was inclined to believe it in the first place. You take a whole lot of convincing, Slocum."

"Yup."

Slocum heard a retching sound, and turned in his saddle just in time to see Patrick vomiting over the side of his horse. Again. Slocum pulled up Cheyenne and Sully reined in Old Scratch, and Old Scratch took the opportunity to amorously swing his neck over Cheyenne's.

At which point, Cheyenne bared her teeth and bit him in the cheek.

"Dammit, Slocum," Sully muttered once he quit swatting Old Scratch over the ears, and ascertained that the bite hadn't broken skin. "Can't you get that mare of yours under control?"

"Seems to me she knows what she's doin'," Slocum said wryly, and gave the mare a pat.

Sully grumbled something that Slocum didn't catch, and which he sure as hell wasn't going to ask Sully to repeat. Instead, he twisted again toward the boys. "You figure that's the end of it, Patrick?"

Patrick didn't answer, just swayed sickly in the saddle, but Tip called back, "Don't see that he could have any more in him. It's just water and bubbles he's pukin' up lately."

Patrick's mouth moved, although Slocum didn't hear, but Tip said, "He's askin' when we're goin' to stop for a rest."

"Another hour ought'a do it," Slocum answered, and Patrick slumped.

"Being a little tough on the boy, aren't you?" Sully asked as they started out again. The dust devils had made a sharp turn to the right, and were spinning away from them at a good clip, tossing gravel and twigs as they went.

"It's a hard land," Slocum said, "and it's gonna get harder. He'd best keep on gettin' used to it."

13

Three days later, they had veered wide to the west of Tucson long before they hit it, and were presently traveling south, with a rugged mountain range between them and civilization.

They had crossed sere desert and traveled some low mountains that Tip, for the life of him, couldn't remember the names of. It seemed they had a chain of the damned hills every four feet in this blasted country, and the ones he was crossing of late were as dry and rocky and uninhabitable as hell itself.

The men seemed to be in a fine fettle, though. Slocum and Sully cracked jokes—most of them at his and Patrick's expense, he was certain. And it seemed to him that the closer they got to the villains' lair, the more jovial the two of them got. It worried him.

They had nearly depleted their water before they came across some scummy, insect-ridden pools of water that Slocum called tanks and seemed glad to find, although Tip privately referred to the water they picked up there as "liquid bugs."

Once, he'd made the mistake of calling it that out loud, and Slocum had snapped, "You'll drink it and be grateful, boy."

For just a moment, he had sounded like Da, yam-

137

mering about the tiny smidgen of mutton or herring
that he'd brought home to the table.

Still, Tip tried to strain it through his teeth when he
absolutely had to take a drink. It was all he could do
to keep the foul stuff down.

The day before, poor Patrick had had a run-in with
the biggest, hairiest, most disgusting fiend of a spider
he'd never hoped to lay eyes on. Nearly the size of a
saucer, it had been crawling across Patrick's neck when
he woke in the morning.

"For the love'a Christ, Patrick, don't move," Tip had
hissed when he spied it. Slocum had brushed it away,
but not before it bit Patrick.

After Slocum—and Sully—had convinced them
both that Patrick wouldn't die, and that the tarantula's
bite was no worse than a bee sting, Pat had calmed
down a bit. But still, he had a gigantic red welt on the
side of his neck, which he probed with his fingers
roughly every five minutes despite Sully's repeated ad-
monitions.

As they neared Mission Springs, Tip found himself
in a strange mood. Until they'd landed in San Francisco, he'd felt a soft driving thing in his belly. At first,
it was the need to escape the law back home, but it
quickly turned into the excitement of an adventure,
with Da being the distant carrot on the end of the stick.

But once he and Patrick had found themselves standing on the San Francisco wharf, that soft, driving thing
had transmuted into something different. It became
more real somehow, this thing they were going to do,
more imperative. And Da, who those last months had
faded to a ghost of himself—in Tip's mind, at any

rate—suddenly began to loom large and monstrous in Tip's nightly dreams.

"Hurry, ye daft buggers," Da would say with a glower, all of ten feet tall and with a face full of fury and indignation. "Hurry your lazy arses along!" And then he would take off his belt.

It was only a dream, but it happened with regularity, and always left Tip wide awake and whispering, "Aye, Da, we're comin', Da. . . ."

But now, only a day away if that, he found himself dragging his feet. Maybe it hadn't been such a good idea, what he and Patrick had done. Maybe he should have just stayed in Ireland and faced the music. Well, no. The gallows weren't for him. But he should have run off to Africa or South America or China or somewhere, even Australia. And he shouldn't have brought young Patrick along.

He had a horrible feeling, deep in his belly, that Da was dead, and that he and Patrick would soon be joining him.

He scouted the distant, featureless expanse, finding no succor in its emptiness.

No Da, no hope.

Nothing.

There it was again. That tiny glimmer on the horizon.

"See that?" Slocum asked. He didn't point, didn't make any gestures. He just kept riding along, nice and easy.

"Yeah," Sully replied, although he too gave no physical indication. "Somebody's watching."

Slocum nodded. "For the last quarter hour or so."

"How far you make it?"

"Mile. Maybe more, maybe less."

"I take it back, Slocum," Sully said. "My apologies to Crazy Earl Lemke."

There was no place to run to on the vast expanse of desert, nowhere to hide. Their best bet was to just keep moving along at a jog until they reached the far hills to the south. By Slocum's calculation, it'd be at least another hour, unless they made a break for it. Which would be a lunatic idea, considering the heat and the distance.

"Maybe, maybe not," said Slocum. "Don't know that it's our fellas."

Sully pursed his lips. "Don't know who else it could be."

Far away, light once again briefly reflected off glass, then winked out.

"There's a place a few hours north of town," Slocum said.

"The old mission," Sully said with a nod. "I know the place."

"They're there. I'd bet my life on it."

"I imagine you'd win that bet," Sully said. "I'm gonna have words with Red Granger once we finish up down here."

Behind them, hoofbeats quickened, and in a moment Tip and Patrick were beside them.

"Did ye see it?" Patrick asked excitedly, waving his arms all over the place.

"On the horizon, over there," Tip said, and pointed.

Slocum batted at his arm. "Knock it the hell off," he barked. "We seen 'em, but you don't need to let 'em know it."

Both boys stopped gesturing. Patrick had the good

grace to look a little embarrassed, but Tip insisted, "It's the ones what have got Da, isn't it? Surely, nobody else would be spyin' and peepin'! Quick, give me your glass!"

"Maybe it is, maybe it isn't," said Slocum. "And I'm not takin' a chance on the glass. If we can see the sun glintin' off theirs, they can sure as shootin' see ours."

"Get your hand away from that spider bite, boy," snapped Sully.

Patrick, who had been unconsciously fiddling with his neck again, dropped his hand. "Sorry, sir."

"No, boy, I'm sorry," Sully said with a sigh. "Those gentlemen with the glass are making me jumpy as all get out. But just don't fiddle with it, all right?"

"If y'all are done playin' doctor," Slocum broke in, "you think we might step this thing up to a slow lope?" He tipped his head to the western horizon. "It's moved."

Whoever was watching their party had indeed moved a short distance south, for the next glimmer came from a new spot. They were being shadowed, no two ways about it, and Slocum felt a familiar warning tingle at the base of his spine.

"Fine by me," Sully replied, then shook a stern finger at both boys. "No racin', you hear?"

"And drop back," added Slocum. "Keep that damn donkey movin'."

They eased into a slow lope, Slocum out front, followed by Sully leading the pack donkey, and the boys right on its tail, urging it to keep up. To an observer, Slocum hoped it would appear that they were just in a little bit of a hurry to reach the meager shade of the hills before they stopped for their midday meal. Not too much of a hurry, though. Just a nice, gentle lope. Easy does it.

And whoever was out there seemed to buy into it. The intermittent glints on the western horizon moved slowly to the south. They kept pace, but drew no nearer.

Who the hell was out there anyway?

When at last they reached the safety of the foothills, and Sully and Slocum had at last decided on a place that was safe enough to stop, Tip fairly jumped off Flannel. He tossed his reins to his brother and began to scramble to the top of a low hill.

He didn't beat Slocum, though. The man was already in place, lying on his belly on the rocky, gravelly crest, and he had his spyglass out.

"Do you see anything, Mr. Slocum?" the boy asked eagerly. Slocum had already told them that he didn't think their party was in any immediate danger. Whoever was out there was just watching them.

For now at least.

"Not yet." Slocum took his eye from the glass for a moment and looked back over his shoulder. "Get down, goddammit!" he growled.

Tip dropped.

Slocum turned back to the glass.

"Ye don't have to be so surly with me," Tip whispered.

Slocum muttered something under his breath.

For fifteen minutes Tip lay there tensely while, in silence, Slocum scanned the hills to the west. At last, Slocum scooted back from the rim and collapsed the glass. "Nothin'," he said. "Least not yet. I'm gonna go see to the horses, if your brother or Sully haven't yet."

He began to slide down the gravel slope.

"Wait!" Tip called incredulously. "Are you givin' up?"

Slocum stopped and shook his head with a roll of his eyes. "Nope. After I check the horses, I'm changin' hills. And I'm gonna grab some grub on my way."

"Well, would ye be so kind as to leave the glass?"

Tip asked hopefully. "You can borrow Sully Washington's. It's better anyway. And I'm wantin' to be of assistance."

Slocum looked at him at for what seemed like ages, and just when Tip was sure the man was going to haul off and hit him for having had the audacity to belittle his spying equipment (a mistake he'd realized a half second after it emerged from his mouth), Slocum crouched down and handed up the glass.

"All right," he said. "Don't suppose you can get into much trouble up here. Just keep low. Stay flat on your belly. And if you see anything, anything at all, slither back down here pronto and tell Sully. You got that?"

Tip hugged the spyglass tight to his chest. "Oh, aye!"

Slocum hesitated for a moment, and Tip was afraid he was going to change his mind. But at last he turned, growling something to himself, and skidded down the slope.

Everyone was getting a little growly and grumpy of late, Tip thought as he eased the glass out to its full length. It was dull brass, the plentiful scratches on its finish attesting to frequent use, and each segment slid smoothly into place with a satisfying *click*.

Of course, Tip thought as he raised the glass to his

eye, it was hard to tell with Slocum so far as growls were concerned. In Tip's brief span of experience with the man, he was most always a bear, even with people he liked.

After a half hour of watching and waiting—and a half hour of nobody thinking to bring him a bit of jerky or hardtack to quiet his poor, aching belly—Tip was about to give it up and slide down to the base of the hill—and food—when a bit of movement caught his eye.

He stared hard at the base of the next hill, holding his breath, and a moment later, it slid back into view again.

One rider. No, two! He could see just the head of the second horse.

The first fellow was a bandit, all right. Tip had never actually seen a bandit—either up close or far away—but this fellow seemed to fulfill all the qualifications. He was a broad-shouldered Mexican man, and he looked fair exotic. Dressed all in dingy gray, he was mustachioed and swarthy, and a big sombrero shaded his cruel face. Ammunition belts, like those that Sully wore, crisscrossed his chest. Pistols rode his hips, a rifle was in his boot, and a hellish-looking blade was strapped to his thigh.

Even the man's horse looked lean and nasty.

Everything about the fellow cried murder. If this was the fellow who had kidnapped Da, then Da was surely long dead!

A shiver ran through Tip, despite the sweat trickling down his back. It was a shiver of despair, but also relief. They could go home. Or go back to Carson City and Fiona.

And just then, the second horse moved forward until Tip could see the rider, until he could see him plain.

Tip swallowed. "Da?" he mouthed silently.

It was himself, Seamus Rafferty Carnahan, in the flesh. Oh, he was dressed differently than Tip had ever imagined him, but setter-red hair poked from beneath the battered Stetson that looked so strange on his head, and his features, though tanned to a copper, were unmistakable.

He didn't appear to be under any sort of restraint either. In fact he was gesturing, as if he was giving the Mexican bandit orders.

Well, this was a fine kettle of fish! Here he and Patrick had come halfway round the word to rescue the old bastard, and there he was, big as life and in no trouble at all, riding around on a grand chestnut horse and telling people what to do!

Just like always. With the exception of the horse, of course. Back home, Da could have no more afforded a fine mount than he could have afforded new shoes for his children.

Tip dropped the spyglass, and it skittered and bounced all the way back down the hill, finally coming to rest against a rock.

His trembling hands balled into fists.

"I could murder ye, Da," he whispered through clenched teeth. "I could just murder ye!"

A mighty surge of energy coursed through him. With no further adieu, he stood straight up and crossed over the top of the hill, alternately running and skidding his way ever closer to those distant riders.

•   •   •

Down below, in the narrow, twisting strip of purple shade between hills, Slocum slid Cheyenne's saddle to the ground while he chewed on a strip of venison jerky. Nobody had hollered yet—and he doubted anybody would.

If those really were Paolo Martinez's boys out there, they'd have no way of guessing that the Carnahans were among their party. And they probably wouldn't bother to waylay such a small party. Old Paolo and his boys did mostly banks and trains and ore shipments. Anything else was beneath him.

Slocum patted the leopard mare's shoulder, then straightened her mane. It was a good chance to let her cool off.

Patrick had already walked out the horses, which had been a little hot from their lope. He'd also watered them and loosened their girths by the time Slocum came skidding down the hill. Patrick was real good that way, being nearly as concerned about their horseflesh as Slocum was. Twice the natural rider his brother was—or ever would be—Patrick had taken part in their care right from the beginning. Slocum remembered how upset the boy had been about that old mare back in Carson City. What had that mare's name been? Susie, that was it. And that old gelding, Buckshot. Tip had never even asked his name.

Slocum shook his head. Well, some folks just didn't care for horses, he supposed. He didn't understand it, but there it was.

"Is it all right for me to be strippin' the tack from the others, sir?" Patrick asked. The welt on his neck had gone down a good bit. Slocum hadn't let on to either of the boys, but he'd been worried about Patrick for the first couple of hours. Tarantula bites were like bad bee stings to most folks. On the other hand, he'd occasionally seen men up and die from them.

"Sure, boy," he said almost kindly. "Sully head up this way?" Jerky in hand, he poked a thumb to the southwest.

Patrick nodded.

"All right. Watch out for spiders."

Patrick grinned. "Aye."

Slocum spotted Sully at last, and had climbed halfway to his perch when Sully suddenly cursed, wheeled round, and came skidding down the hill, out flat and feet first, holding his spyglass wide and high above the ground. Slocum narrowly avoided taking Sully's boot heels to his head, and caught the man by the sleeve.

They both skidded a few feet further, in the process spinning halfway around, and came to a stop all caddy-wampus and hard against a boulder, still partway up the hill.

"Jesus Christ, Slocum!" Sully spat, and checked his spyglass for scratches, then his blue and blousy sleeve for tears. "You nearly ripped my shirt!"

"Woulda been a real shame," Slocum replied dryly, and picked a sharp rock from under his back, then sat up. The whole damn hill was made of the sharp little bastards. "Why the hell you comin' down in such an all-fired hurry?"

"If you'd been doing your job, I wouldn't've had to!" Sully shouted.

"What you gettin' mad at me for?" Slocum shouted back.

Sully looked at him as if he were a prize idiot. "I thought you were supposed to be watchin' Tip."

Suddenly, Slocum had a very bad feeling. "What the hell'd he do this time?" He glanced over toward the hill to the west, where he'd left the boy, but boulders obstructed his former perch from view.

"He ran out there," Sully said, pointing back over his shoulder. "Straight into the arms of two of Paolo's men."

"He did what?" Slocum roared, but by then Sully had dug in his butt and his backside, and was sliding down the steep hill again.

Cursing a blue streak, Slocum followed.

The men hit the narrow valley running, Slocum just a length behind Sully. They nearly bowled over Patrick in their hurry to get to their mounts.

"What?" Patrick cried. "What is it?"

Slocum cinched up Cheyenne's girth and moved to the pack donkey. "Get your horse saddled, and Flannel too. *Move!*"

Patrick did so without question, and Slocum proceeded to quickly strip the donkey of what was left of their supplies, which he tossed atop Flannel. He shooed the donkey away. There wasn't that much baggage left to haul, and the donkey would slow them down considerably.

"But where's Tip goin' to ride?" Patrick wailed as Slocum swiftly secured the last water bag.

"He's gone," Sully said tersely. He swung up on Old Scratch.

"Gone?" Patrick turned in a circle, looking frantically up at the surrounding hilltops. He ran to the base of the hill Slocum had climbed with Tip, and bent to pick up something. Slocum's spyglass. Forlornly, Patrick looked up the hill. "Tip? *Tipper!*"

Slocum stepped up on Cheyenne. "Mount up!" he barked.

"But where's me brother?" Patrick wailed. "What have ye done with him?"

For just a half second, Slocum felt sorry for the kid, but anger toward his idiot brother overshadowed it. He growled, "He ran off to Paolo's men. Now, get up or we'll leave you. And bring along that spyglass!"

Patrick looked up at him, blinking back tears of anger and resentment and worry. "I'm comin'," he said, trotting back, and stuck a foot in the stirrup.

14

When they rode up to the crumbling church, Da barked, "Git ye down, Tipperary!"

Tip did, slithering to the weedy ground. He wished his father would explain these shenanigans. Why was Da riding with the Mexican bandit, for instance, and why hadn't he spoken a word since he'd ordered Tip up behind him on the horse? That had been almost an hour ago.

Now Tip found himself standing in the dusty courtyard of what must be, he thought, an old Spanish mission. Here and there, weeds grew up through the cobblestones that surrounded an old well. The adobe church was before him, its cross still intact, and a second building, long and low and roofless, was to his right.

Both buildings bore the scorch marks of long-ago fires, and the glass in their windows, if indeed they had ever owned any, had long since been broken out. The little mission yard was an island of green in the rocks. A thick grove of paloverde—sulphur yellow with spring flowers and interspersed with other, much taller trees—grew round the church itself and spread toward the other structure. It reminded Tip a little of the ancient places back home, all gone to rack and ruin, but left standing for centuries in their crumbling glory.

"Da?" Tip said as the Mexican man led his father's horse and his own away. "Da, what is this place?"

Seamus Rafferty Carnahan didn't answer. Instead, he cocked hands on his narrow hips and angrily said, "Jaysus Christ, Tipper! Who brung ye to this distant land?"

Anger bubbled in Tip, but he tamped it down as best he could. "You did! You wrote, Da, or don't you remember? It was money you were wantin', money to set you free."

"Aye, money," Seamus spat. "Not some whelp, still wet behind the ears."

Tip could hold it back no longer. "Where's your captors then?" he shouted. "Where's this terrible fellow Martinez? We were picturin' you bound in chains, for the love'a Mike!"

"We?"

"Mum and me. Patrick and the girls. Or don't you recall their names?" he added sarcastically.

Seamus lifted his chin. "Moira, Iris, and Siobhan," he said curtly. "Siobhan must be near three by now. How do they fare?"

Tip sniffed. "Don't pretend you're carin'," he muttered, but he winced in pain when Seamus suddenly slapped him across the face hard.

"Don't be takin' that tone with me, boyo."

His cheek was bright with pain, but Tip held his ground. "I'll take any tone I please, old man."

They stood there for a minute, staring at each other while each tried to decide who was the angriest.

Tip felt that he was winning. He had grown inches taller since he'd last seen his father, and now he looked down on him, where before, back home in Ireland, he'd had to look up. He found it made a good bit of difference, this new perspective. Either that, or perhaps it was the time they'd spent apart, or his father's tan or foreign clothes, or his Stetson hat.

Whatever the reason, Seamus Carnahan didn't frighten him anymore, not by half. Who could be afraid of a funny little scarecrow, even if the blasted terrier of a man had poached and swindled and thieved his way across half of Ireland, even if his threats and his fists had cowed the whole family for years?

A grin spread over Tip's face. "You don't scare me, Da. Not anymore."

Seamus's hands twitched at his sides, and that familiar look—the one he used to get right before he took off his belt—overtook his features. But his fingers didn't go to his buckle. Instead, he said, "You don't know what scared is, bucko."

And then he hauled off and punched Tip square in the jaw.

As Tip was falling backward, he had just enough time to think what a grand thing it was that such a tiny man could have such amazing strength—and then he cracked his head on the side of the old well.

Everything went black.

When he woke, he found they'd dragged him inside the church. A few broken or half-burnt benches lay about, and they'd tied him to one of the last still in one piece. He was alone with his head throbbing to beat the band. Gingerly, he twisted about, trying to get his bearings.

The door was at his back, and he sat in the center

of the place, on a floor strewn with old bottles, straw and kindling, and some broken tack. Here and there, a stray weed peeked up through the cracked floor. The windows were all smashed away and the trees were growing in right through the open sashes, but one section of glass remained.

In the upper left-hand corner of what had once been a great stained-glass window above the altar, bits of blue and red twinkled brightly. The sun streamed through them, turning them to glittering jewels, as if to tell him that there was always hope.

"The hope of more horse manure," he muttered bitterly, then licked at his dry lips.

Again, he twisted toward the door. He could see but a slice of the courtyard. He couldn't see the well at all, and could hear nothing save for the wind softly whistling along the cobblestones and sighing through the windows.

"Have you gone off and left me then, you old coward?" he whispered.

Suddenly, he paled, for he'd just realized that all his pockets had been turned out, the ones he could see anyway. He bent one knee and stamped his foot on the floor, then bent the other one and did the same.

He relaxed, and let his head fall back. He still had his money. At least he wouldn't die poor.

And it would be just like Da, wouldn't it, to abandon him in this state. After all, the old git had run off to America without a word, and left poor Mum with five mouths to feed plus her own. The only reason he'd taken Fiona along was so he'd have something to sell. The filthy bastard had probably sold her a hundred times on the crossing, and more on the way to San Francisco.

For the very first time, Tip realized that his anger, all the rage he'd felt toward everyone from sailors to sheriffs, to Slocum, to his own sweet brother, to Mum and Fiona and everybody in between, was directed at Da. It was the old man that he'd been so royally pissed at all these years. Not fat men with fatter purses on the docks, not seamen showing Patrick how to do scrimshaw. Not the constabulary, nor that poor fellow back at Murphy's Tavern. Not even cheating old stable men.

It was Da. It had always been Da.

He should have had a father like Sully or Slocum. Da wouldn't have trailed them clear across a mammoth canyon and shot that vile cougar. Da wouldn't have taught him how to shoot with his very own rifle, given to him by the territorial governor of Colorado. Da would have been off drunk somewhere. Or in jail.

Suddenly, he brightened. Why, they'd be coming to save him, Mr. Slocum and Mr. Washington! Da and that Mexican might have ridden off with nary a thought for him, but Slocum and Sully and Patrick would be coming along any minute now.

Oh, he knew they'd have a few choice words for him—Slocum the worst, if he didn't miss his guess—but they'd come, and they'd set him free. They had every time since he'd met them, hadn't they? He'd explain about Da, and then they could all go back.

He wasn't quite sure where they'd go back to, but he reassured himself that it'd have to be a great deal better than this. At the moment, he would have paid five dollars for a single drink of that bug-ridden water.

He straightened at the sound of hooves on cobblestones. Sully and Slocum and Patrick, come to save him already! He must have been unconscious longer than he thought.

He strained to hear the leather-creak sound of a man dismounting, and then the soft and steady *ching-ching* of spurs drawing nearer. It wouldn't be Sully then. Sully wore those short little spurs, the kind with a little round knob on the end and no rowels.

"Mr. Slocum?" he called, doing his best to be polite as well as grateful. He'd been a fool again, and he knew it. "I'm in here, sir!"

But the man who walked through the mission door wasn't Slocum, and Tip slumped against his bonds in disappointment.

"Slocum, is it, Tipperary?" said Seamus with a frown. "Seems to me I've heard of this Slocum character. Was he one'a the fellows you were with then?"

Tip didn't respond, only turned his head away. Da might have fought his way free of Paolo Martinez, but he was a dangerous character to strangers and family alike. And by the looks of him, he'd gotten more so. Tip didn't think bandying Slocum's name about would be too smart at this juncture. Fiona had said he was practically famous, after all.

Seamus crossed the room and knelt at Tip's side. He produced a knife, and involuntarily, Tip flinched.

Seamus smiled nastily. "Ye'd think I was goin' to cut you, boyo," he said, and deftly severed the rope that bound Tip's hands.

Free of the bench at last and rubbing at his wrists, Tip scrambled to his feet. "Why'd you tie me in the first place, Da?"

"Why, so you wouldn't run off, lad! Jorge and me—

self had a bit of business to attend, and we didn't want you vacatin' the premises before I had a chance to talk to you about old times."

Once again, Tip remained silent. Old times? What could they possibly have to talk about? The belt? The beatings? The drink and Da's long absences from home—either self-inflicted or insisted upon by the local authorities?

Tip had hated him and idolized him at the same time. It was beyond comprehension that such a thing could be, but it was there nonetheless.

"Care for a wee nip?" Seamus asked, and pulled a flat silver flask from his back pocket. He took a long pull himself, then held it out to Tip. "I'm thinkin' you're of an age now."

When Tip didn't respond, Seamus wiggled it and sternly said, "Take it, boy!"

Old habits died hard, and Tip took the flask. Eyeing it for a moment, he at last lifted it to his lips and took a swig.

The liquor—he didn't know what kind—seared his mouth and burned its way down his throat, and he sputtered, his eyes tearing.

Seamus laughed and slapped his thigh. "You're still a babe, lad. Can't hold your liquor."

Tip handed the flask back. Hoarsely, he said, "Ye haven't changed a whit."

The irony of this statement was apparently lost on Seamus, who grinned at him, took another sip, then pocketed the flask. "Jorge!" he called.

The Mexican man came through the door. Somehow, he looked even fiercer than he had before. He was taller than Seamus, but still no more than medium-sized in height. Broad was another matter. The man looked like he battled bulls with his bare hands, and his fists were the size of small hams.

Seamus babbled something at him in Spanish and Jorge babbled something back, and the only word of it that Tip understood was "Slocum." The Mexican looked curiously upset at the mention of it too.

"You'll have to be pardonin' old Jorge," Seamus said conspiratorially. "The heathen bastard don't speak a word of English."

He sat down on the bench Tip had been tied to and relaxed in a slouch, his arms spread wide along the back rail. "So tell me, Tipper, who were these other two sods ye were ridin' across the desert with?"

"First, you tell me somethin'."

Seamus shrugged. "Fair's fair."

"Why?" Tip said. "Why'd you write that letter? Ye sent the selfsame message to Fiona as you did to us, but not a word that you'd got yourself free from Martinez. Didn't you think we'd be worried sick and scared to death, Da?"

In truth, nobody had been all that worried, but Tip, being a true Irishman and a good Catholic to boot, knew to lay on the guilt when he had a chance.

"Did ye give a thought to poor Mum," he said, "workin' her fingers to the bone, and with the added misery of you, a continent away, in the hands of thugs and villains? Why didn't you write us again, you bleedin' bastard?"

Tip's timbre had risen a good deal more than he'd planned, and trembling, he closed his mouth with an audible *click*.

But Seamus didn't jump up and hit him again, a move for which Tip had been tensed and ready. Instead, he grinned wide. "Why, I never got free of Paolo Martinez, Tipper, darlin'."

"What? But you said he was goin' to be killin' you! You said—"

Seamus waved a hand lazily. "Oh, a man will say plenty of things when there's money to be had and he's in need of it. I thought for sure Fiona would provide, but the ungrateful bitch didn't give me so much as the pleasure of tellin' me to sod off. But you, Tipper, darlin', you've done me proud. You did bring it, did ye not?"

Tip glared at him.

Seamus smiled. "Ye've got it, all right. Just not on your person. It's back with the other three, isn't it? Well, soon enough, soon enough. And I think you'll be needin' some convincin' about this other matter." He turned his head and spoke in Spanish to Jorge, who grinned, stepped forward, and snagged Tip by the collar of his shirt.

"Now," said Seamus, who hadn't budged from his seat on the pew. "Who were those other two gentlemen?"

When Tip didn't answer, Seamus signaled to Jorge, who cuffed Tip across the back of his already throbbing head so hard that he saw stars.

"Oh, he won't kill you," Seamus commented. Through eyes seeing triple, Tip saw all three of him dig into his pocket for the little silver flask.

"You might find yourself wishin' you were dead," the wobbling triplets said, "but he won't be puttin' you in your grave. Least not a'purpose. You're me son, after all. And now," he said, leaning forward and propping sharp elbows in his bony knees, "I'll be after tryin' again. Who were those other two fellows?"

15

"Give me a pistol!" Patrick demanded.

"For the third time, no, dammit!" Slocum hissed. "And get the hell down!" He leaned over, placed his hand atop the boy's head, and shoved him down below the level of the old, eroding sill.

They had left the horses well back, hidden around the base of a rise, and Sully had scouted the lay of the land. At the moment, Slocum and Patrick were in the long, low building that overlooked the courtyard. By now, Sully would be across the way, around the side of the old mission, hidden in the trees.

Two horses waited beside the well. Two riders. And since the structure in which Slocum and Patrick were crouched looked to have been recently used for a barn, Slocum didn't figure there were any more.

Faintly, he heard intermittent voices coming from inside the church. Not words, just sounds. Not angry exactly, but raised.

The voices came again, and Patrick whispered, "That's Tipper!"

Slocum rechecked his pistols. "Yeah," he said.

He dropped the Colt back into its holster, then slid the smaller pistols home, into their cross-draw rig. He turned to Patrick.

"Listen, kid, and listen good. I want you to stay put, you hear? Stay here and stay down."

"But—"

"But nothin'," Slocum said sternly. "Your sister wants you and Tip back in one piece, and I aim to get you there that way."

Patrick's round face puckered with worry and his blue eyes were shiny with unshed tears, but roughly he said, "Aye, sir."

"Good boy," Slocum said, and slipped out the back way.

Why is it that I'm always talking to these kids like they're a couple of damn dogs in training? he wondered as he crept from tree to tree. He had drawn his Colt again. It was ready.

He had just reached the side of the church, and plastered himself against the rough, scorch-marked adobe wall, when he heard Sully's signal. That was fine for Sully, he thought in irritation. Sully probably had a nice big tree over there. He'd probably already shinnied up it and was staring in the window, ready to hop inside with his guns out.

Slocum, on the other hand, found himself about two feet below the nearest window, and the only trees around were scrawny paloverdes that wouldn't have held his weight if he'd paid them. He could jump up and grab the sill, all right, but the noise he'd make clambering up to get through it would pretty much defeat the purpose.

"Shit," he whispered, and then he signaled back at Sully, a soft whistling quail call that they'd agreed upon. The signal said, "Hold up, I've got a problem."

He began to work his way forward, edging his way

quietly along the wall toward the front of the church. Ancient broken glass crunched softly under his boots, but he figured the fellows inside were making enough noise to cover it.

And then suddenly, he stopped and really listened. He could hear most of the conversation plainly now, and all of that Irish brogue wasn't coming from Tip.

The old sonofabitch! Slocum ground his teeth. Tip was in there with his own father and some *bandido*, and they were both against him, by the sound of it.

"Damn it, boyo!" he heard Seamus suddenly shout. "Button salesman, me foot. Ye've surely got your mum's stubborn streak!"

In Spanish, he heard the *bandido* say that the boy wasn't going to talk, that unless Seamus wanted him dead, he'd better think of another way.

What information could Seamus want badly enough to endanger his own son's life?

Well, there wasn't time to sit and mull it over right at the moment. Slocum started moving again.

Just as he eased up to the corner of the building, the *bandido* emerged, headed for the well. He was muttering and he carried a wooden bucket. By the sound of him, the boy had passed out again, and the *bandido* was growing weary of it.

Slocum didn't hesitate. He leapt forward and grabbed the Mexican around the neck, yanking him off his feet at the same time he brought down the butt of his pistol on the man's skull. As the unconscious *bandido* fell back on him—and the bastard weighed nearly as much as a yearling steer—Slocum managed to swing his arm out in time to catch the empty bucket just before it could clatter to the cobblestones.

As quietly as he could, he shimmied out from beneath the *bandido*. Plastering himself to the wall outside the door, he put fingers to his lips again and softly whistled. He was ready.

When the birdcall came in reply, Slocum swung into the open doorway, his pistol cocked. Tip lay on the floor, semiconscious, and his father stood over him, blinking in surprise.

The shock on his face swiftly gave way to a cocky grin, however. He looked a great deal like his sons, but there was a lot more mileage—none of it good—on his face. He was a great deal better armed too.

"Ye'd be Slocum then?" he said.

"I would," Slocum replied, and kept his gun pointed straight at Seamus's forehead. Where was Sully? He should have come leaping in that window straightaway.

"Unbuckle your gunbelt and let it drop," said Slocum.

Seamus did so without argument. "I'm thinkin' that you're the selfsame Slocum that cramped those rogue strikebreakers up in Crown City," he said as his gunbelt slid to the floor. "The one who gunned down Pedro Diaz, and who was after that Louis Sanchez fellow. You catch him, bucko?"

Slocum said nothing.

"I may be new to this grand country of yours," Seamus confided, setting his hands on his narrow hips, "but I keep me ears open. It's quite the reputation you've got, sir."

Slocum remained silent and kept his eyes on Seamus. Where the hell was Sully? Not that he was worried about holding one shanty Irishman at bay, but it wasn't like Sully to just disappear.

"Well," Seamus continued, pursing his lips, "I didn't believe the lad a'tall, a'tall." He pointed down at Tip, who was just trying to lift his head. He didn't look good. "He was tryin' to tell me that you were some fellow named Festus Slocum," Seamus continued. "A button salesman from Frisco, of all things! Said he was travelin' down from Dirty Dog with you and two of your pals." He laughed. "Got the gift of blarney, that boy'a mine. Course," he added, pulling himself up a mite, "he's got to get a lot better at it to run the course with yours truly."

"Move away from him," Slocum said, and moved the barrel of the gun, just slightly, for emphasis. He didn't like this Irish sonofabitch, didn't like him one bit, and suddenly, he had a lot more insight into what made these boys tick.

Seamus spread his hands, palms wide. "Oh, be glad to, be glad to!" Smiling, he stepped carefully to the side. "Would this be far enough for ye? Say, you wouldn't by any chance be in charge of carryin' my money, would you? The lad told me he'd left it back with his party."

"Mr. Slocum?" came Tip's weak voice. "Would . . . would that be yourself?"

"Stay put, kid. And you, Daddy," he added as he deftly unwound a bit of rope from the back of a bench, "over here."

"Certainly, certainly!" Seamus said, walking nearer. "Would you be wantin' me to sit down then?"

Cocky little bastard! Slocum shot out a hand and shoved Seamus down on the bench, then tied his hands behind his back and secured the rope to the pew. He seated his Colt back home in its holster with a quick snap of his wrist, then went to Tip.

"Oh, he'll be fine," Seamus said happily. The lilt was even stronger in his voice than in his sons', and for some reason Slocum couldn't fathom, that pissed him off as much as anything else.

"We Carnahans have strong skulls, we do," Seamus added.

Slocum lifted the boy's head. Tip was still dazed, but he smiled up weakly and whispered, "Ye've come for me then."

Slocum looked up and shouted, "Sully! Get in here, goddamn it!" and then gently he laid the boy back down. "Got a little business to attend to," he said, thinking it'd be time for that *bandido* to be waking up pretty soon. "You just stay put."

"No, *señor*," said a new voice from the doorway.

Slocum's hand went to his gun, but a slug, echoing thinly in the roofless mission, spat into the clay floor beside him, and he stilled his hand.

A Mexican stood in the doorway, and he was holding a bound and teary-eyed Patrick by his collar. Grinning, he wiggled the barrel of his gun. "Better," he said.

Seamus twisted toward the door. "Why, Patrick!" he said, shocked. "I thought I told you to stray no farther from home than Kelly's farm!"

"Sorry, Da," said Patrick miserably.

Seamus turned back toward Slocum, and he was shaking his head. "Children," he said. "They don't listen to a word you say. Well, it's likely my fault. It takes a lot of the belt to raise up a child right, and I'm afraid I've not been home of late to administer it."

From the floor, Tip tried to bark, "You bastard." It came out more as a whimper.

"And they've got shitty mouths too," Seamus said with a scowl. "What'd I tell you about that, Tipper?"

The sound of a squeaking wooden wheel scraping over the cobbles caught Slocum's attention, and he looked toward the door just in time to see two splinted legs poke through it. The rest followed directly.

"Paolo Martinez," Slocum said curtly.

The man in the wheelbarrow, his broken legs stretching stiffly into the air before him, held a hand up to the *bandido* who was steering him through the door. "It is I," he said simply.

Martinez was rough-looking, with a stubbly beard and a big mustache, and he wore clothing that was dusty and nondescript, being neither wholly Mexican nor American, but half of each. A welted scar ran down his face from just above his eyebrow to the line of his chin, and had drawn his eyelid down like the flap of an envelope.

"And who would you be, *señor*? Surely you are not the son of our Irish friend."

"His name's Slocum," said Seamus. "The one and only, if I'm not missin' my guess. Slocum, I've got to tell ye—for a lad with a good Irish name, you're not even a wee bit talkative."

"It is an honor, Señor Slocum," Paolo Martinez said, and tipped his head in a bow. "I have heard stories about you. All of them bad, of course."

"Ones I heard about you were pretty much the same," Slocum said. The *bandido* he'd clubbed over the head was now standing in the doorway, behind Martinez and his carter. He had his hat off, and rubbed at his skull. If Sully was outside, now would be a real good time for him to come barreling through the window or over the wall, guns blazing.

"Are you wondering where your big black friend is?" Paolo said suddenly, as if he were reading Slocum's mind. "We have heard of him also. Señor Sullivan Washington, *El Negro Grande*. He is *muy malo*, no?"

Slocum was getting itchy. While Paolo was speaking, he'd heard a number of horses—and what he was certain was a wagon—being led or ridden over the cobbles and up to the door. He wasn't having the most hopeful thoughts about Sully either.

"Ah, so that's the fourth fellow!" Seamus exclaimed. "A filthy bounty hunter! Did ye catch him then, Paolo? And if it wouldn't be too much of a bother, could one of you lads be untyin' me?"

The big man who'd come through the door first made a move toward Seamus, but Paolo raised a hand, stopping him. Seamus's brow furrowed. He opened his mouth in a question, but Paolo spoke first.

In Spanish, Paolo told the lummox that Slocum had knocked cold to go find some rope. While the *bandido* fetched it, Paolo said, "I'm afraid this friend of yours has come upon a great misfortune, Slocum. In fact, he may be dead. Esteban tells me that when he left him, he was not sure whether he would survive to tell the tale."

The man who'd come in the door wheeling Paolo smiled and gave a small nod.

"Of course," Paolo continued, "Esteban did not wish to spend a bullet and alert you. Esteban apparently forgot that he had a knife. Or hands."

Esteban suddenly stopped smiling.

"But we do not wish to harm you, Señor Slocum," Paolo went on.

"All we want is me money," said Seamus. For a man that was tied up, Slocum thought he was talking awfully big.

Paolo cocked a brow. "They did not have it?"

"The boy didn't," Seamus replied. "I'm not knowin' about the other whelp. Or Slocum."

The man who had Patrick began to turn out his pockets. The boy squirmed, and the *bandido* boxed his ears a good deal harder than was necessary.

"Stop it!" bellowed Slocum, and took a step forward.

The sound of Esteban's pistol cocking stopped him. Patrick was unconscious by that time anyway.

The ape who had gone for rope was back, along with two new *bandidos*, both with their guns drawn.

"You will not do anything foolish, *señor?*" Paolo asked. The question was entirely rhetorical, and when Paolo signaled him to unstrap his guns, Slocum slowly dropped his pistols to the floor.

"Back away," said Paolo.

His jaw muscles working, Slocum did.

"Paolo, me darlin'," Seamus said, "these ropes are beginnin' to chafe at me."

"Uno momento," Paolo said, and as three men descended on Slocum, tied his hands behind his back, and patted his pockets, emptied them, and threw his possessions on the floor—and pocketed his compass and his watch—Paolo whispered with Esteban, who left directly.

Satisfied that neither Slocum or Patrick had the money they were looking for—although they took the four dollars and change that Slocum had in his back pocket as well as his guns—they tossed Patrick's unconscious body next to Slocum, and hog-tied Tip too. The poor kid had passed out again.

Esteban was back. *"Nada,"* he said.

"It has to be there!" Seamus roared. "Check again!"

"Ah, *amigo,* I am afraid that you are unlucky today," Paolo said with a shake of his head. "No money on the boys or this man, and I am told that Señor Washington had less than fifty dollars as well. And no money in their saddlebags."

Slocum jerked against his ropes, and felt a swift kick to the backs of his knees in response. He fell forward, landing on his knees with a *thud* that sounded a hell of a lot duller than it felt.

Seamus laughed nastily.

"You are in a good mood, no?" Paolo said to Seamus as Slocum gritted his teeth and more men crowded through the door. There had to be at least ten that he could see. Only the Lord knew how many were still outside on the courtyard. He cursed himself for not being more careful, for not figuring the two that they'd followed to have backup.

"No, I'm not," Seamus replied, suddenly sober again. "I want me two thousand. And I'd be most appreciative," he added, half-shouting, "if somebody'd step forward and start sawin' at me ropes!"

Paolo adjusted one of his legs. It was a downright weird sight, him in that wheelbarrow. It must be damned uncomfortable. At least, Slocum hoped that it was.

Paolo grunted at his leg, then looked up at Seamus. "No, I do not believe I will set you free. I grow weary of you, my Irish friend. Ramon tells me there was a small question of an extra bag of gold in Poplar Flats."

For the first time, Seamus looked nervous.

"And as I remember, the count came up short after the Kingman job, did it not?"

Behind Paolo, two men nodded grimly, and another curled fingers around his rifle.

"No," said Paolo with a shake of his head. "I think you are retiring, Seamus. I think this is what they call an enforced retirement."

"But—"

"Shut up," snapped Paolo. "And you, Señor Slocum? I think we will be magnanimous today. I think we will let you live." He fussed at his leg again. "I thank you for the horses, by the way. Two of them are very nice. I think maybe I will be riding the Appaloosa mare very soon. I think she suits me."

Anger, white hot, surged through Slocum's veins. Bad enough that the sonofabitch'd had his own kids beaten senseless; worse yet that his *bandido* friends had likely killed Sully. But to leave them high and dry with no horses, almost twenty miles from the nearest town over a harsh desert?

He didn't know which made him madder, the fact that Paolo was abandoning them all to a slow death— or the next thing to it—or the fact that the bastard was stealing his horse.

He ground his teeth.

While Paolo had been giving his nasty little speech, the ape from the courtyard had walked up behind Seamus, who was frantically twisting against his bonds. His hat had fallen off with his gyrations, and his red hair was dark with sweat and slicked to his head.

"Paolo, darlin', surely ye must be havin' me on!" Seamus cried, a quaver in his voice. "Ye can't kill the sole father to these poor boys! What will the lads do without my encouragin' presence?"

Calmly, Paolo said, "Jorge."

A grinning Jorge raised his pistol, pressed the barrel against Seamus's sweat-streaked temple.

"Are ye mad?" Seamus whispered, and his eyes had gone wild. He was shaking now, shuddering so hard the bench clattered against the floor.

Slocum whispered, "Don't, Martinez."

Paolo said, "Jorge."

Jorge pulled the trigger.

16

With a pounding head and bleary eyes, Tip slowly regained consciousness to find the bandits gone. Like Tip, Slocum was bound hand and foot, except that Slocum was struggling to reach his own boot. Tip counted himself lucky that he was just seeing one of Slocum instead of three, although the one he was seeing was damned blurry.

"Mr. Slocum, sir?" he said through a dry mouth and cracking lips. "Could I be assistin' ye in some way?"

"About time you came round," Slocum grumbled, and scooting forward on the clay floor, he repositioned himself. He shoved his boots behind Tip's back, next to his bound hands. "There's a knife in there, kid. Get it out."

Tip began to fumble clumsily with the boot top. "Are the brigands gone then?" he asked.

" 'Bout twenty minutes, by my reckoning. No, not there, dammit! Can't you feel, for Christ's sake? To your left, and yank up the cuff of my britches."

"And Patrick?" Tip said as his fingers finally claimed the grip of the knife. He began to work it free. "Does he fare well?"

"He's breathin'," Slocum said.

The knife slid out at last, and Tip scooted up until

he felt it pass to Slocum's hands. He sagged against his ropes, exhausted, his head pounding in time to his heartbeat.

"Where's Da then?" he asked, his cheek against the cool of the clay tile floor. "Gone too, I suppose. Gone off and left us. Again."

He heard a rope tear and pop, then heard Slocum sit up. And begin to work at the rope binding his feet. Another pop, this one faster. As Slocum finally began to saw at the rope binding Tip's hands, he finally said, "He's outside."

"Outside?" Tip shouted, and was immediately sorry. Not only did the effort scrape a razor of pain up his throat, but the sound of his own voice felt like a thousand sledgehammers, all intent on pounding his brains to a pulp.

More quietly—and through gritted teeth—he said, "You mean the old crook's right outside the door and bein' no earthly help to us? Did they go off and leave him too?"

Tip's hands came free, and clumsily, he brought them around in front of him and began to rub at his wrists. Slocum moved toward Patrick. He appeared to be out cold, but his sides were moving with each breath he took. He was alive, all right. Tip began to work at the ropes round his ankles.

"Well, did they?" Tip insisted, tugging at the knot.

Slocum paused with his knife. "In a manner of speakin', son."

Tip tensed. It wasn't like Slocum to speak so kindly to him, and his tone had been smooth as silk. Not like him at all. And he'd called him son. . . .

"No," Tip whispered. A ripple of disbelief passed

through him, and then a terrible, heavy sadness. "No," he repeated, and he felt his head slowly moving back and forth.

"I'm sorry," Slocum said softly. "There was nothin' I could do." He looked at Tip a moment longer, the look saying more about pity—and about getting on with things—than words could have managed, and then he turned again toward Patrick's ropes.

Numbly, Tip finished untying his ankles and slowly got to his feet. Wobbling as much from his head wound and the lack of circulation to his feet as from shock, he followed a smeared trail of blood that began at the bench and led out the door.

And then he stopped, leaning heavily against the wide door frame. There was Da, lying face-up in the sun. Somebody had crossed his arms neatly over his chest. The head wound, the one that had left all that terrible blood, wasn't anywhere near so tidy. Half his face was gone, and the flies lazily buzzed over it.

Tip slowly slid down to the front steps, his eyes riveted on his father. "See, Da?" he whispered as tears slowly streamed down his cheeks. "See what you've done, you poor, lunatic fool of an Irishman?"

Slocum found Sully in an arroyo behind the mission. When he first saw the body, he was sure Sully was dead. There were signs of an ambush—of four men who had hidden in the brush—and a brief tussle, and then it looked like Sully had rolled or fallen back down into the wash. And he hadn't gotten up again. The wash was steep-sided, and the tracks of the other men didn't venture down after him.

Slocum skidded down the side of the arroyo, nearly

losing his balance and taking a tumble himself before he came to a halt a few feet from the big man. The bandits hadn't stripped Sully of his guns. Likely, he'd fallen before they had a chance to grab anything but his wallet, and in their hurry to steal the damned horses, the *bandidos* had forgotten all about going back for his guns.

Slocum knelt next to the body. Sully was lying face-down, but he was breathing. With some effort, Slocum got him rolled over. He'd smashed his head good, all right. The bandits had smacked him over the back of the head with something that had left a rising goose egg, and the stone against which he'd landed against hadn't done him any good either. It was covered in blood, and Sully's right eye and cheek dripped with it.

"Shit," Sully groaned suddenly, and Slocum jumped.

"Jesus, Sully!" he breathed. "You tryin' to give me an apoplexy?"

Slowly, Sully opened the eye that wasn't full of blood. "Goddamned sonsofbitches," he growled. "What happened? You get 'em?" He tried to prop himself up on his elbow, but fell back again.

" 'Fraid they got me," Slocum said.

Sully closed his eye again. Angrily, he muttered, "There were only four of the weasels, goddammit. Couldn't you handle four, you sissy?"

Slocum grinned. "Well, hell, Sully! The four of 'em took you out, didn't they?"

"Cheated," came the reply. "The bastards whacked me with something." He lifted a hand and gingerly felt the back of his head. "Must have been a goddamn anvil."

"Front of your head's fair banged up too."

Sully's eye opened again. "I know that, you idiot. Stop blabbin' and help me sit up."

By the time Slocum got Sully up the side of the arroyo and back to the ruined church, he'd filled him in.

"And next time," Slocum added as they emerged from the trees and came out on the courtyard, "could you pick a goddamn birdcall that ain't so common?"

As if to punctuate his comment, a quail, somewhere back in the cover of the trees, whistled softly.

Sully began to chuckle, then suddenly stopped. Whether it was the pain in his head or the sight that greeted them in the courtyard, Slocum never knew.

Patrick was awake. He sat beside his father's body silently weeping, oblivious to everything else. Tip was in exactly the same place that Slocum had left him— in the doorway of the church, with his shoulders slumped and rounded. He wasn't crying at the moment, but the pale, dry tracks of tears were upon his dusty cheeks. Forlornly, he stared at Patrick, and at Seamus's body.

"That's a sorry sight, Slocum," Sully said softly.

"Got a feeling it's gonna get worse," Slocum replied. Besides stealing the horses, Paolo Martinez's men had taken everything on them, which included Slocum's folding shovel. They were going to have to carry a lot of rocks to get Seamus underground, and none of them were in the greatest shape.

Best to get on with it, though.

The old cemetery was still there, although it was overgrown with brambles and spring weeds, and most of the markers were so eroded that they defied you to read them. He set Patrick to work clearing a place while he lugged Seamus's corpse out there. Sully had volunteered, but the big man was still weak from the blows he'd taken to the head. He stayed in the shade of the well, washing his face from the bucket Slocum had drawn.

After Patrick and Tip had scooped a shallow trough from the hard ground and Slocum had gathered the biggest stones he could find, they buried Seamus beneath a gravelly cairn of limestone and shale. Slocum topped it off with a layer of the big rocks he'd brought up. He hoped they'd keep the coyotes out.

And then the three of them just stood there, staring at the mound.

"Tip?" Slocum said at last. "Patrick? You want to say some words?"

"Aye, I will," Tip said. He looked past Slocum toward Sully, who was slowly making his way toward them. "We'll be waitin' for Mr. Washington."

Sully arrived, sat heavily to straddle a limestone marker, and nodded at Tip. His moist bandanna was pressed to the side of his face, and when he removed it momentarily, Slocum saw that his eye was swollen shut.

With his cap curled between his fingers, Tip began. "Heavenly Father, if you don't mind, I'd like to be sayin' a few words about Da. He was a right bastard, Da was. He was always slappin' our mum about, and us too. Seldom did he have a kind word for another soul, unless he was thinkin' they could do him some good."

Perplexed, Slocum looked up at Tip, but the boy was staring at the grave, sober as a priest. Beside him, Patrick did the same, except that he was nodding along with his brother's words. Seamus Rafferty Carnahan had been a royal pain in the ass from what Slocum had seen, but these boys had come halfway around the world to rescue him. A man would think they'd have something kind to say about him, even if they had to make it up!

"Da was in the jail as often as he was out," Tip went on. "He was fair cruel to man and beast alike. But, Dear Lord, he was Patrick's da and mine too, not to mention Fiona's and Siobhan's and Iris's and Moira's. Oh, he sold poor Fi into a life of degradation, and surely would have done the same to the other girls had he lived long enough. Well, if he'd still been in the same country with 'em.

"But now he's dead, Lord, and he was our da, and we're after askin' you to forgive him. If you're not minding a recommendation, Sir, I think a long stint in Purgatory would do him a world of good. Amen." He slapped his cap atop his head again.

Patrick too slid his hat back on. "Amen," he said tearily. "God rest him. That was grand, Tipper, just grand."

Sully slowly shook his head in disbelief, and Slocum saw him mouth, "Jesus Christ."

Slocum didn't say anything. He simply settled his hat back on his head and walked back up to the church. They had a very long hike to the town of Mission Springs, and he had to prepare for it. Morning would have to do, since Sully was in no shape to go anywhere tonight, and evening would be upon them in a couple of hours. But Slocum figured to find something besides that damn bucket that could carry water, even if he had to hollow out chunks of tree trunk.

He was going to get to Mission Springs, get himself another mount by hook or by crook, and go after Paolo Martinez.

And make him very, very sorry that he'd ever messed with a man called Slocum.

The next day found the foursome trudging southeast under a beating sun and a vaguely troubling sky. Slocum had managed to find three ancient gourds and an old whiskey bottle, and Patrick had come up with a frayed water bag, which he had repaired during the night. It leaked a little, but it was good enough.

They rationed the water and took turns carrying the heavy water bag, and even though they were slowed appreciably by Slocum's increasingly aching legs—and Sully's too, though the bastard would never admit it—they had made a good eight miles by noon.

The land around them had gradually changed from rock and gravel and sun-shimmered earth to the pale green of decent grazing land. Well, decent for southern Arizona. The hills had vanished as well, and had been replaced by gently rolling land. Here and there a stunted tree sprang up, and they walked past thick groves of prickly pear.

The sky too had changed. There was a faint yellow ochre cast to it that Slocum didn't like, a yellowish cast that could promise either fast, unforgiving winds or beating rain—or nothing at all. The Arizona Territory was like that.

On the other hand, at about mid-morning they'd found a road. It wasn't much of a road, granted, but it meant they were on the right path. Slocum hoped it also meant that some fool had put Mission Springs on a stage route. He kept his ears and eyes open for any sign of an approaching coach. One had better show up pretty damned soon, he thought. Each step he took was agony, and that sky wasn't looking any better. If it let loose, he hoped it let loose with rain. They could use some extra water right about now.

But he kept on moving, with Sully and the boys trailing behind, strung out like pack mules on a line. Nobody spoke. About an hour ago, one of the little peckerwoods had started singing—and he'd had a pretty good voice too—but Slocum had snapped, "Shut up!" over his shoulder. "Keep your damn mouths closed and breathe through your noses."

He hadn't heard a peep out of them since.

Actually, he was sort of sorry. He could have used some music right at the moment. It would have taken his mind off the skies, and the growing humidity.

Using Sully's pistol, Slocum had shot a few quail the night before—and gladly, considering that it was them he'd been whistling signals at, like a certified idiot—but they hadn't eaten since. His belly was beginning to hurt as bad as his calf muscles.

They stopped to rest for five minutes roughly every hour, but their pace had slowed considerably since morning. Also, their water supply was dwindling fast, due in large part to the repairs to the water bag having come undone. For poor Patrick, this was nearly the last straw. He trailed along behind the rest of them, head down.

"I'll not drink another drop then," he'd croaked when the bag had broken and gushed their precious water down into thirsty soil.

"Yes, you will," Slocum had said. "Still got a couple of gourds left."

"No, sir. I won't."

Slocum had been in too much pain to argue. These boys might be used to traveling shank's mare, but he figured it was going to take him a month of bed rest before his legs would be halfway back to normal. And he was goddamn thirsty.

At about two in the afternoon the clouds, which had been slowly inching toward them, moved in and the wind came up. It started out soft, and Slocum was glad for the light breeze, although he knew what was certainly coming. At least it dried the sweat on his face and kept him feeling a little cooler, even if it did speed up the men's dehydration.

But within a half hour, the pale clouds that had overtaken the sky were shouldered aside by darker ones, the color of dirty nickel. They rolled in fast, and the wind was rising. The men had to hold their hats down to keep them.

"No place to shelter," Sully croaked, squinting at the sky with the one eye that would open.

"Gonna have to make do," Slocum shouted over the wind. It had rapidly grown downright hostile, carrying bits of sticks and gravel, and increasing in velocity with each second. "Was there a ditch on your side'a the road back aways?"

Sully nodded, and without speaking, began to dog-trot back the way they'd come.

In the time it had taken them to speak a few words, the sky had gone from dirty gray to charcoal, and Slocum found that he could barely see Sully, who was only fifteen feet ahead of him. He too picked up his pace, although his burning thighs argued against it with every move.

"This way!" Sully shouted as a sapling blew past his ear.

Through the blow, Slocum spotted him up ahead. Tip was under his outstretched arm, and Patrick was holding onto Tip's belt for dear life.

Sully waved, and shouted again. "Down here!"

Slocum, leaning against the raging wind, followed.

He nearly fell over them, for he hadn't seen the edge of the shallow ditch, and that first step was longer than he'd anticipated. But he managed to miss them, and fell in a heap on Sully's far side.

Sully pulled Patrick's bandanna up to cover the boy's face. Tip watched and followed suit. Sully shouted, "Sonofabitch sure moved in fast!"

"Here she comes," cried Slocum, and ducked his head.

As the sky went black, the two men and the two boys covered their heads and huddled together. Bits of rock and brush and cactus pads came at them as if fired by a cannon, and Slocum felt a sting as something cut into his cheek.

They couldn't talk over the roar of the dust storm. They couldn't do anything but wait it out.

Which was just fine with Slocum. At least it got him off his aching legs.

As the wind whirled around him, pelted him, pulled at his clothing, and turned exposed skin into rawhide, Slocum considered that this could go on for a couple of hours. He was hot and tired and thirsty, and most of all, he was ticked off that any of this was happening at all.

That his horse had been stolen three times in as many weeks when, by rights, he should have been sitting at a poker table in the back of a barroom somewhere, was unconscionable.

And that he should have been deprived of female companionship for this long? Well, that just made him madder. When he caught up with Paolo Martinez, he was, by God, going to strangle him.

And when he got back up to Carson City, he was going to have a few choice words with Carmella too.

17

A sweet sound came to Slocum. It was a familiar sound, a comforting sound: the sound of a woman humming softly.

He was dreaming. He didn't want to open his eyes.

And then a cool cloth covered his brow. Carefully, he opened one eye.

"Welcome back, stranger," the vision said.

He knew he was dreaming now. "Dulcie?" he croaked. There she was—Dulciana Forbush—in all her blond and full-busted glory. He hadn't seen her for years, not since the last time he'd visited Daisy's House of Comfort, which was the best whorehouse in all of Dodge City. He wondered why, if this was a dream, she was wearing clothes at all, let alone men's work clothes! She wore a denim work shirt and denim britches, and it seemed to him that she should have been naked if his mind was arranging all this.

She smiled at him. She looked a little older, but the years had been kind. "Now, what the hell were you doin' out there with no water, you big ol' bear?" she purred. "You lost your senses along with your horse?"

"Out where?" he asked, and tried to sit up. The ache that shot through his stiff and sore muscles told him that this was no dream. He remembered the desert, the boys, and Sully—and that goddamn horse-thieving sonofabitch Martinez—all in a rush.

Now, just how in the world Dulcie had gotten here was a big question, but first things first. "Sully and the kids?" he asked.

"Just dandy," she said.

She had yellow hair—paler now than he remembered it, likely from the Arizona sun—but she also had the darkest, longest lashes he believed he'd ever seen.

She dipped the cloth in water, wrung it out, then replaced it on his brow. "You're not doin' so fine, though. That was quite a blow you took."

The last thing he remembered, he'd been hunkered down in that ditch, collar up, bandanna snugged over his nose, with his face turned into Sully's back and away from the pummeling wind.

Which did nothing to explain how he'd gotten to this neat, whitewashed, and lace-curtained room.

He said, "What blow?"

"Sully didn't figure you'd remember," she said. She had long, graceful fingers, with which she stroked his cheek. "You recall the dust storm?"

"Yeah."

"That's something anyhow. I tell you, Slocum, we get the next thing to twisters in these parts. Sully said you got bashed pretty bad in the back of the head. Said the storm picked up a sapling and whacked you with it."

It figured. What else could go wrong?

Gingerly, he lifted a hand and felt the back of his skull. There was a good-sized goose egg there, but it didn't hurt as much as he expected. His brow furrowed.

"How long?"

"Two days," she replied. "Been pourin' water and broth down your gullet like nobody's business. Honestly, Slocum, I know Paolo stole your horse and killed those boys' daddy, but anybody else would have just stayed put and waited for the stage to pass by."

"What stage?" he roared, and his head started to pound in punishment.

She clucked her tongue. "The road runs right past the old mission. Well, almost. A mile west. There's a coach once a day, runnin' between Mission Springs and Los Lobos."

"Now you tell me," he muttered. His head was quieting down some, and he asked, "What about you, Dulcie?"

She shrugged. "Oh, we picked you up after the storm. Or I did leastwise. Sully threw you across my horse and we started walkin'. Good thing we were less than a mile from the house."

"What house?"

She snorted. "This one, you big silly. Me and Joyce Marie—you remember her?"

Slocum shook his head. He just couldn't reconcile Dulcie with her present surroundings, or her wardrobe. All he could think about was Dulcie, all those years ago, sitting on top of a piano and surrounded by admirers. She'd been wearing a bright pink dress, and she'd been laughing. And she'd thrown him a wink. It was a world away.

"Well, come to think of it," Dulcie said, pushing up the sleeve of her work shirt, "she was after your time. Anyway, we decided to break it off clean with the sportin' life. Joyce Marie's fella sent for her, you know? I just come along. I had me a little stake built up, and I figured, well, it was time."

She changed the cloth on his forehead again. " 'Cept about three weeks after we got here and Joyce Marie got hitched, her husband up and got himself killed. Got bucked off a horse and busted his fool neck. So Joyce Marie and me decided to make a go of his place. We're small, we only run about a hundred sixty head. Well, a hundred eighty, but about twenty of 'em are like pets."

She lifted the cloth, refolded it, and put it back in place. "Anyhow, that's where you are now, Slocum. The Double R, for Richard Riley. That was Joyce Marie's fella's name."

Slocum listened in silence. He could not, for the life of him, picture Dulciana Forbush—the daintily scented lover of lace hankies and silk sheets and bawdy barroom songs and slippery sex—shoving a bunch of cows around. At last, he said, "You serious?"

"Hope to kiss a pig, I am," she said with a grin. "This here's our third year. We're makin' money. Not much, but enough. Well, it would be enough if . . ."

She paused, then turned her head slightly and gave him a sly look. "How you feelin', honey doll?" She bent toward him. "It's been a mighty long dry spell for me. Mighty long. All the menfolk around here are either married or plug ugly or dumb as dirt." She leaned closer and cooed, "Remember all those high times we had back in Dodge?"

He pulled her down to him and kissed her long and slow, and suddenly, his legs didn't seem all that stiff. He thumbed open the bone buttons on her worn, blue shirt and tugged her camisole free of her britches, running his hand up under her clothes, up over her stomach and ribs, to clasp her round, full breasts.

"I guess you do," she whispered, her hand gripping his already stiff cock through the covers. Her mouth, bow-shaped and full, twisted into a grin. "You feel like makin' an old ranch woman happy, Slocum?"

"Reckon I could fit it in into my schedule," Slocum rumbled, and lifted the camisole to expose her. Her nipples, shell-pink and tiny, were already darkened and knotted hard with desire. He sucked one into his mouth, and Dulcie hissed.

"Good boy," she whispered. "Nice Slocum."

He wasn't going to be good for much longer. He felt exceedingly bad, but in the best way possible.

With his teeth, which were digging softly into her nipple, he held her tethered while his hands ripped at her belt and the buttons on her britches. Breathing hard, she helped him and kicked her way clear of them, as well as her underdrawers.

"Leave go for a minute," she whispered, and he unclamped his teeth so that she could sit up and divest herself of the shirt and camisole.

She ripped back his covers, and he wasn't too awful surprised to find that he was stark naked beneath them.

As she joined him on the bed, he said, "You been nursin' me exclusive-like, Dulcie?"

He slid a hand between her legs. She was already slick. Her inner thighs were moist, and when he slipped a finger inside her, it was like putting it into a jar of warm honey.

"Nobody else, Slocum," she murmured, and squirmed down against his hand.

He figured it had been so long for her that she was

about to pop, so he did the gentlemanly thing. He dipped his head, took her nipple in his mouth again, and began to suckle it deeply, roughly, and all the time he stroked her, petted her, teased her in that honeyed place. And just as he had expected, she spasmed almost immediately, craning her head back, the muscles in her neck straining as she locked her arms about him. He slid three fingers up inside her, and felt her muscles involuntarily clenching and unclenching around his hand.

He waited a moment longer and then he mounted her, pulling her knees up and wide, sinking his cock deep inside her with a sigh of pleasure.

Her eyes were slitted, and she whispered, "Why, Slocum, you nasty ol' cowboy . . ."

He ran his tongue along her throat, up that tanned column, along her jaw, and found her lips again. As he began to move, he kissed her deeply, and she clung to him, teasing his tongue, then sucking it as she moved to his rhythm.

He began to speed his thrusts slightly, and she wound her legs around his waist, urging him on. Soon he was riding her like there was no tomorrow, and the time for kissing was past. They were both caught up in some primordial haze, both back in time, back in Dodge, both racing toward the ultimate explosion of flesh and blood and consciousness.

She reached it just before he did, tensing unconsciously into a posture that left her pelvis tilted and wide open to him, and he took full advantage. He didn't wait for her, not by a long shot. He pounded into her, pumping just as fast and as hard as he could, until he too exploded with a loud groan.

Two more thrusts, and then he was still.

After a moment, he rolled off her. She was staring at him through slitted eyes, smiling, toying with a lock of her sweat-dampened yellow hair. "Jesus," she said, her breath still coming in tiny pants. "How much would you charge to stay around for a year or two?"

He grinned back at her. "You got anything to eat, Dulcie?"

"Besides me, you mean?"

He rubbed his hand over her belly, teasing at the damp curls at its base, then slid it up along her body to cup a breast. He leaned his head over and kissed the underside, then lipped the nipple. "That's dessert, honey."

She gave him a sly smile, then reluctantly sat up. "Well, I reckon if you're well enough to do what you just done, you're well enough to eat somethin' besides beef broth."

She stood up, stark naked, and picked her trousers up off the floor. She had one leg in before she stopped. "You gonna get the hell out of that bed and come get fed, or you gonna sit there for the rest of the afternoon starin' at my tits?"

He stuck his hands behind his head, the elbows pointing out like wings. "Tough decision, Dulcie."

She dropped her britches, yanked a pillow from beneath his head, and swatted him with it.

Laughing, he grabbed her arm and pulled her down on top of him. "I guess I ain't all that hungry, Dulcie," he said as he wound his arms around her waist.

"I ain't in that much of a hurry to cook either," she replied, and giggling, kissed him.

• • •

It was a good hour before they emerged from the bedroom into the house's large main room, and Sully was sitting in front of the fluttering yellow curtains, his feet propped up, reading a book.

He glanced up. " 'Bout time," he said. And then he took one look at Slocum and another at Dulcie, and in a disgusted voice said, "Christ. Don't you ever quit, Slocum?"

Slocum shrugged and swatted Dulcie on her rear, and Dulcie stuck her tongue out at Sully before she went to see what was in the larder. Dragging over a chair from the big oak table that centered the room, Slocum sat down on it backward and rested his forearms along the top of the back. "Where're the kids?" he asked.

Sully tipped his head toward the windows, through which Slocum could see a great stretch of land, bordered by distant hills. "Outside. Down at the barn. Joyce Marie had a late foal born last night. Quite a girl, that Joyce Marie."

Slocum cocked a brow. "Do I sense somethin' more than admiration for her foalin' skills?"

"I'm a gentleman," Sully replied archly. "I do not kiss and tell."

"Oh," Dulcie called from the stove, "they been doin' it like a couple a cats in heat ever since we found you boys. Been drivin' me peach-orchard crazy, if you wanna know the truth." She put something into a hot skillet, and it sizzled. "If you hadn't woke when you did, Slocum, I would'a raped you in your sleep."

Sully laughed. Slocum had the good sense to look sheepish. "Sorry I didn't come round sooner," he said.

"Actions speak louder than words," she replied.

"You can apologize again after you get your belly full'a vittles."

To Sully, Slocum said, "She ain't changed a whit. Well, except for the clothes. She fills 'em out nice, though."

"That she does." Sully put his book aside and leaned forward. "She tell you about Paolo Martinez yet?"

"No, I ain't," Dulcie called, and slipped something else into the skillet. Slocum could smell it now. Ham and potatoes! He hoped there'd be a few eggs to go along with it.

She continued. "There's only been so much time, Sully. And when he did wake up, it was first things first."

"My dear Dulciana," Sully intoned, "must you talk entirely in cliches?"

Ignoring him, she said, "Slocum, I don't know how you put up with this ol' owlhoot chaser. Ever since he's got here, he's either had his face in a book or in Joyce Marie, or he's been givin' me a hard time."

Slocum sighed, and grinned. Dulcie might have changed her wardrobe and her locality, but she was still the same old back-talking gal. He liked that. "If you two are done sparrin'," he asked, "would somebody tell me about Paolo Martinez?" He looked over at Sully. "You got a clue which way he went off to?"

"Nope," Sully said. "But I got a real good idea of where he's headed."

Slocum tensed. "Where?"

"Right here," Dulcie said brightly. "How many eggs you want?"

18

"Here?" Slocum said, and stood up so fast that the chair nearly went flying. "What do you mean here?"

"Just what I said," Dulcie replied. "How many eggs, dammit?"

"Dulcie . . ." he grumbled.

"Seems our boy Paolo and his gang have been availing themselves of the hospitality of these young ladies," Sully said. He had his fixings out, and rolled himself a smoke as he spoke. "Completely uninvited, of course," he continued. "According to Dulcie and Joyce Marie, he shows up about every nine, ten days. Takes a hog or a steer, plus other assorted grub, spends the afternoon with Joyce Marie, and then he disappears again for another ten days."

Slocum turned toward Dulcie. "You didn't think to mention this to me?"

She shrugged. "Well, I started to, but you were so damned cute. . . . And if you're not gonna say how many eggs, I'm gonna make you six. You want any more, and you can make 'em yourself." With a curt wave of her spatula, she turned her attention back to the skillet.

Well, she *had* said something about how they weren't making as much money as they should. . . .

"Cute?" he said. And then something else sank in. "Sully, you're diddling Paolo Martinez's gal?"

"Not his gal by choice, Slocum," Sully replied a little indignantly. "According to her, these gals flipped for it and Joyce Marie lost."

They both turned toward the open door at the sound of boot scuffs. A woman stood there, tall and slender and dressed in much the same manner as the more petite Dulcie. Her coffee-with-cream skin and her regal face told Slocum that she was most likely octoroon— what the boys in Louisiana would have called "high yaller." She peeled off her work gloves, tipped her head toward Slocum, and said, "He's up, I see."

Slocum went toward her and stuck out his hand. "Joyce Marie?"

She took it and shook it firmly. "The same. And Sully's telling you the truth. I lost the damn coin toss, all right, and now I'm stuck spreadin' 'em for that smelly dirt-bag Paolo three times a month." She turned her head toward the kitchen area. "Dulcie, why're you cookin'? I thought I had kitchen duty tonight."

Dulcie was busy scraping the last of the fried potatoes, crisp and golden, onto a plate. "Just makin' Slocum a little snack." She lifted a slab of ham from the skillet and laid it beside the potatoes. Slocum was already salivating.

Joyce Marie frowned, and a little furrow appeared between her delicate brows. "Snack? Christ on a crutch, girl, you keep feedin' him like that, and between him and Paolo, we're not gonna have any livestock left on this place inside of two months."

Then she looked over at Sully. Her face softened,

and in a completely different tone of voice, she purred, "Hiya, sugar."

"Hi, baby," Sully rumbled, and held out his arms and motioned to her.

Joyce Marie took him up on it, languorously melting down into his lap just as Dulcie slid Slocum's plate onto the table. No, plates. The ham and potatoes were on one, the six eggs—cooked over easy, just the way he liked them—were on another, and a third held half a loaf of bread and a pot of what looked like blackberry jam.

He was close to drooling, for two days without solid food had left him ravenous. He pulled up a chair, grabbed a fork, and started to wolf it down. Dulcie slid a cup of coffee—and the pot—onto the table, then down next to him.

She propped her chin in her hands and cocked her head. "Slow down, sugar pie," she said. "Paolo and his boys ain't comin' for another week or so. And I got a question for you."

He grunted, because his mouth was full of eggs.

"Do you boys ever get hit anywhere but on the noggin?" she asked brightly. "I never in my life seen such an assortment of goose eggs and lumps as on you fellas' skull bones!"

Patrick leaned back against a hay bale. "It's surely different from the stables back home," he said.

Tip knew what he meant. At the last place his mum had rented for them—the last place that had had a barn, that is—the stable was a stone affair. Its floor was two feet lower than the surrounding terrain, the result of a century of horses and cattle with digging hooves and men mucking out after them. Its interior had been dark and cool. This one was made of whitewashed adobe, so light and airy that it nearly made him dizzy.

"Aye," he said, then pointed at the filly. "She's goin' to be a grand one, isn't she?"

Patrick grinned. "As if you'd be knowin'."

Tip scowled, but it was only make-believe. "Horses, horses, horses. A fellow can make do in the world without 'em, you know."

"Aye," said Patrick, "but he'll have a hard time gettin' from point to point." He picked up a bit of straw from the floor and stuck it between his teeth. Around it, he asked, "What are you thinkin' he's goin' to do when he wakes up?"

"Himself?" asked Tip. "I'm thinkin' that's already been decided. Mr. Sully Washington, he's got just as big a stake in this as does Mr. Slocum. He's out for the reward, and a grand lot of money it is too. Push comes to shove, I'm stayin' with him."

Patrick eyed him.

"What?" said Tip.

"You can't pull the wool over me eyes, Tipper," said Patrick. " 'Tisn't those thieved horses you're aimin' to go after."

Tip looked away. "Somebody has to do it. By rights, it should be meself."

"Or me," Patrick said.

"You're too young," Tip replied. "Mum'd skin me if harm was to come to ye."

Patrick sniffed. "And if harm was to come to you, don't you think she'd be chasin' me with an ax from here to Dublin?"

Tip grinned. "That's a lot further than it used to be, Pat."

"Aye," said Patrick.

Inside the stall, the filly twitched her tail, took a few faltering steps on stilted legs, and began to nurse again. The boys remained silent for a moment, watching her.

"Where will ye be when they come, Tipper?" Patrick asked finally. "Miss Dulcie says there's better than a dozen of the bastards."

Tip looked up at the low rafters, and at the barn's many windows. "Not in here, I'm thinkin'. Maybe up top. I dare say I could hit three or four of 'em before they saw me."

"And that leaves eight or nine."

Tip frowned. "Stop bein' so pessimistic."

His brother took the straw from his mouth and waved it at him. "I'm not bein' pessimistic. I'm just not wantin' to haul you back to that crumblin' church and bury you next to Da, that's all." He grinned suddenly. "It'd be an awful lot of work and bother, Tipper. I'm wonderin' if you're worth it."

Tip set his mouth. "Don't want to be spendin' my hereafter next to Da. Ship me home in a box."

Patrick rolled his eyes. "Ye don't wish to be buried next to him, but you're after gettin' your revenge? What goes through your head, Tip? I say we just let Mr. Slocum and Mr. Washington get on with it. Why, either of them's got as much grudge against this outlaw as you or me!"

"He didn't kill their da, Pat."

"That's right, Tipper, he didn't. It was ours he was killin'. Our da, who beat us bloody all our lives and sold Fiona's body, who gave poor Mum more bruises than you could shake a stick at, and broke her poor arm twice that I can remember! We never would've given another thought to him when he ran off, and never thought twice when we got that damned note unless it was to say 'three cheers for the bandits,' except that you had that little problem at Murphy's Tavern."

Patrick shook his head sadly. "I was grieved to the core when he got himself shot, Tipper. You know I was, same as you. Even if Da was a right bastard, he was the only da I knew. But I say we let our betters handle Martinez. I say we stand aside and let them have at him."

Tip stared at his shoes. Words welled up in him, so many that he couldn't straighten them out.

He wanted to tell his brother that the "little problem" had been that he'd killed Flynn O'Toole, killed him dead in front of a crowd of witnesses at Murphy's. He wanted to tell Patrick that he loved him dear, and was heartily sorry for having brought him along on this fool's errand. But he couldn't. Pride—and shame—wouldn't let him.

But there was something else, something he could tell. He blurted out, "Paolo Martinez killed Da, Pat, killed him most cruel. Da was a thief and a scoundrel, all right, and woe be to the women that came under his influence. But he was our da. He was blood, and blood needs avengin'. That's all I'm sayin'."

Patrick sighed long and hard. "Ye'll not be dissuaded then?"

"No." For once in his life, Tip had to do something right. He had to see something through.

Patrick stood up and dusted hay from his britches.

"That's it then," he said, looking toward the foal.

"Aye, that's it."

Across the yard, the dinner bell clanged repeatedly. Tip got up too.

Patrick said, "I wonder if Mr. Slocum is awake yet. Two days is a terrible long time."

"Doesn't matter," Tip replied as they started toward the house. "We've got another week till the brigand Martinez shows his cowardly face."

"I'm thinkin' you'd best be payin' Mr. Slocum for our horses, Tipper."

"In time, Patrick. In time."

Slocum was all for going into Mission Springs and rounding up a posse. After all, it was only three miles, and he figured that he and Sully could handle twelve ordinary men, but Paolo Martinez's men were far from ordinary.

Sully, however, was inclined to disagree.

"Those bounties are mine, Slocum," he said that night. "Well, I'll split 'em with you," he added reluctantly, "and I'll give those boys a token if they help, but I'll be damned if I'll cut a bunch of sheriff's deputies or badged-up farmers in on it."

The boys had gone to bed an hour past, and Dulcie, curled next to Slocum in one of the big chairs by the hearth, said, "You couldn't even if you wanted to. Get deputies, I mean."

Slocum arched a brow. "Why's that?"

"No sheriff," Dulcie replied.

Both the women had changed clothes. Dulcie wore a pretty green cotton dress, not too low-cut, but it showed off the curve of her bust nicely, Slocum thought, as well as her tiny waist. Joyce Marie had changed too, but into pants again. Clean ones, though, and a short-sleeved man's shirt that was far too big for her.

Presently, Joyce Marie was slouched back against Sully's broad chest. She sat between his splayed legs in the wide chair, and he had slid his hands inside her baggy sleeves. He played lazily with her breasts as they talked, and the movement of his big fingers beneath the fabric—and knowing what they were moving over— had Slocum pretty well aroused. He was anxious to take Dulcie down the hall.

But not anxious enough to leave before they had this thing settled.

"No law at all?" he asked.

"Closest is forty miles northwest," replied Dulcie, her eyes on Sully and Joyce Marie. "And that's no good, 'cause Paolo's got them in his pocket too."

"Got most everybody around here in his pocket," added Joyce Marie softly. Her eyes were slitted, and her head lolled back. Softly, she whispered, "You're such a pretty badman, Sully. . . ."

He murmured something into her ear, and she smiled drowsily and whispered, "Yes, baby . . ."

He looked up at Slocum for a second. "They leave him alone, and he leaves them alone. Doesn't rob 'em." His hands moved again beneath Joyce Marie's shirt, and she let out a tiny hiss.

Slocum shifted in his chair.

"We're the only ones with any reason to want him dead," Dulcie said. "This year anyhow. The year before it was the Martins' livestock he was siphonin' off, and the year before that, Joe Carter's. They're both outta business, gone back East. Next it'll be us, and he'll have to pick somebody new to leech off." She tugged at Slocum's sleeve. "Let's go to bed, honey."

But Slocum wasn't done yet. He said, "You mean to tell me there's nobody around here who wants Martinez outta their hair for good?"

"Not enough to do anything about it," said Dulcie, and she pinched his arm. "Don't you want to go to bed, darlin'?"

Sully had slid one hand free of Joyce Marie's shirt and stuck it behind her, between their bodies. The sonofabitch was undoing his pants, right out here in front of God and everybody!

Well, Slocum was pretty damned sure that was what he was doing anyway.

More urgently—and through clenched teeth—Dulcie whispered, "Honey?"

"Just a minute," he muttered, having forgotten Martinez entirely.

Sully curled one of those giant hands around Joyce Marie's hip and rested it on the fly of her trousers. He twisted the top button between huge fingers, playing with it.

Grinning, he said, "Forget it, Slocum. There's nobody. We're on our own." He undid the top button of Joyce Marie's britches with a flick of his fingers. "Now, you want to do what the lady says and get the hell out of here, or you gonna stay and learn something?"

"*Slocum!*" Dulcie hissed.

As he reluctantly left the room, he heard Sully say, "Shuck 'em, baby," and turned in time to see Joyce Marie kicking the britches down over her legs, in time to see Sully lift her a good foot into the air and ease her down on what appeared to be just about the biggest cock he'd seen outside of a corral.

"Christ!" he breathed, and then Dulcie dragged him down the hall.

He had his pants off before he reached the bedroom door, and took a very willing Dulcie standing up against the hallway paneling.

19

Slowly, the week passed.

Summer was coming, and during the days the temperature climbed well past one hundred on Dulcie's porch thermometer, but at night fell to what felt like a frigid seventy. The boys, unused to the climate, baked during the day and sat out on the porch in the evenings, while Slocum and the others stayed inside, by the fire.

Not that Slocum got all that much fireside-sitting done. For all of Dulcie's complaints about Sully and Joyce Marie, she was all over Slocum night and day.

She didn't have Carmella's creative flair, but her sexual appetite more than made up for it. Slocum was more than happy to appease her.

As the days passed, Slocum posted guards in shifts, just to be on the safe side. The men and the boys took turns climbing up to the adobe house's flat roof, from which the surrounding terrain could be seen for miles during the days. At night, a man listening closely could hear a coyote skulking along or a scurrying jackrabbit far off in the distance.

And Slocum and Sully planned. Dulcie and Joyce Marie said that the bandits couldn't be counted on to come in from any particular direction, which fit with what Slocum had heard about Paolo. He was always moving, and apparently his broken legs hadn't stopped that, except possibly at first.

Oh, Sully and Slocum found a number of hiding places—an arroyo to the south, a little knoll far to the northwest, a grove of paloverde to the east—where they might have lain in wait for the bandits. But since they had no idea where Paolo would be coming from, the point was moot.

"The house and barn are the best," Slocum said on the fifth day, and probably for the hundredth time. He was tired of waiting, tired of rehashing this plan. Rolling a quirlie, he leaned against the corral, wishing they could just get on with it.

Sully spanked the backside of the gelding he'd just unsaddled. As it slowly trotted off, he grabbed the top rail of the fence and climbed out.

"As much as I hate to admit it, Slocum, you're right," he said once his boots hit the ground. He peeled off his leather gloves and secured them through the back of his belt. Since they'd arrived at the Double R, he looked more high-tone than ever. Joyce Marie kept those goddamn powder-blue pirate shirts of his freshly laundered and pressed.

"Just wish there was more cover around here," Sully continued, and stretched an arm out wide, sweeping it slowly along the line of the horizon while Slocum lit his quirlie.

"Any cover at all! Flat as a damn pancake," Sully said. "Nothing but those two cottonwoods up by the house and this little ironwood down here." He poked a thumb over his shoulder at the tree that shaded the corral. "Unless you count the chicken coop or that hog sty, which I don't. Smokehouse doesn't amount to much either. Joyce Marie's late husband should have thought ahead, picked a better place to build. Christ, you'd think he would have been worried about Apache!"

Slocum shook his head. He blew out a plume of smoke, saying, "No, the place is too new. Four years at the most, I figure. The Apache were pretty much corralled by the time he got around to throwing this place up. Did a nice job of it too."

Nodding in agreement, Sully stared off into the distance. "He must've loved Joyce Marie a powerful lot to build this place for her," he mused.

Slocum took a thoughtful drag on his smoke, studying Sully's tone. Brows arched and half-teasing, he asked, "You're not gettin' any ideas about settlin' down, are you? It'd ruin my whole month."

Sully pulled himself up, which was an impressive sight. "Me? You crazy?"

"Probably," said Slocum, and tried not to smirk. He'd been watching Sully, who gave every appearance of a man who was smitten, not a fellow who was just fooling around with some ex-whore.

"What do you think?" asked Sully, effectively changing the subject. "The barn or the house?" And then, without waiting for Slocum's answer, he said, "I'm thinkin' both."

"Agreed." Slocum tossed his butt down into the dust and stomped on it for good measure. "Figure maybe we should put one man in the house, one in the barn, and one up top. The fourth up in one'a them cottonwoods maybe," he said, pointing. "Dulcie and Joyce Marie in the house too. They can both shoot. Don't know how they'd feel about shootin' a live human, though."

"They'll shoot," Sully said, as if there was no question. "The boys too."

The women had two rifles, a shotgun, and three pistols. Sully still had his arsenal, with the exception of his rifle, which had been on Old Scratch when Paolo made off with him. That gave them plenty of guns, and they'd been molding lead all week. They'd have a surfeit of ammunition when the time came.

"The boys are a little too willin', if you were to ask me," Slocum said.

Sully nodded. "Tip. He's a bloodthirsty little peckerwood. Got it in his head that he's going to get Paolo."

"If he does, you gonna let him collect the reward?" Slocum said with a grin.

Sully sneered at him. "Anybody ever tell you that you're a real card, Slocum?"

"Just askin', that's all."

Sully grunted. Slocum knew that he'd be about as willing to share in the bounty on Paolo as he'd be to walk stark naked up the main street in New Orleans.

Actually, if he knew Sully, he'd do that street stroll in his skin a lot sooner than he'd hand over the cash. Sully had pride in his profession, after all. Bringing in the big-money corpses was a point of honor with him. And while Slocum knew that Sully lived pretty high back in New Orleans, he also figured that the man must have built up one beautiful bank account over the years.

But these were powerful odds they were facing. He hoped Sully would live to go back home and spend some of it on fancy cigars and fancier women. Hell, he hoped he'd live through it himself. Time and time again, he'd asked himself if a spotted horse was worth getting shot up over. And time and time again, he'd had to answer yes.

Sully had pride in his profession, but Slocum had principles too, goddammit.

"I figure one'a the boys in the barn, and the other up a tree," Slocum said.

"Yeah," Sully answered. "Let 'em flip for it. I hate to get them into this thing, Patrick especially, but it can't be helped. Thought about sending them into town, but . . ."

"They'd run right back the second we dropped 'em off," Slocum said. "Plus which, they'd probably open their mouths, and one of those townies would tip Paolo. Besides, the way I figure it, this whole deal is pretty much the boys' doin' anyway."

"My thoughts exactly."

"You want the house or the barn?"

Sully pursed his lips. "The house. That's where Paolo's going to go. I'm thinking that we just let them ride in, all easy-like. Let 'em get comfortable. I'll take out Paolo with a knife and hope he doesn't make a fuss. Then I'll signal to you."

"If you're gonna suggest another damn birdcall," Slocum growled, "I swear, Sully, I'll kill you where you stand."

Sully grinned. "You just won't let go of that, will you?"

"It was a stupid idea, dammit."

Sully cocked his head slightly. "Well, I suppose I've

had better," he admitted, although that look said that he wasn't a damn bit sorry.

Slocum grunted. "Just don't shoot my mare once this thing gets started."

Although he tried not to show it, Slocum was concerned about the mare. He didn't figure Paolo to be a stupid man, and therefore he didn't figure him to be one who'd mistreat a good horse, especially one as good as Cheyenne was. But still, Paolo quite literally wasn't on his feet. It would fall to his men to take care of the horses, and they hadn't looked like they gave a damn.

Also, what little Slocum had seen of their horses through that church door hadn't bolstered his hopes. They were a scrawny, unkempt lot. The steer tied to the back of their wagon—the steer they'd just picked up at Dulcie and Joyce Marie's—had been the best-looking animal of the lot.

Dulcie and Joyce Marie, on the other hand, knew how to take care of livestock. They had two good geldings—which he and Sully had ridden on their scouting forays—and two mares with foals at their sides. He'd spent some time with the newest foal, the little bay filly. She was going to be a keeper, all right. Dulcie said she'd bred the filly's dam to a quarter horse stud.

"Feller came through last year, on his way to a race in California," she said that night in bed. She smiled. "I couldn't help it if my Tess was in season, could I? I couldn't help it if I sorta forgot to latch that old stud's stall. . . ."

"Hell, Dulcie," Slocum said, bunching the pillows behind his head. He slung his arm around her shoulders. "Why didn't you just ask the man nice?"

"I did! But he was wantin' a hundred and fifty for the fee. Or he said he'd take it out in trade." She made a face, and then she shuddered. "He was just terrible ugly, Slocum! All elbows and buckteeth, what there was of them. I came out to Arizona so that I could pick and choose. So far, I hadn't seen anything I was willin' to drop my drawers for, and I wasn't about to make an exception for the likes of him!"

He stroked her arm. "You ever find anybody, Dulcie?"

She smiled slyly. "Not till you, darlin'. You make me sorry I didn't hang on to that ol' pink dress of mine. I'd like to wear it for you." Her hand came up, and she stroke his face. "You ready for another go-round, boy?"

"Don't you ever get tired, Dulcie?" he pretended to complain.

Her smiled widened. "Not around you, honey."

By the eighth day, Tip and Patrick were nervous as a couple of chained owls. To escape the constant scent and sight of women, which was grinding on them harder than either one wanted to admit, they spent the majority of their free time in the barn. While Slocum was up on the roof with a rifle and Sully was up at the house doing Lord knows what with Joyce Marie, Patrick had nearly brushed both mares bloody, and the path Tip paced in the aisle was slowly turning into a trench.

"I been thinkin', Tipper," Patrick announced.

Tip kept pacing. "What's that, Pat?"

"I been thinkin' over how we should dig some holes."

Tip stopped, his eyebrows wiggling. "Are you daft? And stop brushin' that mare. You're after givin' her a condition."

Patrick put his brushes down and moved the foal out of his way. "I'm not daft," he said, and came to lean his elbows over the wall of the stall. "I read about it once. See, these fellows, back in the olden times, dug these holes. Deep enough to stand in, they were, like a grave set on end. They got themselves down inside, and pulled some wood over their heads. . . ."

"Like kindlin'?" Tip asked, half-teasing.

Patrick rolled his eyes. "Faith, no! Like a panel, don't you know. And then some other fellows threw dirt over the tops. To disguise 'em, like."

Tip sat down and kicked idly at a hen, which had wandered in out of the sun. It squawked and flapped away before he could make contact. "And what were they after doin' it for, other than to amuse themselves?"

Patrick threw up his hands, and the mare tossed her head and backed off. "Why, to ambush the other side, Tip! It's clear as day! They'd wait for the other side to near, then pop up all of a sudden, wavin' sabers and shootin' arrows and such."

"Ah, now I see," Tip said with a nod of his head. Patrick had come up with some corkers these past few days—out of nervousness, Tip supposed—but this was the best one yet. He stretched his arms thoughtfully, and said, "Would you be comin' out here, Patrick? I'm wantin' to show you somethin'."

While Patrick let himself out of the stall and latched

the door behind him, Tip went to the corner of the barn and grabbed a shovel. Saying, "Follow me, boyo," he walked outside. Ceremoniously, he presented the shovel to Patrick. "There ye be," he said. "Dig."

"Here?" Patrick shook his head. "It doesn't seem quite strategic, Tipper."

"I'm tryin' to prove a point. Dig."

Patrick shrugged, then flipped the shovel around and drove it down. It glanced off the surface, barely disturbing the top layer of hard clay and gravel.

While Tip covered a widening grin with his hand, Patrick frowned at the earth, then jammed the shovel down again, this time with all his might.

This time, he made nearly half an inch's progress. He stood on the shovel with one foot, then jumped on it with both, and managed to drive the blade down another quarter inch before he lost his balance.

"Shite!" he muttered before he looked up. "Mayhap it's different up by the house?"

Tip shook his head and held his hand out for the shovel. "More'a the same," he said. The shovel went over his shoulder, and he went back inside the barn.

Patrick trooped after. "Never seen the like!" he said.

"Mr. Slocum says it's what they call caliche," Tip went on. "You can cut it and build houses from it— just like bricks, I'm told—but you can't be diggin' it 'less you've got a great lot of time and water both. Didn't you hear Miss Joyce Marie tellin' about how her late husband had to blast for the well water we're drinkin'?"

"Foul stuff if you ask me," Patrick interjected, and made a face. "Tastes funny."

"Well, she said he couldn't so much as set a corral

post till he had the water. And the reason it's tastin' funny to you is because a thousand years' worth of sheep dung hasn't been leachin' down into it."

"Tipper!"

Tip laughed, and set the shovel back in its place.

"Well, couldn't we be wettin' down a couple places and . . ."

"No, Patrick," Tip said with a shake of his head. "There's too many of the vandals comin' down on our heads. All ye'd do is give them a neat place to aim their pistols at."

Tip slumped down on the hay bale again, the reality of their dilemma closing in on him anew. A dozen ruthless bandits were on the way, and there were only the four of them to hold them off. He didn't figure he should count the women. And even if Mr. Slocum and Mr. Washington were worth at least two men each, and trusting that he and Patrick could hold their own, the odds still seemed fairly hopeless.

What had he gotten them into anyway?

They'd gone over and over the plan until his ears were blue from hearing it. He was to be in the barn. Yesterday, they'd sent Patrick up one of those big cottonwoods just to see what would happen, but there wasn't enough foliage to hide him. And besides, he couldn't get down once he got up there, and it took Slocum standing on a saddled horse to ease him back to earth. They had regrouped, and now Patrick was to be stationed on the roof of the house.

And absolutely, positively no shooting until Mr. Slocum gave the word. Or shot first.

It wasn't a very good plan, to Tip's mind. He would've preferred it if Paolo Martinez would ride up to the Double R as big as life—and all alone and demanding his tribute. He'd dreamt it over and over. And then Tip would step out on the porch, as bold and brave as the new head of the Clan Carnahan should be, and say, "I'm here to avenge me father, you larcenous bastard!" and fire his pistol. Martinez would crumple to the ground, everybody would get their horses and guns back, he could go back to Fiona and Carson City a hero, and that would be that.

Except it wasn't going to be that way, was it? Mr. Washington was going to kill the rogue Martinez, and then Slocum would get off a few shots. Patrick would freeze in fear and the women would cry, and even though Tip himself—having proved his marksmanship on that deer in the mountains—would probably take down five or six of the desperados, the rest of the bandits were going to cut them into mincemeat, and just because Mr. Washington had made them mad.

Well, no, that wasn't exactly true. But his heart told him that it was fair close to the facts.

"Tipper?" Patrick said, slicing rudely into his thoughts.

Tip stared at the floor. "What?"

"I've been thinkin'."

"Good for you, Patrick."

He looked up. Patrick was scowling at him. "Stop it, Tip! It's dead serious I am!"

Tip sighed. "Sorry, Pat. What is it that you've been mullin' over?"

"That maybe," Patrick said, "when Miss Joyce Marie's late husband was blowin' up dynamite to dig that fine artesian well, that maybe he didn't use all he had. The dynamite, I mean."

Tip opened his mouth, then closed it again. Underneath that floppy, stained hat of Patrick's, there was a lovely, conniving, darling mind.

"Where do you think he would have put it then, Patrick?" he asked, grinning wide.

20

On the ninth day, the men took up their positions. Slocum told them that it would be just like Paolo to show up a day early—or a day late—and Sully agreed. They put Tip in the barn, and at the last minute put Patrick down under the raised porch, where he complained and swatted spiders for the first hour.

Tip only heard about this later, of course. At the moment, he was busy searching the barn.

The day before, after they'd looked in every nook and cranny of the barn, the henhouse, and even the small, low smokehouse, Patrick had given up.

"He's used it all up, he has," he'd said in defeat as, in answer to the dinner bell, they'd walked up to the house. "The selfish bastard."

But during the night, Tip had been awakened by a sterling thought. They hadn't checked the small feed room. "After all," Patrick had said to him, "what idiot would be after blowin' up good oats and corn, even accidental-like?"

But Tip figured to check it today anyway. He was that desperate.

Once he heard Slocum's feet go still on the roof, and heard the soft, overhead *thump* as Slocum lay flat and settled in, Tip set his rifle aside and quietly went to the feed room.

It wasn't a room exactly, being more like a closet. There were barrels and bins of grain, and shelves to hold all manner of potions and balms to doctor sick horses, or make their coats or hooves shine. He didn't recognize many of them. He supposed that Patrick would have. But after going through every box on the shelves and peering behind the barrels, he had to admit defeat. There was nothing even remotely incendiary.

Dejectedly, he returned to his post and picked up his rifle. He could have proved himself with that dynamite. He could have done them all proud. And he knew something about blasting, having helped Sean McBride blast the rocks from his field two summers past.

He knew about fuses and timing, and about the deadly nitro that sweated from the sticks if the dynamite was old enough. Sean's had been old indeed, having been purloined from a defunct mining concern's storehouse. They'd carefully wiped the nitro from the crumbly old sticks with their fingers, then flicked it at one another's feet, laughing like fools when the droplets exploded with a great white flash and boom.

Stupid, he thought with a shake of his head.

Well, he'd only been fifteen.

Damn Joyce Marie's late husband for not having saved back a wee bit!

"No," he muttered. "Stop that. Ye mustn't think ill of the dead. Especially when you didn't know them while they were livin'."

In case Paolo and his men were watching from afar, the women had been instructed to go about their business as usual, and soon Miss Dulcie came out of the house carrying a bucket filled with breakfast scraps. She stopped on the porch and had a good stretch, then made her way down to the barn, pausing to slap a stray steer on the backside or flank and move it out of her way.

The cattle, which had been far off in the thin and distant pastures, had slowly moved up toward the house in the last few days. This morning, about fifteen head of scrawny, spotted cattle—steers, cows, and calves—were milling about the yard. Not like range cattle at all, but like pets. The rest were farther out: scattered, grazing speckled dots in the distance.

Miss Dulcie turned to saunter down toward the pigsty, the bucket of leftovers swinging from her hand. It never ceased to amaze Tip that this land could be so bounteous. What Miss Dulcie threw to the hogs each day could have fed him and his for a week.

And often had.

He watched her, turning his head to follow her lovely form as she crossed in front of his window— pretending to take no notice of him, but tossing him a sly wink—and made her way to the hogs. And as he looked at her, and tried not to think about what she and Slocum did while they were alone, the corner of his eye once again lit upon the feed room.

Or rather, the place *over* the feed room.

All through the interior of the barn, walls and stalls went up no higher than about eight feet or so, being securely nailed to airy cross beams. Above that, the entire place—except for a small open loft that he and Patrick had scoured the day before—was clear for another seven or eight feet, all the way up to the great pole-and-plaster ceiling. Well, Tip thought it might be plaster anyway.

Except that the entire ceiling *wasn't* open. Why had he not noticed it before? In the corner, at the back of the tack area, the feed room's walls soared all the way up to the roof.

It was very odd, if you asked him. The little room hadn't seemed that tall when he was in there. Why, it should have seemed as if he were in a long vertical chute, and he was fairly certain he would have noticed that!

He glanced out the window again at the clear horizon, then rested his rifle against the wall and walked back to the little feed room. Sure enough, the walls stopped about eight feet up, ending in a wooden ceiling. There were seven or eight feet of space unaccounted for.

Clambering atop the oat bin, he peered up and clucked his tongue. "Tipperary Carnahan," he muttered, "you're six hundred kinds of a fool." It was right there in plain sight: a little trapdoor, just big enough for a man's shoulders to fit through!

He pulled open the latch, and it swung down immediately, and narrowly missed clipping his nose. The dust didn't miss him, though. It billowed out and down in a cloud that left him sneezing and rubbing at his eyes.

Once the dust settled—and once he stopped coughing—he inched his foot onto one of the shelves, tested it, then pulled himself up.

No good. Utter darkness.

He fumbled in his pocket for a sulphur tip, popped it with his thumbnail, then gingerly raised it above the level of the trapdoor. And there, covered in cobwebs, was one single dusty crate of dynamite.

Whispering, "Thank you, Jesus," he quickly checked for any spiders that might wish to take a bite out of him, then shook out the match and tucked it into his pocket.

Carefully, he inched the box toward him, then eased it through the trapdoor. He peered inside. The little crate was lidless. The old sticks were covered in a thin dew of nitroglycerin that had seeped through the thick layer of dust, and more than half of them were gone, but a good-sized coil of dusty fuses lay to the side.

He smiled, just as the shelf he was standing on gave way.

It seemed to him that it took a very long time to fall, although it was likely a fraction of a second. Instinctively, he held the box away from himself. A stab of pain went through him as his back glanced off the oat bin, and he lost the box for just a moment.

But when he landed, head in the aisle and feet in the feed room, he held the crate in the air, and let his elbows act like springs to cushion its landing.

Ignoring the pain in his back and holding his breath, he peered inside.

Tiny wisps of smoke curled off the dynamite—the nitro really—and for a moment he couldn't have breathed even if he had wanted to.

But then the smoke stopped, thank the Lord (which a trembling Tip was doing enthusiastically and without cease), and he gingerly carried it out into the barn. His heartbeat slowly returning to some semblance of normal, he went back to his window perch, hurriedly checked the horizon again, then took count.

Seven sticks of the stuff. Plenty of fuses. He could cut them to any length, time them to the second.

Of course, the dynamite was old as the hills. It had only been sitting out here for four years or so, but maybe this troublesome Arizona weather was hard on it. Or maybe Joyce Marie's late husband had lifted it from somewhere. Tip could time the fuses all he wanted and throw it with the greatest of accuracy, but the concussion when it hit the earth would set off the nitro, which would naturally explode the rest of it.

And then, perhaps it wouldn't go off at all.

He scowled, but then the scowl relaxed. Even if the damn stuff wouldn't explode, the bandits didn't know that. He supposed even the bad sticks, if there were any, would create a goodly amount of panic if he were to use a long enough fuse.

Then again, he thought, a person couldn't really tell whether a stick was good or not until after he'd lit it, could he?

Carefully, he set the crate aside, nestling it well out of the way in a bed of straw. He didn't want to look at his back, but he thought he'd scraped it raw when he fell. The sharp pain had fallen back to a biting sting over a dull ache.

Picking up his rifle, he settled back to stare at the horizon.

At noon, Slocum watched as Joyce Marie strolled down to the barn, carrying a deep pan. She paused along the way, dipping in her hand to throw feed to the chickens, and pushing a cow or steer out of her path. He heard her when she stepped into the barn for a moment, heard her say something to Tip (although he couldn't understand the words), and then she was outside again. He heard her scuffing along, softly calling, "Chick, chick, chick!"

And then she was at the rear of the structure, and he heard her call up, "Your lunch, Slocum. You want to come down, or you want me to send it up?"

He called softly, "I'll come down. And tell Patrick to pull back a little. I can see the sun shinin' off his rifle barrel every now and again."

"Will do," Joyce Marie said, and he heard her footsteps slowly moving off.

Slocum turned in a slow circle on his belly, spyglass to his eye, making one last check.

Nothing.

It was good to get down off the barn and stand on his own two feet again. The sun was scorching, and his belly was sore from lying all morning on the rough adobe. It was also good to find that Joyce Marie had brought him a thick ham sandwich, wrapped up in brown paper, and a jar of lemonade, along with a slice of Dulcie's almond cake, also wrapped in paper.

Joyce Marie was gone by the time he slithered down, of course. Her back turned to him, she walked leisurely up the yard, scattering grain, calling, "Chick, chick! Chick, chick!" The cattle followed her, cleaning the cracked corn and rolled oats off the ground before the chickens had a chance at it.

He picked a few stray bits of cracked corn off his sandwich and wolfed it down, thinking all the while that Sully sure had it easy up in the house. The sonofabitch was sitting at a table instead of standing in a patch of shade next to a rain barrel. He lounging on padded furniture instead of lying flat out on a rooftop, with the sun scorching his back.

And Slocum was thinking that if Paolo Martinez didn't show up today, he and Sully would have a little talk about tomorrow's waiting arrangements.

He sidled over to a window, and called, "How you doin', Tip?"

From inside, a voice—speaking around a mouthful of food—said, "Fine, sir." Or at least, that's what Slocum thought he said. "Joyce Marie says that Patrick was swattin' spiders for nigh on an hour," the boy said after he'd swallowed. He chuckled. "She said he was complainin' most bitterly. Him and his spiders!"

Tip seemed in altogether too fine a mood for someone who was expecting a dozen armed men to ride down on him at any moment, and it grated on Slocum.

"You do what you were told, you hear?" he warned the boy. They'd gone over this time and time again, but it bore repeating. He didn't want any heroics. "If things go sour, you climb up into the rafters and hide. You got that?"

When the boy didn't answer, Slocum said, "You listenin'?"

"Aye."

"You gonna mind?"

"Aye, sir. Have faith."

Slocum didn't believe him for a slap second, but there was nothing that could be done. He was fairly certain that he'd convinced Patrick to lay low if it went bad, but Tip, damn him, was another animal entirely. Half the time Slocum thought that he should've just bound and gagged the boy and shut him up in the smokehouse for the duration.

He needed level heads now, not wild-eyed children with their heads full of romantic notions about avenging their daddy's honor.

"As if the old sonofabitch had any," he whispered, then took another bite of his sandwich.

From inside the barn, he heard the sound of paper crinkling, then a jar lid being turned. It reminded him to take another gulp of his lemonade.

He watched the western horizon, and what he could see of the north and the south. Down here, the house blocked the view to the north, but he had a pretty good reconnoitering place from atop the barn. Which he should be getting back to.

He crumpled the brown paper from his sandwich and stuck it in his pocket. No sense leaving Paolo any more clues than he had to. He recapped his lemonade jar, giving it a hard twist before he wrapped his bandanna around it and gently tossed it up to the roof. It landed with a dull *clunk*. He'd have the rest of it—and his cake—up top. Paolo wasn't coming today anyhow.

"The bad guys," he muttered as he lifted his boot to the top of the rain barrel, "never come when you're ready for 'em."

But just as he was about to transfer his weight and climb up, Tip hissed at him.

"They're comin', sir!" the boy said, and his voice was full of fear as well as excitement. "They're comin' from the east and there's thousands of 'em!"

21

Slocum hopped back down and peered around the edge of the barn. Through gritted teeth he growled, "Shit!"

They were coming in at a fast gallop. Not twelve—and not thousands—but fourteen, no, sixteen! And they were coming in fast enough that if he were to try and climb up on the roof again, one or more of them would be bound to spot him.

He'd have to do what he could from ground level.

"Keep steady, boy," he said to Tip. "Hold your fire."

A wagon bearing Paolo Martinez and a driver galloped in the lead. Riders surrounded it on three sides, and dust billowed back in a choppy cloud from the horses' hooves and the churning wagon wheels. Slocum saw that his fine leopard mare had been forced to new depths of degradation—she was one of the horses hitched to the wagon.

His nerves had already been riding the edge, but this new affront—Cheyenne, a cart horse!—made him just plain mad. And when the riders and the wagon slowed to a halt in front of the house, and he saw that she was thin and her coat was caked with dirt, his anger rose to a whole new level.

"Mr. Slocum!" Tip whispered. "Your poor mare!"

"Quiet!" Slocum snapped. If even Tip had noticed it, it must be worse than he'd thought.

The *bandidos* began to dismount. Two men lifted Paolo's wheelbarrow from the wagon, then eased him down into it. While this was going on, Dulcie and Joyce Marie had come out on the porch. Joyce Marie engaged in a brief conversation with Paolo, although Slocum couldn't hear them well enough to make out the words. She appeared to be welcoming him, though. Dulcie stayed up on the porch, fiddling with a dish towel. It was the only thing that gave away her nervousness.

Slocum hoped that Paolo wouldn't notice.

He didn't appear to. While Joyce Marie walked at his side, one bandit wheeled him up to the porch steps, and then another trotted up to help lift the wheelbarrow the two steps to the porch.

Except Paolo wasn't going inside—where Sully was presumably waiting in Joyce Marie's bedroom, with his knife drawn and ready. No, the bastard had himself wheeled around, like the master of the manor surveying his property, and parked next to the spare table the girls kept on the porch.

Nonchalantly, Paolo waved a hand at Dulcie, who nodded and went inside, and then motioned for Joyce Marie to join him at the table.

Half the bandits were leading all the saddle mounts—Old Scratch among them—down toward the corral, and Slocum knew he had to move before they got any closer. He left his position at the edge of the barn and hurried along the south side. Hiking himself up, he crawled in a stall window.

"What are you doin'?" Tip hissed when Slocum hit the floor.

"Up!" Slocum ordered quietly, and pointed. He shoved the mare out of his way. "Up to the loft. They're comin'."

Tip didn't ask any questions. He bent over and fussed with something in the hay, then skittered up to the loft like a rifle-packing monkey. Joining Slocum against the back wall of the loft, on the opposite side of the wide second-story hayloft door, he whispered, "Are ye thinkin' they'll come inside?"

In answer, they heard approaching voices.

"Down," whispered Slocum, and quickly reached across the opening to shove the boy's head down into the hay.

Beneath the loft, three bandits entered the barn—at least, three that Slocum first heard, then could see. They sauntered to the far stall, where they leaned over the railing and commented, in Spanish, about the new foal. One of them started to light a cigarillo, and another slapped it from his hand and stomped it out with a comment of *"Estúpido!"*

Outside, Slocum heard the sounds of the gate being opened and horses filing into the corral, and then four more men joined the other three.

This wasn't going the way it was supposed to, not at all. He glanced down at the north-facing window, but the angle was wrong. He couldn't see the porch from up here, couldn't even see the house.

The conversation on the floor of the barn escalated into an argument over the filly. Her legs were too long or they were too short. She'd be fast as lightning. She'd be too slow to pace a tortoise. Her color was wrong, and she had two white feet, which everybody knew (said the last man to come inside) meant that her hoofs would split. She was a fine filly, said another, and maybe they should steal her when she was a little older.

There were seven of the thugs down there, which was roughly half the total, Slocum figured. If Tip wouldn't panic—or try anything heroic—he might just be able to make the odds a lot more even.

Either that, or get them all killed.

He lifted his head and silently signaled to Tip to take a look out the high loft window. Amazingly, the boy seemed to understand, and quietly edged around. After a moment, he spread his hands to indicate that all was clear.

It was a step in the right direction.

Next, Slocum signaled the boy away from him, toward the far side of the loft. Whatever the kid had been doing in Ireland, it must had been sneaky, because he didn't make a sound.

Then Slocum slowly crawled forward. The bandits, intent on their argument, hadn't looked up. But they did, all at once, when he cocked his rifle.

"Hands up," he said in Spanish. "Real quiet now, boys."

Two of the men hesitated, but the sound of Tip's rifle cocking at the other end of the loft convinced them.

"Turn around," Slocum said. "Face the rear of the barn."

They did.

Signaling to Tip to stay put, Slocum swung down to the wall of a stall, then to the floor. He disarmed the three men closest to him, putting down his rifle in favor of one of the men's pistols, which just happened to be his own Colt.

"It ain't nice to steal a fella's guns," he growled, and cracked the man over the skull. The bandit crumpled to the straw-strewn floor.

"Tip," he said curtly, and the boy climbed down the ladder. With Tip covering him, he disarmed the rest of the men. After Slocum reclaimed his cross-draw rig from a fat-faced *bandido* and his derringer from a man with a scar bisecting his mustache, the bandits' remaining guns and knives were temporarily placed in the oat bin. All seven were gagged with their own scarves or bandannas and tied securely, hand and foot.

Satisfied that these seven were out of the way for the time being, he went to the window and looked up at the house. Paolo Martinez was still sitting on the goddamn porch, sipping what looked like lemonade, with his splinted legs sticking out before him like the twin prows of a boat.

On the steps sat five of his remaining men, and one of them cradled Slocum's rifle. The wagon was still there, and Cheyenne was still in the traces, along with a horse he now recognized as Patrick's gray gelding, Flannel.

Dulcie was handing out glasses of lemonade, and when one of the bandits grabbed her backside, she hurled the contents of a glass in his face. Slocum's muscles tensed, but instead of retaliating, the men only laughed and playfully pushed their offending compatriot off the steps.

Another bandit was watching the last two lead a placid steer up to the house and the wagon. Dulcie pointed at it and yelled, "Take one'a them steers out there! These are like pets!"

The men leading the steer ignored her, and secured the animal to the rear of the wagon.

"I said, you're not takin' old Deuce!" she shouted plain as day, and started marching straight for him.

"Look out!" Tip suddenly hissed, and shoved Slocum over to the side.

"What are you doin'?" Slocum whispered angrily, and turned back to the window. *Don't do it, Dulcie!* he thought. *Can't you just wait a few minutes longer?*

"Ye nearly blew us all to kingdom come!" the boy said testily.

"I what?" Slocum twisted toward the boy just as one of Paolo's men grabbed Dulcie's arm and started dragging her back up to the house. She was pitching a fit, and another of the bandits came off the porch to aid the first one.

"Nearly blew us to the heavens," Tip was saying. He carefully picked up a box from the floor.

Slocum knew what it was before Tip got it all the way to him. The little wisps of smoke rising from it told the whole story.

Stepping back involuntarily, Slocum said, "Where the hell'd you get that?"

Two of the bandits were staring at the box as well, their eyes wide. They knew what was in it too.

"Not a peep," Slocum threatened in Spanish, "or I'll leave you in here with it."

"What did ye say to the rascals?" Tip asked in a whisper.

Slocum peered down into the crate. Seven sticks and

plenty of fuse. "I told 'em I was gonna tan your jackass hide. Now, where'd it come from?"

He took another look up at the house. Dulcie had won her point, although he didn't know how. She was back up on the porch, arms crossed over her bosom, and the men were untying the steer and shooing it away. A man Slocum recognized as Esteban had his hands on the grips of the wheelbarrow, in anticipation of moving Paolo through the front door.

"I found it," Tip said tersely. " 'Twas hid up over the feed room. And why are you gettin' so blasted angry at me?"

"Nothin' kid," Slocum said soothingly. The last thing he needed was Tip getting a bee in his bonnet.

Paolo disappeared into the house, and Joyce Marie went in behind him.

Carefully, Slocum picked up the crate.

"Hey!" Tip hissed. "Where are you takin' me dynamite?"

"I'm gettin' it out of the barn," Slocum replied, his eyes on the window from which Sully was supposed to signal. "This is dangerous stuff, kid."

Tip rolled his eyes. "Don't you think I'm knowin' that, for the love'a Mike?" he whispered. "Don't you think I'm knowin' that a wee bump could set the whole lot off?"

"I'm gonna try to prevent that wee bump," Slocum said. "Now, stay put and watch for Sully's signal."

"But—"

"No buts. Just do as I say." And Slocum exited the barn the same way he'd come in—through the back window.

• • •

Tip was fair disappointed, and fair angry too. The way he saw it, that was his dynamite, to do with as he was pleased, and he was pleased to set it off underneath those rapscallious bandits' feet. But now Slocum had made off with it, and in doing so, had made off with the glory.

Behind him, one of the *bandidos* mumbled something into his gag, and Tip whirled around. "Shut up, damn ye!" he hissed, and raised the butt of his rifle in a threat. The man quieted.

He turned back toward the window. He couldn't see Slocum anywhere, but this didn't surprise him. Neither could he see Patrick's rifle poking from beneath the porch. The seven bandits that remained outside the house had spread out some now. One, halfway between the house and the barn, was kicking at chickens that happened to peck their way too close to him.

Another bandit—the squat brute Jorge who had beaten him at his father's command—was urinating on the side of the house, and two had walked around the structure's far side, and hence out of Tip's line of vision. Three more were on the porch, wolfing down the last of the sandwiches Miss Dulcie had brought out with the lemonade.

They ate like pigs, he thought.

Esteban, the one who had pushed Paolo Martinez's wheelbarrow, came out the front door and gestured angrily at the sandwich-eaters. They backed down the steps, grumbling, and he sat sideways on a chair and picked up the meal where they had left off.

Tip wiped the sweat from the palms of his hands one by one, never once putting down the rifle.

And then Sully appeared in the window. He waved

once, very slowly, then pulled the curtain. Paolo Martinez was dead.

Something in Tip went flat.

He had no time to dwell on it, however. He raised his rifle to his shoulder, letting the barrel rest on the wide windowsill. His hands had begun to shake. He didn't know when, but he suspected it had been the moment when, up in the loft, Slocum had cocked his rifle and all the bandits had turned their faces up.

He took three slow, deep breaths. The shaking slowed, then stopped. Not altogether, but enough. With great care, he aimed past the closer chicken-kicker, and sighted down on that head-thumping jackal Jorge. He waited for Slocum to fire the first shot.

From the back corner of the barn, Slocum saw Sully signal, and knew that Paolo Martinez was either dead or incapacitated.

Quickly, he once again surveyed the situation. One man in the middle of the yard, three on the steps; Esteban was on the porch, and two more were out of Slocum's line of vision, on the other side of the house. Jorge was just buttoning up his pants at the front of the house.

The way they were spaced out, he figured the best Patrick would be able to do was shoot a few of them in the ankle. He could take out the hombre in the yard, but the others would all dive for cover.

And now that he had this damn dynamite, what the hell was he going to do with it?

Get it away from the buildings, that was for sure. Tip had surely disturbed the stuff when he moved it, and it wasn't a bit happy being jogged and jiggled around. It was smoking feebly again, and Slocum knew that a good jolt would set it off. He wished he could just stick the whole damn thing in the rain barrel. Unfortunately, there hadn't been any rain for some time, and the rain barrel was that in name only. For the time being, he carefully set the crate against the outside barn wall, in a patch of shade. First things first.

He was drawing a careful bead on the man in the yard when the front door opened. He checked himself. Dulcie stepped out on the porch, said something to Esteban, who'd been shoveling food into his face. Dumping his napkin to the floorboards, he rose and followed her inside.

That was good. Sully could take care of him too.

The man in the yard started walking up toward the house again, and shouted in Spanish to the others to unhitch the team.

Slocum, who had sighted again on the bandit, lowered his gun. Let them get Cheyenne and Flannel clear of the traces. It would save him shooting around her. And when one of Paolo's men led them to the corral, he'd be able to take him down, out of sight of the others.

Slocum crept back to the window, and pulled himself inside again. Seven bound and gagged *bandidos* eyed him with less than adoration. He stepped around them.

"Why aren't ye shootin'?" Tip asked angrily. "And where's me box of dynamite?"

"Don't be so goddamn anxious," Slocum whispered, and crossed to the barn's front doors. He positioned himself against the wall, behind the door, his Colt in his hand.

"What's happening out there?" he hissed to Tip.

"A fellow's leadin' the horses down."

"Just one man?"

"Aye."

"How big's he look to you?"

"I beg your pardon, sir?"

Slocum rolled his eyes. "Is he 'bout my size?" The seven they'd already corralled were too scrawny, to a man.

"Close, I'd say. But why—"

Slocum waved his hand, silencing Tip in mid-question. He could hear the sound of approaching hooves now, and hear a bandit, in Spanish, call down from the house, "See what's keeping Ramon and the others!"

"I bet you a hundred pesos those lazy shits are asleep in the shade of the barn!" came the shouted reply, much closer, and then a laugh.

One of the *bandidos* behind him rustled the straw, and before Slocum could react, Tip swung his rifle around, whispering, "Quiet, you heathen!"

Slocum listened as the corral gate opened, then closed again.

The door creaked open. "Hey, Ramon! Did you—"

The man suddenly saw Tip, saw his bound *compadres,* but before he could put a hand to his holster, Slocum stepped from behind the door and brought the butt of his pistol crashing down.

" 'Quiet, you heathen'?" Slocum asked as he quickly started stripping the bandit.

Tip shrugged.

"What's happening?" Slocum asked.

Tip glanced through the window. "The two that were around the house are back," he said.

Slocum began pulling on the bandit's clothes over his own. The man was smaller than he was, but at least he'd worn baggy clothes. "Tie him up," Slocum said, settling the filthy serape over his shoulders. It smelled of old sweat and sour vomit.

Tip's expression had gone from curious to concerned. As he deftly tied the unconscious bandit's hands to his feet, he asked, "You're not thinkin' to just walk up there, bold as you please!"

Mimicking the boy's lilt, Slocum said, "That I am, boyo," and put on the bandit's sombrero. He tilted the brim so that it would shade his face. "Patrick can't get a decent shot at any of 'em. If I know Sully and them gals, Sully's taken out Martinez and the other one, and now him and the girls are just sittin' there with their guns aimed at the door, waitin' for us to start shootin' and drive the rest of 'em inside."

He straightened and looked out the window. "Trouble is, where two of 'em are standing, they're more apt to go round the house and cut back on us. And another's bound to head straight under the porch and right on top of your little brother. Now, I'm gonna try walkin' up and hope they don't look too close. But if they do, you aim for the one leanin' up against the rail. That's the one that'll throw himself down and roll straight for Patrick. You get him before he can get there."

Tip swallowed. "What if I miss?"

His hand on the latch, Slocum said, "You won't. You're a good shot, Tip." And then he smiled, just a little. "But if you do, just keep on firin' till you hit him."

He opened the door again, stuck his hands beneath his borrowed serape, and started toward the house. He made it—completely unchallenged, with no one saying so much as a word to him—and wandered lazily to a point ten or twelve feet in front of the porch steps.

And then all hell broke loose.

22

The front door burst open—broke into splinters, more like—and Sully came flying through it, back first, and landed flat on the porch, his head hanging down on the first step.

The boys who had been on the steps jumped back in surprise—one right into Slocum—and Slocum managed to clip the man over the head before he could turn around.

Slocum brought his pistol to bear on Esteban, who was just coming through what was left of the door, his pistol drawn. Esteban had no eyes for anybody but Sully, and his intentions were clear. But behind Slocum, from the barn, a single shot rang out before Slocum could get one off. Esteban, looking vaguely surprised, crumpled.

Slocum was just thinking *Good boy, Tip!* when somebody grabbed him from behind, grabbed him around the throat, and he felt a pistol digging into his back.

He didn't think. He just reacted, twisting his body slightly and swinging his gun hand from right to left.

He fired the Colt directly behind him and so close to his side that he felt a sear of heat when it went off. As the bandit fell to the ground, the man's gun discharged. The shot, intended to sever Slocum's spine, went harmlessly into the dirt.

The front porch was a hive of activity. Sully was up and had taken his knife to the throat of an unfortunate *bandido*. He used the limp body as a shield against another bandit, who was mindlessly backing down the length of the porch, emptying his pistol into the body.

Slocum caught just a glimpse of another bandit rolling beneath the porch, and heard a muffled gun report almost immediately. He sure hoped it had been Patrick who fired, but there was no time to take a look.

There were two of the *bandidos* left, by Slocum's count. One of them, the man who had been firing at Sully, suddenly found himself out of ammunition. He dived over the porch rail and started running. Sully tossed his limp and bloody shield aside and took out after him, headed north toward open pasture.

It crossed Slocum's mind that this particular bandit must only have an "alive" price on his head, else Sully—the greedy sonofabitch—would have simply pulled his gun and finished it.

The other bandit—Jorge, Slocum thought—was nowhere in sight.

"Patrick!" Slocum shouted as he ran to the front wall of the house and peeked around the south side. Where was that bastard? "Patrick! You okay?"

"Aye, sir," came the crackling reply. "C-can I be comin' out?"

"Stay put," Slocum said curtly, and eased around the side of the house. All the bloody activity out front had taken place in less than fifteen seconds, but by now the surprise of it had worn off. The missing Jorge had had time to think.

Tossing his sombrero aside, Slocum edged along the wall beneath the tall cottonwoods, his Colt raised and ready. He paused when he came to the corner, hanging back, listening. He jumped a little when he heard a far-off shot, and then Sully's distance-muffled "Shit!"

Whether Sully had got the bandit or the bandit had got Sully was a question that was going to have to wait.

Slocum eased around the corner, muscles tensed, and then he paused. He stood erect. No bandit. Where the hell could he have gone?

And then he felt a bit of gravel pelt down on him from above.

He didn't think. He just threw himself backward and started firing as he fell.

His first shot didn't kill the bandit on the roof, but his second—and third, and fourth—hit home. A good thing too, for as he watched Jorge tumble from the roof, he became aware that something was very wrong with his own shoulder.

He muttered, "Jesus!" at the same moment Jorge's body hit the ground beside him, and at the same time realized that Jorge hadn't drawn his gun. A gun barrel glinted in the window, and Slocum rolled to the side just as he heard the gun's report. A new slug splatted into the ground inches away from him.

Despite the pain in his shoulder, he kept on rolling until he was behind the house, out of the range of that window.

Paolo. It had to be Paolo, unless Slocum had fouled up his count of the bandits, unless somebody else had managed to get into that house without him seeing.

Quickly, he lifted the serape and checked his shoulder. The joint still worked, and there was blood on the back of his shirt as well as the front. The slug had gone right through, and hadn't hit anything more than the meat. Satisfied that he was going to live—even though he was going to hurt like hell for a while—Slocum crept along the back side of the house, keeping low, until he came to the next corner and spied Sully.

Sully was walking toward the house, dragging the dead bandit by his collar as easily as a giant would drag a gnat. But Sully was hurt. The bandit whose throat he'd slit hadn't made such a good shield after all, and spreading bloodstains covered his pretty blue shirt in three places.

Slocum waved his good arm, gesturing frantically. Somewhat reluctantly, Sully dropped the Mexican and wearily dog-trotted over. "What, goddammit?" he panted once he was within speaking distance. He touched one of the bloody places on his shirt and winced. "I just lost five hundred dollars."

"You hurt?"

Sully gave a little huff. "No, I just bleed for the fun of it. Of course I'm hurt!"

"Not bad enough to soften your personality," Slocum said wryly. "Well, you're coming out on top in the long run. Got eight of the bastards hog-tied in the barn. Where's Martinez?"

Sully brightened. "Well, that was very kind of you, Slocum. Believe I might cut you in after all. I left Mr. Martinez in the bedroom, with Joyce Marie holding a gun on him," he said, still fingering his wounds and wincing. The blood was spreading fast. "Goddammit! You know how much these shirts cost me?" He looked up. "And then that sonofabitching lieutenant of Paolo's slipped his ropes somehow. I guess you came in about there."

"Well, Joyce Marie don't have that gun anymore," Slocum said curtly. He flipped out his Colt's cylinder, dropped the spent cartridges to the ground, then thumbed new ones from his belt and reloaded.

"That crafty old sonofabitch," Sully grumbled. "This'll teach me to have a heart. Thought I'd let him live long enough to hang. You want the front or the back?"

Slocum tried to move his shoulder around and succeeded, although painfully, but he figured to be in better shape for cottonwood-climbing than Sully. He appeared to be losing more blood by the second.

"Back," Slocum said.

Sully nodded.

Slocum holstered his gun and stared up the toward the roof. "Gimme a boost," he said.

"Jesus, Slocum," Sully said as he cupped his hands and Slocum put his boot in them. "Can't you do anything by yourself?"

Slocum scrambled up and took a last look down at Sully. The pain showed on Sully's face for a moment, but then he saw Slocum looking at him and it vanished. "What?"

"Just remember, at least one of those gals is in there with him."

Sully frowned. "As if I could forget it . . ." He stalked off, staggering slightly, toward the front of the house.

Slocum moved across the roof as quietly as he could, and came to the place where the cottonwoods overhung the house. Easing himself onto a sturdy limb, he climbed out and down a bit. His shoulder complained with every move he made, but he moved from limb to limb until he had a decent view through Joyce Marie's bedroom window. Looking down, he could see Joyce Marie, sitting on the edge of the bed, but he couldn't see Paolo Martinez.

"Hey, Slocum!" the bandit called. "You still out there? You in that cottonwood? I can hear the rustle of the branches. Slocum, I like your spotted mare. She pulls the wagon very good!"

"Screw you, Paolo!" Slocum shouted back. He wanted to keep Martinez's attention toward him and away from the door. He leveled his pistol at the window.

Paolo Martinez laughed. "You are very good, Slocum. How many of my company have you killed? Four? Five?"

"Every last mother's son of 'em, Martinez," Slocum lied. "You're on your own now."

For a moment, there was silence.

Just chew on that for a while, Slocum thought. Where the hell was Sully?

"You there, Martinez?" he called at last.

As though in reply, a shot exploded the silence, and Slocum heard a *thud,* and then a wail. Joyce Marie. He couldn't see her anymore.

"Your big friend should not bleed so much, *señor,*" Martinez said after a moment. "I saw it drip to the floor before I saw him. By the looks of it, my men did a fine job of turning him into a strainer for the chicken bones when you make soup, no? I think he is quite dead now, though."

Slocum closed his eyes, silently cursing.

"These ladies tell me that you and this black-skinned giant came alone," Martinez went on. "They say they know nothing about any boys."

These ladies. He had both of them in there with him then. "They lied to you, Martinez," Slocum said. "They're right out here with me, and they're both armed."

It had the desired effect. Martinez laughed again. "It is a nice try, *amigo*, but I do not believe you. You and I are both alone, but I have your women. And if you wish them to stay alive, this is what you will do. Hitch up my team and lead the wagon to this window. You understand?"

"I understand. But you'd best understand something too, Martinez. You touch one hair on either of those gals' heads, and I'll track you all the way to Bolivia if I have to."

Paolo Martinez chuckled ominously. "They are far too pretty to harm. Unless you cross me, *amigo*."

"Don't do it, Slocum," cried Joyce Marie's disembodied voice, and then there came the sharp sound of a slap.

"Go!" Martinez barked. "Go now!"

"Keep your goddamn splints on," Slocum muttered, and started climbing down from the cottonwood.

He trotted down toward the barn, holding his arm and half-expecting to be shot in the back at any moment. But the shot didn't come, and he slipped into the shelter of the barn. The *bandidos* were still hog-tied, although another one lay slumped in his ropes, unconscious.

"What in the name of St. Michael is goin' on?" Tip half-shouted.

"Shut up!" Slocum hissed. "This ain't over yet. You okay?"

Tip nodded. "What about Patrick?"

"He's just dandy." He tipped his head toward the unconscious bandit. "You do that?"

Tip lifted his chin. "He was annoyin' me."

"Hold tight," Slocum said, and pulled back from the door before Tip could respond.

He picked out the two of the most slab-sided, flea-bitten horses in the corral, one of which was an old pinto he remembered having glimpsed before drawing the wagon back up at the mission.

At least one of them would be harness-broke anyway.

The corral, which ran halfway down the south side of the barn, was shielded from the house, and he quickly slid though the far side of the fence, out of the corral, and went to the corner of the building. On his hands and knees, he crept around the corner to the rain barrel, and gingerly picked up the crate of dynamite that sat in its shade.

Taking care not to jostle it, he backed up, keeping low and hoping that the barrel would block him from Martinez's view, and hoping too that Martinez was mistaken about Sully. He'd thought he'd killed him once before, and had been wrong.

Sully was pretty hard to kill.

But still . . .

Once he reached the corner of the building and drew back around it, he stood up again. Carefully, he brought the crate with him and slid back into the corral. Next, he went to the horses, which he'd tied to the corral fence. Placing them between himself and the house, he led them out of the corral and up toward the wagon.

When he reached it, he slid the crate, as gently as he could, into the wagon's bed, using the horses' bodies for cover.

"Hurry, *amigo!*" he heard Martinez shout. "I am growing weary of waiting!"

Slocum buckled the last strap into place, then patted the pinto on its shoulder. "Sorry, old friend," he said, then grimly led the team forward.

The wagon just fit between the trunk of rearmost cottonwood and the house, and as per Martinez's shouted instructions, Slocum led the horses forward until the rig's high seat was roughly level with Joyce Marie's windowsill.

Martinez's head was in the window now, and he gestured at Slocum with his pistol. "To the side, *amigo*. Drop the guns."

Slocum obeyed.

His gun outstretched, Paolo Martinez heaved himself onto the windowsill, then out onto the wagon's seat. He paused. "They are harnessed good, *señor*? No tricks?"

Slocum nodded. "They're harnessed good."

"Step back."

Slocum did.

Martinez eased himself the rest of the way into the wagon seat. The wooden splints on his legs thumped the windowsill, grated along the armrest.

"Now you, *querida*," he said. When nothing happened, he angrily added, "Now, or I will kill your friend Slocum where he stands."

Sullenly, Joyce Marie crawled through the window

after him. She'd been crying, Slocum could tell, and her cheek was still bright from that slap Paolo had doled out earlier, but there was still some fight left in her.

"In the back," Martinez ordered. "You will not grab my reins. I know how you women are," he grumbled. "All the time, it's pull the hair, grab the reins, stomp on the foot. . . ."

She climbed over the seat and into the bed, and Slocum nearly cried out when she almost stepped on the crate.

She looked down, and recognition, then horror, overtook her features.

Martinez picked up the reins, and in the second that he looked away from Slocum, Slocum mouthed, "Jump!" at Joyce Marie.

She understood, and nodded.

"I see you, Slocum," Martinez said. "Sooner than you think, I bet." He fired his pistol—not at Slocum, but into the air.

The team leapt forward.

Before it had gone twenty feet, Joyce Marie rolled off the back and sat up, cradling her arm. She stood up then, and scrambled back to Slocum.

Forty feet, a hundred feet, two hundred feet it traveled, and Slocum was just about to shake his head and count Paolo Martinez as among the luckiest bastards to ever cross the face of the earth when, about three hundred feet out, the dynamite went up.

There was a deafening *boom*, and a black cloud of smoke filled with flaming boards and bits of metal. Wheels and splintered wood rocketed up and out, and

Martinez's body sailed along with them, twisting like a child's doll.

The blast had separated the hitch from the wagon, and the horses galloped away wildly, their tails smoking and sparking.

Martinez, minus his splints and one leg, landed two hundred feet from where he'd started in a smoldering, contorted heap, as twisted chunks of metal and flaming splinters rained down over Slocum. The other leg, still in its splits, landed twenty yards to the side a second later.

Slocum didn't bother to go out and check. He didn't need to kick the body to know that Paolo Martinez was dead, and he had other things to attend to.

Calling the boys from their hiding places and helping Joyce Marie—who was holding him up as much as he was her—he went around to the front of the house.

The bandit he'd knocked cold was just coming round, but a boot heel to the head settled him fast enough. "Find something and tie him up," he said to Patrick. The poor kid was filthy and sweated through, and sticky black-widow webs adhered to his pants and shirt.

But he said, "Aye, sir," and took off in search of rope. Game kid.

To Tip, who was just trotting up from the barn, he said, "Saddle up a couple horses. You and Patrick go fetch that team, if they haven't run clear to California already."

"But—"

"Do it!"

Slocum and Joyce Marie went inside. While Joyce

Marie untied Dulcie, Slocum bent to Sully. The big man had fallen in the doorway of the bedroom, and Slocum had to pull him through it before he could turn him over. Slocum's shoulder complained—loudly— with every tug.

But he put his ear to the big man's chest, and was gratified to hear his heart beating.

"He'll be fine," Slocum announced, sitting back on his heels.

"But the blood!" cried Joyce Marie. His entire shirt-front was soaked with it, and there was a new slug hole in his side, just beneath his ribs.

"Reckon these other ones—plus chasin' after the *bandido* that shot him—weakened him enough that when Paolo shot him in the side, he just keeled over," Slocum explained. He ripped open Sully's shirt, and sure enough, the three slugs that had peppered him through the body of the *bandido* didn't appear to have done much damage. In fact, he could see metal peering from one of the wounds, and thumbed out the impact-deformed lead.

Joyce Marie scurried off for water and bandages.

Dulcie pulled Slocum up to sit beside her on the bed. Her wrists were red and chafed, and she rubbed at them. "What about you?" she said, wet-eyed, and stopped fussing with her wrists to unbutton his shirt. "What about the boys? And what happened to those other *bandidos*?"

"Down at the barn," he said, and winced when she pulled the shirt free of his shoulder. "We got lucky."

Her lip caught in her teeth as she studied his wound. "I'll say, honey," she whispered. "I'll say."

23

Night had fallen on the desert, and the Carnahan brothers sat alone on the front steps of the adobe house. The boys were both as full as ticks after having inhaled one of Dulcie's steak dinners with all the trimmings, and bone-tired to boot.

After all the excitement of the early afternoon—Tip had been amazed, when the smoke cleared and the shooting stopped, that so little time had gone by—they'd at last tracked down and brought in the unfortunate team of horses. They turned out not to have been as unfortunate as Slocum had originally thought.

The brown one had its tail nearly singed away, but there was no damage to the beast's hide. The other one, the old pinto, had a bit more hair on its tail, and just a few tiny burns scattered over its backside. A little unguent, and Patrick pronounced them fine and dandy, if a tad odd-looking.

Tip imagined, however, that today was the last time either of the brutes would stand still for hitching. He couldn't say that he'd blame them.

After they brought the horses back and settled them in, the boys helped Slocum scrape up what was left of Paolo Martinez. Grisly, that. They never did find his right ear.

Patrick had vomited, and Tip himself had felt a strong urge to copy him. Later, they had wrapped the bodies of the dead *bandidos* in blankets, piling them into Dulcie and Joyce Marie's flatbed wagon like so much kindling.

Finally, along about dusk, Slocum had butchered out the one poor steer that had been hit and killed by shrapnel from the blast.

Thus the steak dinner.

"I swear, Tipper," Patrick groaned beside him, his hands on his belly, "I can't move. I would have sworn on Mum's soul that I couldn't be eatin' a thing, but there I was, wolfin' it down till I was fit to burst." He looked over. "It doesn't seem Christian somehow. I mean, after killin' a man and then sortin' through all that carnage."

"Appetite's got no conscience, Patrick," Tip said quietly. "And besides, you had to be killin' that man. He would've surely killed you had he the chance."

"Still, I pulled the trigger," Patrick said. He shook his head. "I didn't think I'd be havin' to do it. After all those lectures Mr. Slocum and Mr. Sully Washington were after givin' us! You know, about keepin' down and where to aim and such . . . well, I didn't really think I'd have to. Even if the man was a right bastard, Tip, I'm feelin' a bit low about it. I'm wonderin' if the Lord'll be forgivin' me."

Tip said, "I know just what you're sayin'."

"Aye," agreed Patrick sadly. "Mr. Slocum told me you shot that villain on the porch. 'Twas a fine shot, Tipper, comin' all the way from the barn. I'll wager it was more than a hundred yards."

Tip stared at his shadowed hands, concentrating on

the bumps of his knuckles. " 'Twasn't me first, Patrick," he said.

"Did you take out another of the brigands?"

Tip shook his head. It seemed the right time for admissions, and he was finally going to get this one out.

"No, Patrick, I didn't. But . . . but I've killed a man before."

Patrick's hand went to Tip's shoulder. "Say it isn't true, Tipper!"

" 'Tis, Patrick, and may God have mercy on me." Tip was staring at his feet now, anything to avoid his brother's eyes. "Back home, that little trouble I had at Murphy's Tavern . . . Well, I got into a bit of a conversation with a few of the boys the night we left for America. We were all drinkin', you know. The talk sort of got heated, and before I knew what was what, Flynn O'Toole came after me with a fistful of darts and a murderous look."

Patrick gasped. "The black-hearted bastard!"

"Aye," said Tip. "But I broke a whiskey bottle over his head." He looked up, looked into Patrick's eyes. "I killed him, Pat. Killed him as sure as I'm sittin' here. Oh, the blood! Rivers of it, there was. . . ." His head dropped into his hands.

He felt Patrick's arm go round his shoulder. "There, there, Tipper," his brother said softly. "Why, anyone could tell it was self-defense. You were attacked!"

"How much damage could he be doin' to me with his poor fist filled with darts, Patrick?" Tip said angrily. "Any magistrate would be hangin' me, sure as anythin'. I just struck out, and I cooked me own goose. And then Royal O'Shaughnessy and Tom Quinn stuck their fists out of the mob and started cryin', 'Murderer,

murderer!' and God help me, I took off runnin'."

Patrick snorted. "O'Shaughnessy and Quinn! Worthless ruffians, the both of them!"

"No matter," Tip said. "The whole tavern had a good look at it." He straightened up, shrugging Patrick's arm away. "I'm sorry, Pat. It's why I was tuggin' you out of bed in the hard, dark center of the night to go to America, and why I dragged you halfway around the world. 'Twasn't Da at all, I'm thinkin'. He was just the excuse. You were right. I give you leave to beat me to a bloody pulp for all the torment I've been causin' ye."

"Oh," said Patrick, "I don't believe I will, Tipper. Why, I'm reckonin' things are just fine."

Tip cocked a brow. "How can ye be sayin' that? I've pulled ye off one continent to a new one, then made you sail around a third. I've made you toil beside me to raise this damned money that's probably crippled us for life, walkin' around on it for so long. I've got you bit by a giant tarantula and knocked silly by bandits. You've nearly died of thirst, been sick as a dog more times than I can count when we were aboard ship, and just escaped havin' your head cracked open back in Boston Town. I've made you break the law by freein' me from jail, and then by stealin' a horse, and that puma could have jumped you as easily as it did me. Now, how can any of that be 'just fine'?"

"Well," said Patrick with a little smile, "you'll have to be admittin' it was a grand adventure."

"Aye," Tip admitted. "It was that."

"And one we'd never be havin' at home."

"True. But it's not over yet." Tip stared down to-

ward the barn, where all the bandits left alive were
spending the night hog-tied.

"Oh, we'll have a grand time takin' them to market,
I vow it," Patrick said, following his gaze. "Mr. Washington says they're worth nearly seven thousand all
told. Can ye imagine the cheerin' when we bring 'em
up to the constabulary? It's like bein' heroes, Tip! Too
bad about Mr. Slocum havin' to blow up Paolo Martinez, though. He was worth three of those other brigands put together."

Tip nodded, and sat silent for a moment. When he
broke the silence, it was to say, "That was fair wizard
of you, Patrick, darlin', thinkin' there'd be dynamite."

"Aye, Tip. But 'twas more brilliant of you findin' it
after I'd given up me own self."

Tip smiled and hung an arm about his brother's
shoulders. "You're a fine brother, Patrick Carnahan. I
couldn't want for a better one."

"I'm thankin' you," Patrick replied. Then hesitantly,
he asked, "Do . . . do ye think there might be some
ladies of the evenin' in the place we're goin' to turn
in these bandits? Miss Dulcie and Mr. Slocum and
Miss Joyce Marie and Mr. Washington are about to
drive me stark ravin' mad, what with all their cattin'
about."

Tip's smile widened into a grin. "Why, Pat!" he exclaimed, and playfully slugged his brother in the thigh.
"And here I was thinkin' you were practically engaged!"

Two days later, they kissed the girls good-bye and traveled north. Cheyenne traveled behind the wagon rider-
less, and Slocum fussed over her constantly, to the

point that Sully and the boys teased him about it something awful. He didn't care. He wanted that mare back to one hundred percent, and she was in pitiful shape.

They went all the way to the town of Eternal Hope before Slocum and Sully felt it was safe to turn the gang over to the authorities. The bandits were past grumpy by this time, and were almost happy to finally shed their bonds and cram into nice, comfortable cells.

Slocum and the others waited around in town—and Tip and Patrick practically lived at the local whorehouse—until Sully had collected his bounties. The authorities failed to pay out on Paolo Martinez, claiming they couldn't come close to an identification from the shreds of flesh provided. Slocum noticed, however, that they tore down Martinez's wanted posters.

That evening in the hotel room, Sully counted out the reward money in front of Slocum.

"Seven thousand, five hundred, and forty," he said with satisfaction, riffling the bills.

"What was the forty for?" Slocum asked.

"For one Julio Jacobson Ruiz," Sully said. "Only a hundred and forty on him." He shrugged. "That was the young fellow in the yellow serape."

Slocum leaned back in his chair. "Maybe you should've thrown him back in the pond. Waited till he got a little size on him."

Straight-faced, Sully said, "You're a funny man, Slocum." He began scooping up the bills.

"I try," Slocum said. "What about the boys? And me, for that matter? Seems like we ought to be gettin' at least half of that."

Sully actually had the gall to look pained. "Why, Slocum! You knew I was going after Martinez in the pursuance of my profession. If you insisted on tagging along, I couldn't help that, could I?"

Slocum just stared at him.

Sully burst out laughing, and the boom of it filled the room. "All right," he said. "Three thousand, and split it any which way you like. But I'm keeping the rest. I'm thinking maybe I'll head back down to Mission Springs. I'm getting too damned old to be traipsing all over the country, and it seems to me that Mission Springs is a town in need of an honest sheriff. Well, any sheriff at all, come to think of it."

Slocum grinned. "And Joyce Marie. Does she need an honest man?"

Sully pushed three thousand dollars at him. "I do believe she does, Slocum. Now, put away your money before I change my mind."

Ten days later, Slocum—riding Cheyenne at last—and the boys pulled into Carson City, and went straight to the sheriff's office—at Tip's insistence. This surprised Slocum. He'd fully expected Tip to throw on the brakes before they reached the city limits. But Tip marched straight in, marched right up to Sheriff Metzger, and stuck out his hands.

"I'm givin' meself up," he announced. "Go ahead, sir. Do your duty."

Patrick aped him and stuck out his wrists too. "And me as well," he said.

And Metzger tossed them in a cell—until Slocum explained, that is. It took twenty minutes, and the boys couldn't hear a lick of it, for the cells were back behind iron doors and upstairs as well. But when Slocum finished, the sheriff unlocked the door, sent a deputy to bring the boys back down, and when they arrived shook hands all around.

"Proud to meet the fellers what took out Paolo Martinez," Metzger said, still pumping Tip's hand. "My congratulations, boys."

"You'll not be jailin' us then?" asked a disbelieving Patrick. He stared at his hand, which the sheriff had just finished pumping.

"Not after what you boys done," Metzger said. "Why, that Martinez was a real sonofabitch! Glad to have done with him. And of course," he confided, lowering his tone and leaning toward them, "Slocum here explained about your daddy. I'm right sorry, boys. Besides," he said, straightening, "the deputy you cracked over the skull, he's fine. He up and quit me, though. Went to California. I say the hell with him if he can't take a little punishment, right?"

Slocum was grateful when the boys just nodded.

Next, they went up to the livery and surprised Jessup, who turned a pitchfork toward Tip and hollered, "Attack me at your own peril, you goddamn shanty Irishman! I ain't responsible for the consequences!"

Slocum wasn't sure who was more surprised—him or Jessup—when Tip swept his cap off his head. "I'm terrible sorry for hittin' you, sir, and I'd like to apologize for thieving these horses. I know Mr. Slocum paid ye for 'em, but would ye consider buyin' 'em back?"

Jessup was surprised, Slocum thought, but he wasn't stupid. He'd charged a pretty penny for those mounts, and he wasn't about to return it. Jessup pulled himself up. "I will not," he said.

Tip didn't argue. "Patrick," he said, "take off your shoe."

Jessup stared at him.

"Then we'll be payin' you, Mr. Slocum," Tip said while Patrick counted out the money. "Orion and Flannel are fine mounts, or so Patrick tells me, and we'd sort of like to be keepin' them. We thought to let Mr. Jessup have 'em back if he was of a mind, but I'm glad he wasn't."

Patrick counted out two hundred dollars, which Slocum quickly stuck in his pocket before the odor had a chance to rise. And then Patrick handed Jessup money for a week's board for all three horses, Cheyenne included, and back board for the ancient Rosie, who was still standing in her stall, asleep. The old gelding, Jessup informed them, had passed away. He tried to make them pay for dragging the carcass down to the butchers, but an evil look from Slocum put the kibosh on that.

"Appreciate it, boys," Slocum said as they walked up the street. He'd been sniffing Carmella for the last two miles into town, and he was past eager to see her again. "There's somethin' else."

He stopped, and the boys stopped with him., He dug into his back pocket and pulled out 2500 dollars. It was a fat roll, and he handed it to Patrick.

"That's from Sully," he said. "Didn't tell you before 'cause I thought I might need it to bribe the sheriff." He winked and grinned at them.

Patrick was busy counting, and Tip took off his cap again. Solemnly, he shook Slocum's hand. "Thank you, sir. We're beholden to you."

"You gonna go back to Ireland?" Slocum asked as they began walking again.

Sadly, Tip shook his head. "No. First, I'm thinkin' we'll get Fiona out of that house. The second thing, we'll think about later."

Slocum nodded just as Patrick finished counting the money. "Jaysus, Mary, and Joseph!" he said softly, his eyes wide, and began rapidly counting again.

Slocum grinned, and opened the door to Carmella's house. "Carmella, honey!" he called before he was all the way inside. "There's a man out here who needs a shave!"

Later, Tip, Patrick, and Fiona sat around the kitchen table, the money laid out before them in neat stacks. With what ransom money they had left over after spending a bundle on the loose women of Eternal Hope (and buying the two horses from Slocum), they had a grand total of 3900 dollars and forty-three cents. And a tuppence.

" 'Tis a fortune," Fiona said thickly. Her eyes were red from so much joyful crying. "It's enough to live on for years and years, enough to get me off me back. It's enough to go back home and live like kings!"

"No," Tip said firmly. "You and Patrick can go for the kingly life, but I'll be stayin' here."

"Why on earth, Tipper?" Fiona asked. "Are you thinkin' to start a ranch? Go into business?"

"Oh, he killed a fellow," Patrick said nonchalantly.

"Pat!" cried Tip, and lurched from his chair. "Don't be tellin' her that!"

"Well, it was over there that you did it," Patrick explained. "This is America. No one's carin' a whit!"

"Slow down," said Fiona, her eyes narrowed. "Just who was it that you killed, boyo?"

Patrick answered for him. "Flynn O'Toole, in a terrible bloody fight up to Murphy's," he said proudly. "Why, I'll wager they're still talkin' about it!" He started recounting the money.

"I'll wager they aren't," Fiona said, and she made a face. "Flynn O'Toole, did ye say?"

Tip nodded. "Aye, Fi. And ye needn't be so bleedin' proud of it, Patrick. It's my hands that murdered the poor drunken sot, not yours."

"Tipper," Fiona said patiently, "I've got news for ye. Mum wrote about four months after the two of you went scamperin' off into the night like you hadn't a care. And she happened to mention that Mr. Flynn O'Toole himself was bringin' her peat for the fire. I'm rememberin' it distinct, because it was an un-O'Toole thing to be doin'. Mum said Flynn was feelin' badly because he thought he had somethin' to do with the two of you fleein' the country. Course, Mum brushed it aside. She thought it was because of Da."

"Well, that too," Patrick said with a shrug.

Tip gulped. "He lives?"

"I hope to be kissin' a pig, he does," she replied with her mouth all set.

"Then all of this was for nothin'?" he asked, his voice rising.

Patrick looked up from the money. "Oh, sit down, Tipper. 'Twasn't for nothin'. It was for almost four thousand dollars and Fi and Da, for the little good that it did, and it was for making us into men. It was for meetin' Mr. Sully Washington, and you learnin' to shoot so fine, and us battling bandits and crossin' the

Grand Canyon all on our own." He straightened the bills, curled them into a roll with some difficulty, and added, "And like I told you before—for all the great, majestic adventure of it. I could write a book, I could."

Tip sat back down and propped his head in his hands. "Poor Mr. Slocum. To think what we put him through! We'll both be after apologizin' come breakfast, Patrick."

Fiona smiled and glanced up at the ceiling. "Oh, I don't think you're goin' to be seein' hide nor hair of him for a few days, Tip."

A corner of Tip's mouth twisted up into a grin. "No, I'm not supposin' we will."

Upstairs, Slocum leaned back against satin pillows and lit a fine Cuban cigar. Life was good again. He had his money back, and he'd kept five hundred dollars of Sully's reward for himself. Hell, he'd probably just lose it gambling anyhow, and he figured the kids could use the extra to make a new start.

He had his horse back, healed up as good as new, and best of all, he had Carmella. So far, he'd had her in the barber's chair, on the fainting couch, and in the bed. *Poor little ol' gal,* he thought with a chuckle as she dozed, naked and relaxed, beside him. *She's all tuckered out.*

He blew a perfect smoke ring toward the ceiling and another one through the middle of it, then placed his hand softly on Carmella's hip.

The wild little gal in Dirty Dog, the Mexican beauty in Phoenix, the brave and bounteous Dulcie, and now the adventurous Carmella again: They were all beautiful, the women in his life.

Every single one of them.

J. R. ROBERTS
THE
GUNSMITH

Delivers more bang for the buck!

To Order call:
1-800-788-6262

(Ad # B111)

LONGARM

Explore the exciting Old West with one of the men who made it wild!